George Barlow

The Pageant of Life

An Epic Poem in five Books

George Barlow

The Pageant of Life
An Epic Poem in five Books

ISBN/EAN: 9783744765206

Printed in Europe, USA, Canada, Australia, Japan

Cover: Foto ©Andreas Hilbeck / pixelio.de

More available books at **www.hansebooks.com**

THE PAGEANT OF LIFE.

THE PAGEANT OF LIFE

An Epic Poem

IN FIVE BOOKS

BY

GEORGE BARLOW

LONDON
SWAN SONNENSCHEIN & CO.
PATERNOSTER SQUARE
1888

NOTE.

My best thanks are due to Messrs. BOOSEY and Messrs. HOPKINSON for kindly allowing me to republish in this volume several Lyrics which have been set to music, and published by them. These Lyrics are as follows :—

MIDNIGHT AT THE HELM (Page 323).
Set to Music by Frank Moir. Published by Messrs. Boosey.

THE SONG OF ABOU KLEA (Page 339).
Set to Music by Hope Temple. Published by Messrs. Boosey, under the title of " A Soldier's Song."

THE PATHWAY OF LIFE (Page 348).
Set to Music by Ernest Birch. Published by Messrs. Hopkinson.

FOR EVER YOUNG (Page 370).
Set to Music by Frank Moir. Published by Messrs. Boosey.

"AH! ONCE I THOUGHT I LOVED THE ROSE" (Page 385).
Set to Music by Arthur Hervey. Published by Messrs. Hopkinson, under the title of " Love Conquers All!"

G. B.

CONTENTS.

BOOK I.

CHRIST UPON EARTH.

BOOK II.

A MASQUE OF HUMAN LIFE.

The Masque.

BOOK III.

CHRIST IN THE HEART.

Songs of the Seasons.

Christ in the Heart.

BOOK IV.

NATURE AND HUMANITY.

I.

Nature.

II.

Humanity

I.

II.

BOOK V.

EXIT SATAN.

I.

II.

III.

PREFACE.

THE poetry of the life of Jesus Christ has never been understood. The existing record of that life is very slight and fragmentary; very conflicting, and in portions very obscure; and it has moreover been so traversed and overlaid by thaumaturgical imagination and theological error that it is very difficult to arrive at the real facts. I have not hesitated, in writing of Jesus, to regard him from the point of view which I imagine will be the point of view of the future; the point of view which seems to me at once the most historically accurate and the most poetically fruitful. I look upon him, that is to say, as a man, and not as a god or a demigod ; as a Jewish prophet and man of genius, enormously in advance of his age—·aye, enormously in advance even of the present age—and therefore enormously, almost incredibly, misinterpreted and misunderstood. I have been careful in my poem to preserve his human nature and his manly integrity. I have not attempted to remove the freckles from his face, or the blisters from his hands, or the love of woman from his heart. I have not attempted to degrade him by bestowing upon him a monstrous and unnatural godhead ; nor to degrade his mother by placing her outside the influence of the sacred natural laws of ordinary maternity ; nor to degrade the woman who—we may reasonably infer—most passionately loved him by reducing her love to an unclean spiritual dream, and her passion to a spiritual nightmare. Such fancies[1] may content the minds of men like Canon Liddon or Canon Westcott : they never contented any poet yet, nor, we may add, any true woman. Least of all (we may still further add) would they have contented the broad noble humanity of Jesus himself, or the true riper womanhood of Mary Magdalene ; the woman whose undying love and unshaken belief in her master are chiefly responsible for the legendary embroidery which, in connection with the story of the Resurrection, has been worked upon the canvas of fact.

---

[1] Fancies which, as Victor Hugo saw and pointed out in his fine poem " *L'Immaculée Conception,*" do in effect aim an insult at every wife and every mother. When women once fairly begin to think for themselves, they will all see this clearly. In fact, even with every possible intellectual and educational drawback, women in general will grasp these points far sooner than men in general will.

I have not attempted to degrade Christ's heavenly Father by supposing him capable of generating only one supreme Son and perfect image of himself; nor to degrade his earthly father by supposing him capable of " taking unto him Mary his wife " under the miserable circumstances reported in the legend; nor to degrade the world by supposing it capable of producing one, and only one, such type of heroic nobleness, instead of giving it credit for producing frequently—as it undoubtedly does, and this in the strangest and most unexpected places—types of humanity which probably excel the Nazarene in actual moral worth, while they certainly surpass him in breadth of personality and totality of mental greatness. My Christ is the Christ of Shelley and Hugo, not the Christ of St. Augustine or of Dr. Manning; the Christ who in the centuries to come will gain inconceivably more (both as a grand poetic figure and as an object of religious veneration) from the right apprehension of his manhood, than he has gained (or shall we not rather say lost ?) during the centuries that are past through the mistaken theory of his godhead ; the Christ who was loved by the men and women who were his companions with honest warm human love, and never approached by them in the Christian Church's subsequent attitude of cringing awe and abject superstition.

I cannot doubt that the whole Christian episode (regarded from the simple human unsupernatural point of view) will one day be rendered in the form of a great drama.[1]   But the time has not yet come

[1] The experiments in this direction which have been carried out from time to time at Ober Ammergau must be looked upon as merely partial and tentative.   When the spirit of religious materialism has finally forsaken the churches, and when the world in general has come

for that : as I was keenly conscious (and even more
keenly conscious of the inadequacy of my powers for
the tremendous task) when I once thought of attempt-
ing it.   But it will no doubt be done by some great
poet of the future.   When biblical criticism has
accomplished its final work, and the form of Jesus
Christ stands out plainly—" *en marbre blanc* " as M.
Renan has it—freed from the swaddling-bands of
ages, simply and majestically human, and therefore
in the highest sense divine, the time will have come
when opera and drama may legitimately do their
work upon the great subject ; may elucidate and in-

to see that it is a higher and nobler reverence to regard Jesus Christ
as a real and natural man than as an unnatural and unreal god, the
time will have come for opera and drama to perform a work far higher
and grander—at once more human and more divine—than has ever
yet been attempted, or dreamed of, in their respective spheres. The
school of music which Wagner founded will then be of infinite assist-
ance in providing music suitable for the immense theme.

terpret the life and the character of Jesus ; may translate them into dramatic action and uplift them into lyric song.

This task, as I have said, is at present an impossible task. The age is not ripe to receive and appreciate such a drama—even were I furnished with the necessary historical knowledge and dramatic power. But this much I have done in the direction indicated, and done, as I think I may claim, for the first time ; I have endeavoured to supply at any rate some suggestion of the love-element in the life of Jesus of Nazareth : I have suggested some motive for the conduct of Judas beyond the utterly inadequate motive (that of mere mercenary greed) usually suggested and implied : I have *not* destroyed (as has always hitherto been done) the whole real poetry of the great Hebrew's life by assuming that the love

felt for him by the women who followed him was
something altogether ghostly and bloodless and
spiritual, and not healthy human love and warm
strong human passion. I have used jealousy in Judas
as the motive of the betrayal : I have used pure and
sweet passion in Mary Magdalene as the motive
leading to her devotion to Jesus and her transformation of character.

Thus far as to the view which I have taken of
Jesus ; the character who represents in the Poem the
widest possible range and the utmost possible height
of human optimism. But no purely optimistic theory,
unfortunately, can embrace or explain fully the entire
series of human phenomena presented to it. Life has
a sombre and tragic side as well : and no poem could
have any pretensions to world-width or real human
significance in which this darker side was not at least

fairly stated and courageously considered   Therefore
I am compelled, in endeavouring to render the life
of the universe into song, to take account of the
phenomenon which we call " Evil " ; the negative and
undeveloped side of things.   This negative or " evil "
side of things I regard, for purposes of poetry, as
personified in a Satan or Prince of Darkness.   But
the world of thought has moved onward since Satan
made his *début* on the Epic stage in Milton's great
drama ; it has taken many rapid strides even since the
Arch-Fiend made his second successful appearance,
with Goethe for playwright and stage-manager, and
under the stage-name of Mephistopheles; he has
become increasingly identified with abstract ideas,
and less and less pungent and personal.   The smell
of brimstone which accompanied the stage entrances
and exits of Goethe's Mephistopheles has died away,

and the shield and sword of Milton's gloomy Arch-Angel no longer impress or terrify us. To-day Satan wears flowers in his button-hole : he loves to gather roses, and is particular as to the relative sweetness of clove carnations and purple heliotrope. A few words of explanation therefore become necessary in introducing this tenacious and persistent player for the third time upon the world's stage.

My " Satan," then, is the modern devil of moral cynicism and religious despair. He is a thoughtful and intellectual devil ; he reasons about God and the phenomena of life. He might even write an article in one of our advanced magazines, or free-thought journals. He can pose as a well-bred gentleman too ; would be welcomed at a West End Club, and would delight the loungers in the smoking-room with his delicately coarse stories. He wears rings, brandishes a Malacca cane, and smokes Larrañaga cigars. You might meet him in Bond Street, or on a summer afternoon in the Row.

Taken more seriously, and regarded from his intellectual side, he is the spirit of negation ; of hate, death, darkness, despair : just as Christ is the spirit of affirmation ; of love, life, light, hope. Of old he put forward the worship of himself as the alternative to faith in God and worship of God. To-day he has grown more cunning. As the alternative to faith in a living conscious God, he suggests faith in the unalterable sequences of God's own apparently pitiless laws, and his chorus of dark spirits follow his lead and emphasize the idea.

In such a Poem as the present it is obvious that Nature must not be left unrepresented. She speaks therefore (in Book IV.) through the voices of the

Flowers, the Rivers, the Stars, and the Sea. The Sea still retains within it somewhat of the soul of rebellion, or of denial; but Flowers, Rivers, and Stars, acquiesce in God's rule, and love and praise him.

The principal divisions of human thought and feeling are represented in the Epic by four groups of singers. The Chant of the Agnostics, or Positivists, leads up to the Chant of the Christians. These latter are penetrated by the Semitic reckless disregard of natural law, and equally reckless belief in supernatural agency. They are followed by the poets — the Hellenistic or artist group—whose whole vision is concentrated sensuously, though not sensually, on the visible side of things; on beauty, and woman its visible expression and incarnation.

To complete the harmony, woman herself speaks.

In the Chant of Women she expresses her own view of life, gives utterance to her own desires, and affiliates herself, by the links of purity and self-sacrifice, to the Christian conception of things.

In the concluding Book, the thought rises into a higher sphere. In Book I. Satan and Christ were introduced upon the scene : in Books II., III., and IV., the whole world of Nature and Humanity has been dealt with—Nature and Humanity as swayed and influenced by the two great dominating spirits ; the spirit of darkness and despair, poetically personified in Satan ; the spirit of light and love, actually personified in Christ, the great social reformer and religious teacher. Now, in Book V., Satan, who has quietly gathered and marshalled his forces for a last fierce argumentative effort, meets Christ face to face— thoroughly equipped with the keenest weapons and the stoutest armour of modern pessimism—and the final struggle begins.   Christ, who had uttered one and only one pregnant word at the end of each satiric dialogue in Book III., again speaks—this time at greater length and in greater detail—and harmonizes, from a higher point of view, several of the preceding apparent discords.   He insists on God's eternal miracle of unchanging law, faith in which in him took the form of a spiritual intuition—faith in "the Father," who to him was spiritual and physical law personified.

He indicates the transition from faith in special will to faith in universal will; will exerted not in special instances, but triumphing steadily and surely along the whole historic line.

The long world-drama is concluded by the Chorus of Spirits of Light.   They point out that life has a joyous as well as a tragic side, and prophesy the triumph of Christ's real ideas, though not necessarily of man's interpretation of many of them. The drama began in darkness. It ends in light. It began with the universal wail of agony. It ends with creation's hymn of praise. It began with the voices of dark spirits, adoring evil and suggesting crime. It ends with the voices of children, happy among the flowers and in the summer fields.

It began with Satan. It ends with Christ.

G. B.

PROLOGUE.

ADAM AND EVE.

THE FIRST NIGHT IN PARADISE.

TIME, B.C.——

ADAM AND EVE

Adam.—O Eve, the darkness deepens.   Yet I see
       Through the tall branches of this flowering tree
           Faint streaks of light. 'Twas there the sun sank low.

Eve.—Adam, the sunshine made the sweet earth glad,
       But now I tremble.   Darkness makes me sad :
           I thought the golden sun would never go.

Adam.— And yet, as fades the sun, the tender light
       In thine eyes, Eve, seems ever to grow bright :
           The sun is little, so that I have thee.

Eve.—Thou art my lord and king.   I cannot fear :
       The deepening darkness draws our souls more near :
           The day was sweet, and sweet the night will be.

Adam.—See—from the branches of the trees depend
       Lamps many-coloured, glowing without end
           From branch and branch,—or are they in the sky ?

Eve.—I know not.   Now, behold, a ghostly sun,
       White in the darkness, rises there alone,
           And, flashing into silver, floats on high.

Adam.— O Eve, the flowers were sweet, the day was bright :
       But is not darkness sweeter than the light ?
           For now our lips seem nearer.   Let them meet !

Eve.—My limbs feel heavy with the sultry day.
There's mystery in that white lamp's glittering ray :
Why does my heart at your lips' pressure beat ?

Adam.—I call these small lamps, stars—that lamp, the moon.
Rest in my arms : the sun may rise up soon ;
More golden than all sunshine is thine hair.

Eve.—I love this darkness better than the light :
I feared to touch thee then. But now 'tis right
In thine embrace to rest. I'm happy there !

Adam.—And, Eve, I worship thee, and not the light.
This darkness, which I call our bridal night,
Is sent by God that I may treasure thee.

Eve.—I love the darkness better than the day.
The fruits my red lips fondled fade away,
And now thy lips assert their sovereignty.

Adam.—Let us pray God the sun may never rise !
I never looked before deep in thine eyes :
I never felt that thou wast wholly won.

Eve.—Adam, God took the sun away for this,
Lest it should wax quite jealous of my kiss :
But, Adam, I love thee and not the sun.

BOOK I.

CHRIST UPON EARTH.

SATAN.

I.

O ye who side with me,
Lords of the land and sea,
   The mountains and the hills ;
Lords of the starlit space—
Rebellious in each place
   The high God's presence fills ;

Lords of the earth and air ;
Spirits who haunt the fair
   Green grass-draped heath or wold—
Who haunt the mountains blue
Where never blossom grew,
   The icy peaks and cold ;

I summon all your strength :
For now the Lord at length
   Designs our power to shake.
In Greece and Rome we won ;
But those old days are done ;
   Another morn will break.

God wearies now at last
Of all his efforts past :

His efforts we have marred.
But now his new design
In genius equals mine :
  Spirits, be on your guard !

He sends a low-born Jew :
No Greek or Roman true ;
  No poet now or sage ;
But just a Jewish man,
To mar and spoil my plan
  And to redeem the age.

A poet would be mine !—
He'd dream of stars that shine
  Within the purple sky !
He'd dream of waves that break
Along the bright-edged lake,
  And not of God on high !

A poet I can win
By fragrance of sweet sin :
  No poet can redeem.
Singers of Greece and Rome,
What were their vows but foam
  Upon a wind-tossed stream ?

Set woman in the way,
What singer strives, I pray,
  For the Lord God to fight ?
All singers I can snare
By meshes of dark hair
  And gleam of bosom white.

All sages I can seize,
And mould them as I please :
  I use their pride of brain.
I move them to rebel :
I curtain my dark hell,
  And let Law seem to reign.

I teach them starry lore :
The waves break on the shore
  With steady rise and fall—
"What God," they say, "is here ?
Ah ! man has nought to fear :
  The priests mislead us all.

"We will be gods indeed ;
We sketch out Reason's creed ;
  We pierce beyond the fair
Still starlit height of blue—
We search it through and through,
  And lo ! no God is there."

So sages say, and boast—
Hunting in vain the ghost
  Of God along the sky.
So poets sing, and fall—
Yea, I control them all :
  To each heart I am nigh.

But now this man may be
Stronger, perchance.—The sea
  And stars may be his slaves.
He may note God behind
The clarions of the wind,
  The trumpets of the waves.

He may discern the Lord
Behind the lightning's sword :
   In God his soul may trust.
I can seduce the wise,
And flash through poets' eyes :
   I cannot harm the just !

II.

Long have I struggled, long !
The Lord of hosts is strong :
   But I am strong as well.
If he can rule the sky,
Pure, starlit, sunlit, high,
   I am the lord of hell.

If he can make the pure
Girl-heart, I can allure
   Fair women to my feet.
I can make all things strange :
The pure heart I can change :
   I can make sinning sweet.

If he can make the wife,
True, yielding up her life,
   Her whole soul, to her king,
I can create in turn
The harlot, whose lips burn,
   Whose ardent kisses cling.

I own not yet defeat.
I can make evil sweet ;

Yes, to the heart of man.
This Jesus—who is he?
Can he lash all the sea
   To madness, as I can?

Can he sting all the heart
By deadly subtle art
   To madness and to lust?
Change Greek or Roman sage
To madman?   Ruin an age?
   Smite temples into dust?

Can he, this Jesus, fill
Through his own force of will
   A pure girl's eyes with light
Impure?—Can Jesus make
The faithful wife forsake,
   Smiling, the path of right?

Can Jesus fill the air
With wild cries of despair,
   When warriors meet and slay?
I am the stronger, I.
This champion I defy.
   My force shall win the day.

Aye : I will tempt this man.
He shall assist my plan.
   He shall be part of me :
Shall know that I am lord ;
Shall bow beneath my sword ;
   Shall humbly bend the knee.

I will create for him
Some woman fair of limb,
   And fair of face, and sweet.
Her face and fair gold head
Shall lure him to her bed ;
   Aye, he shall kiss her feet.

Jesus !   Thou shalt redeem
The world ?   O futile dream !
   Yet dream,—yea, dream thy fill.
Dream thou that God is great ;
Then find, and find too late,
   That I am greater still.

Find, as ten thousand hearts
Have found, that God departs
   When Satan waxes strong.
Mine is the force that wins :
Man seeks me when he sins,
   And never seeks me long.

And woman seeks me too.—
Some girl, with eyes of blue,
   Stands at her mother's door.
She'd like a sweetheart ?   Well :
That's the first step to hell !
   I bring her one,—and more.

Yea, step by step I sink
Her soul, till on the brink
   Of hell she pauses, white
With dread.—Another year
Will see her laugh and leer
   With harlots, through the night.

So need I in this hour
Fear Jesus, dread his power?
   Nay, I will bring him low!
One moment he shall reign:
Then 'mid the world's disdain,
   Rejected, he shall go.

O God, O Lord of hosts,
Thine armies are as ghosts,
   Pale spectres in the sun!
Always that spirit can win
Who will tempt man to sin,
   For man and sin are one.

SONG OF THE STAR OF BETHLEHEM.

Lo! this night the Lord descending
  Comes on earth to dwell.
Evil's bitter reign is ending,
  And the power of hell.

Neither Greek nor Roman poet,
  Great-souled though they be,
Read God's secret.—Who shall know it?
  Darkness, or the sea?

Greek and Roman, full of learning,
  Full of strength and might,
Sought for God, their strong hearts yearning
  Godward in the night.

Wise men worshipped God for ages;
  Builded temples grand:
Graved their souls on deathless pages;
  Wrought in many a land.

All these sought for God, and found him,
  In a measure,—each:
Sought for God, and loved, and crowned him;
  Secrets all could teach.

But to-night the love immortal
　Through the gate of time   .
Passes : makes life's fleshly portal
　Evermore sublime.

Woman now is pure for ever,
　No more man's sad slave.
Let man's heart disdain her never
　Whom God bends to save !

Through her sweet lips cometh sorrow
　Sometimes—let that be !
When the bright dawn breaks to-morrow
　Over land and sea ;

When we weary stars are turning
　Homeward to our rest ;
When the golden sun is burning
　On the mountain's crest ;

Light yet nobler this shall presage :
　For to-morrow morn
Through the world shall thrill the message
　" Jesus Christ is born ! ".

III.

THE FOUR TEMPTERS.

1st Spirit.

'Tis the old story!   God in heaven is weary.
He finds the converse of his angels dreary :
  So stoops again to earth, and longs to save.

2nd Spirit.

Yes, the old story.   The same end will follow.
Christ will trust man ; will find each promise hollow :
  Then hear man's laughter ringing round his grave.

3rd Spirit.

So many spirits have failed !   Great souls have spoken.
Strong souls have loved the race,—have died heart-broken.
  This Jesus !   Joseph's and pale Mary's son !

4th Spirit.

He'll fail, as all have failed.   I'll set before him,
When eighteen years have winged their swift way o'er him,
  A woman.   Then his task will soon be done.

1st Spirit.

Thou dreamest ever thus !   The old plan thou bringest.
Ever of woman's eyes and lips thou singest.
  What if he be impervious after all?

4th Spirit.

Was ever man impervious yet to beauty?
Did ever sweet love fail to conquer duty?
What man yet failed to answer woman's call?

2nd Spirit.

There is a method surer.   I will proffer
Kingship and power supreme, and by mine offer
The heart of Jesus will be straightway caught.

3rd Spirit.

Thou knowest nought!   I've watched his mother, Mary.
In no large point the son's desires will vary.
He will love simple ways, and quiet thought.

1st Spirit.

Nay! for his father, though his means be meagre,
Hath ardent brain, and spirit rash and eager:
Jesus will glow with philosophic pride.

3rd Spirit.

Fool! I will bring him blossoms from the meadows.
Stars shall he study 'mid the night's dark shadows:
Flowers shall he gather from Gennesaret's side.

2nd Spirit.

Power is the best of all, the gift most luring.
Wealth gives a man the best means for securing
Both women-flowers and flowers that gem the grove.

4th Spirit.

No flower within the woods hath half the splendour
Of woman, when her fragrant lips surrender.
   Christ will succumb to the old strong god—Love.

1st Spirit.

Rather I'll set his eager swift brain working :
Develop every germ of wild thought lurking
   Therein, till seed-thoughts rise into a tree.

4th Spirit.

Philosophy is like a clear swift river :
It bounds along ; its reeds and rushes quiver.
   Thought is the stream.   But passion is the sea.

3rd Spirit.

I'll lead him forth beside the bluest fountains :
His feet shall brush the dews upon the mountains :
   He'll count the stars through the clear Syrian air.

4th Spirit.

And when he beds upon the sand at nights,
How he will weary of your cold delights !
   How he will wish to find a woman there !

1st Spirit.

Fail—this he must.   The world is in our power.
Greece sank.   Rome sways and founders at this hour.
   God dreams that he through Christ will make all new.

2nd Spirit.

God ever dreams ; and, while he dreams, we labour.
His angels sing : but we wield spade and sabre.
  We drive fierce keels across the tossing blue !

3rd Spirit.

Ah ! how we maddened when the Roman legions
Made the red streets of Carthage like to regions
  Infernal—those we know and love so well.

4th Spirit.

Yes : not entirely has our vigour vanished.
If but this Christ can be destroyed, or banished,
  Earth will be nearly as sweet a home as hell.

2nd Spirit.

Try him with woman, try him with temptation
Persistent.   Let him save from degradation
  Some woman.   Then let her degrade in turn.

4th Spirit.

I have my scheme.   He shall redeem from sorrow.
She whom he saved shall love him on the morrow.
  Her very saviour shall with passion burn.

1st Spirit.

But keep the fiery thought of passion hidden ;
Till suddenly, awake, alive, unbidden,
  Hot passion bounds upon them like a flame.

4th Spirit.

Trust me.   I gave Delilah strong-armed Samson.
His kisses crushed her red mouth like a damson.
    Ah ! . . . she lay still.   But yet the morning came.

3rd Spirit.

And if thou failest, I will bring a quiet
White blossom.   Not perhaps by passion's riot—
    Perhaps by simpler means—this man will fall.

Enter Satan.   *He speaks.*

Peace.—I will win by strategy supremer.
I will do homage to this prophet-dreamer.
    He shall be worshipped as the king of all.

Then, when far lands have owned their lord,
    And worshipped him from sea to sea,
I'll change his sceptre to a sword,
    Man's worship to malignity.

Yea, friend from friend shall break and part,
    Mother from son, and man from wife,
And tender heart from tender heart :
    The love of Christ shall 'gender strife.

Blood shall be poured upon the land
    (All in the name of Christ and God).
A sword shall flash in every hand :
    Deep-red shall be Christ's future road.

This is my victory.   Tempt him not :
  Or strive to tempt him—as ye please.
I'll build him fanes in every spot,
  And win the world by means of these.

He shall be worshipped far and wide,
  Aye, till the very ends of time.
He shall be set on high beside
  The Father, on a throne sublime.

Then man shall cease to see the eyes
  Of God, shall watch Christ's eyes instead :
Shall dream of heaven and golden skies,
  And quite forget earth's sunsets red.

No inspiration ever yet
  Of grander import stormed my brain
Than this,—to let the people set
  Christ beside God, to let him reign.

Let Christ man's endless idol be !
  Let man forget the truths he taught !
So shall eternal victory
  Be mine, beyond our highest thought.

IV

SONG OF WOMEN-SPIRITS.

God at last has heard our crying.
　Through the ages past
We have sought him, groaning, sighing :
　He has heard at last.

Man has mocked us through the ages,
　Goaded to despair.
Poets, thinkers, soldiers, sages,
　All have called us fair.

All have praised our lips and tresses,
　Golden locks or black :
All have sought our love-caresses :
　All have held us back.

All have checked our souls' aspiring :
　All have dreaded this.
This has tired men, never tiring
　Of the lips they kiss.

All have dreaded lest the morning
　Which should find us free
Would be wild with note of warning
　Rung by land and sea !

Not one noble soul has trusted ;
   Roman, Jew, or Greek.
Many and many a sword had rusted,
   Had they let us speak !

Many and many a fierce old quarrel
   Had been lulled to rest !
Ours the myrtle, man's the laurel,
   Man's the battle-crest.

Half the spears that maddening hurtle
   Through the loud rent air
Still had rested, had our myrtle
   Seemed to man's heart fair !

Had man listened to our pleading,
   To our age-long cry,
Battle-fields where he lay bleeding,
   Waiting there to die,

Had been fields of corn and clover,
   Full of peace supreme :
Had but man, our age-long lover,
   Listened to our dream !

For our dream is sweet and holy,
   Full of peace and grace.
Slowly, slowly,—slowly, slowly,—
   We shall win our place.

We shall win man's adoration
   In a nobler sphere,
Rule through him some future nation :
   For our Prince is here.

God, in sending Christ, is sending
　　Woman victory.
God at last is mixing, blending,
　　Strength and purity.

Not their old song-god Apollo,
　　Bright of face and limb,
Is the god for us to follow :
　　Nay ! we need not him.

Songs are sweet, and singers sweeter :
　　Full of charm was each
Old-world bard, and old-world metre,
　　Yet they fail to reach

Woman's soul as Christ's deep phrases
　　Reach her heart and ear.
Every word of his amazes :
　　Rings out pure and clear.

Woman loves at last—who waited
　　Through the ages long,
Weary, saddened, worn, ill-mated,
　　Void of heart for song.

God, who gave the generations
　　Of the past most dim
Unto man, gives future nations
　　Not, oh not, to him !

Woman's is the future season.
　　Christ's and woman's day
Dawns at last : the end of treason,
　　Swords and spears that slay.

Lord, we thank thee that thou hearest
  Woman's piteous prayer.
Christ's chief word, his message clearest,
  Sweetest and most fair,

Is the news that woman never
  Now need dread man's scorn.
Woman now is safe for ever:
  Jesus Christ is born !

V

MARY MAGDALENE.

I fall, O Lord, before thy feet,
For thou hast taught me things most sweet
      Most pure, most grand.
Behold! I longed to conquer thee;
But am content—if this may be—
      To kiss thine hand.

I dreamed of love, and passion wild,
But now, O Lord, am reconciled
      To loveless hours.
Thou art so vast in purity!
I dreamed of sin; but, thanks to thee,
      I dream of flowers.

Thou art my God: for thou hast taught
Truths reaching far beyond man's thought,
      Deep truths and grave.
While other men defile, deflower,
Thou usest thine immortal power
      To lift and save.

As man had made me, lo! I came,
A woman full of sin and shame
      And woe and care;

With but one sweet thing left to show—
The endless glory and the glow
    Of my gold hair.

This, therefore, Lord, I give to thee :
The one sweet pure thing left in me,
    Golden, divine.
These locks that once were wanton gold
Around thy sacred feet I fold
    For loving sign.

As man had made me, unto thee
I came : paths of iniquity
    My feet had trod.
Shameless I was, and lost alas !
As thou hast made me, I can pass
    Straight up to God.

VI

THE FOUR WATCHERS UPON CALVARY.

I.—SATAN.

Thus ends the solemn farce.—He dies.
The same stars watch him from the skies
    Who watched the death in deserts lone
Of Arab kings, his ancestors :
He passes to the unknown shores,
    And ends his mission with a groan.

The stars are ever unto me
Subservient ministers. The sea
    Is ever my subservient slave.
The stars have watched so many die !
The sea has choked so many a sigh
    With its unsympathetic wave !

But neither stars nor moon nor sea,
Though all are ministers of me,
    Have ever watched a death like this.
The Son of God who came to reign,
Writhing in agonies of pain,
    Expires, with that damp sponge to kiss !

Stars, shining over deserts lone,
Behold your Saviour on his throne !—
  Moon, glimmering over wastes of sea,
Behold his pain-drawn, bloodless face !
Mock, moon, with leering white grimace
  The silent corpse on Calvary.

II.—JUDAS.

She will not love him now.—He hangs,
Pierced by the red nails' iron fangs ;
  A sight to rouse a woman's scorn.
A corpse ? No woman cares for this !
They love warm living lips to kiss.
  They love the rose, without its thorn !

He loses, and I win, the day.
When she and I are old and grey,
  What memory will abide of him ?
His corpse within the tomb will rot,
And she and I above the spot
  Shall wander through the moonlight dim.

She loved him. Now her love is mine.
By all these bright glad stars that shine,
  For ever she is mine alone !
I win the woman by my deed.
Where Jesus failed, I shall succeed,
  And draw her sweet lips to my own.

He loved as dreamers love. But I
Who feared no thunders of God's sky
  So only that my love was won,

While he in dismal realms below
With white ghosts wanders to and fro,
    Shall walk with her beneath the sun.

III.—MARY MAGDALENE.

He dies, and I am left alone.—
The man to whom my soul was known
    As no man else will know it now
Hangs bleeding there, in death-like swoon.
I watch his pale face 'neath the moon,
    And watch the red drops on his brow.

Jesus : thou canst not hear my cry !
O silent height of starlit sky,
    Bear witness that I loved him well !
He lifted me from depths unknown,
And raised me to a spotless throne,
    And did not loathe the soul that fell.

Bear witness, moon, and stars, and sky,
That I will love him till I die !
    A woman, when she loves, is grand.
A man is sometimes strong : but oh !
When woman loves, she worships so
    That angels stoop and kiss her hand.

Could I but bring him back to life !
Then lead him from the paths of strife,
    And watch once more spring's flowers in bloom
His brown eyes gazed so straight in mine,
With love so perfect and divine
    It seemed to reach beyond the tomb.

IV.—MARY, THE MOTHER OF JESUS.

Had he but listened to my plea !—
He trusted his own brain, and he
    Upon the dismal dark cross dies.
The Holy God of Israel's race,
From whom he turned aside his face,
    Would have sent angels from his skies !

But no : he lived and thought, alone.
He set a new God on the throne
    Of the Eternal, Israel's King.
The old traditions to despise
Is never safe, is never wise :
    With unchanged notes the young birds sing.

Each summer, the same flowers are fair.
The same sun kisses the same air
    To warmth and beauty, every June.
Yes : over thunderous Sinai,
Through awful depths of lurid sky,
    Once glittered this, to-night's same moon !

But he, my Jesus, would have nought
Save of his own creative thought,
    And now that thought's strange task is done :
The " Father "—whom he sought by night—
Has robbed the world of genius-light,
    And robbed a mother of her son.

THE RAPTURE OF MARY.

I sought the rock-hewn sepulchre :
　　Beside the dead is woman's place.
I chafed the dead hands, pale and fair :
　　I kissed the fair dead face.

What mattered it ? my lord was dead.
　　Upon the cold damp rock he lay.
I gathered to my breast his head,
　　And brushed the earth away.

It was so sweet to be alone
　　At last, though utterly forlorn,
With him—my darling, yea my own !
　　My king of all men born !

It was so sweet to feel that now
　　I quite might love him, quite might kiss
The dead white glory of his brow :
　　That God had given me this.

That God, who gave me many a time
　　Live love, and turned my love to scorn,
Had given me now a love sublime—
　　Sublime, and crowned with thorn.

That God had led me past the alarms
  Of earth to this calm marriage-room,
And placed my husband in my arms;
    Here, in this darkling tomb.

Beyond all words it was divine,
  Divinely glad, divinely sweet,
To know that now he was quite mine ;
    Mine, head and hands and feet.

I kissed the death-print of the nails :
  I tore the shrouding cloths aside.
My lips went travelling past the veils
    Of death.   I was his bride !

Quite fearless now, I kissed the bloom
  Of his dead lips.   I kissed them hard.
I was his wife within the tomb.
    I kissed the forehead scarred.

He was so cold to hold and kiss !
  I warmed his bosom with my own.
" By this perchance," I thought, " by this
    I may at last atone !

" I was a harlot in my life :
  The love of man brought shame and grief.
But now in death I am a wife,
    And oh the vast relief !

" I found no husband in the days
  Of youth and joy and girlish bloom :
But now my husband's hand I raise,
    And kiss it in the tomb.

" Upon the earth I was most fair.
   Men loved me, in their fashion—yes !
But now I spread my golden hair,
   Just like the sun's caress,

" Upon the cold dead breast adored
   Which now, at last, I love alone.
In life he was my far-off lord :
   In death he is my own."

BOOK II

A MASQUE OF HUMAN LIFE.

DIALOGUE

BETWEEN THE SPIRIT OF LOVE, THE SPIRIT OF LIFE, AND THE SPIRIT OF DEATH.

DIALOGUE.

Spirit of Life.

Through all that is I pour my being's sweetness :
  I fill earth's grassy floors that stretch afar
With heavenly blossoms, rounding to completeness
  Each golden sunflower, each white clover-star.

From hill to hill I pass.   The blue clear fountains
  Admit my touch, and leap up every one.
I wake the buds to life.   I thrill the mountains
  With morning kiss of the voluptuous sun.

I speak.—Flowers rise, snow-petalled, crimson-hearted.
  Birds carrying sunset stamped upon their plumes
Flash through dark groves where sunlight never darted.
  I point.—Gold lichen gilds the very tombs.

Spirit of Love.

And I add colour deeper far, and sweeter,
  Than any flowing from thy hand, O Life !
Thou art the poet.   But I choose his metre.—
  Thou mould'st the husband only : I the wife.—

Thou leftest Adam in the garden olden,
   Lonely among the gem-like flowers and fruits
But I brought Eve with gracious locks all-golden ;
   I gave the birds their passionate harps and lutes

What is thine evening worth ?   What joy comes after
   Thy cold white moon above the garden gleams,
Unless a woman's eyes and loving laughter
   Fill man with joy, and all the stars with dreams ?

Spirit of Death.

And I wait silent,—I, the spirit deathless.
   I slay the sunset at each set of sun.
Ah! Life, my cold breath leaves your blossoms breathless :
   Ah ! Love, I kiss before man's kiss is done.

Ah ! Life and Love—ye twain may struggle forward,
   Your offspring may clasp hands within the ship ;
One breath of mine can hurl the vessel shoreward
   And fix it in the black rock's iron grip.

I watch your work.   Your tale of love and passion
   Is sweet.   Yet anguish racks the human breast
In such fierce earnest, such tempestuous fashion,
   That in the end all hearts shall love me best.

Spirit of Life.

I gain my strength, O Death, from combat endless :
   My mighty valour springs from hate of thee.
All suns and stars adore me.   Thou art friendless :
   Lost as an iceberg in a shoreless sea.

Struggle.—Thy challenge I accept for ever.
　Through ceaseless æons thou and I contend.
Aye, it may be the blood-stained duel never
　Shall wholly close, till one of us shall end.

I mass my conscripts drawn from strange far regions ;
　I range my squadrons on time's boundless plain :
I hurl the force of my imperial legions
　Against thee, Death, again and yet again.

Spirit of Love.

These shall not conquer.　Love is conqueror solely.
　Not by brute force is Death the king disarmed.
The sword and trumpet fail.　Thine host fails wholly.
　In front of thee Death wears a cuirass charmed.

Love conquers Death.　Death's warriors, fierce, vain-glorious,
　Thy stern embattled hosts shall not dismay.
Death met by blood and death must be victorious :
　Death shrieks with rapture in the foremost fray.

Death only once has failed.—When hate infernal
　Against the Christ ranked Roman spear and sword,
Hate helpless fell before the love eternal
　And Death cried, "Love, thou art my rightful Lord !"

Spirit of Death.

And if I failed, O Love and Life, to cheer me
　The centuries bring me victims hour by hour.
What mattered one man, if whole nations fear me ?
　I shatter suns and stars.　What of a flower ?

One man escaped?　I revel in destruction
　　Of races whom their Father cannot save.
The ironclad ship sinks at my white waves' suction :
　　Your noblest hero blenches at his grave.

Thou singest, Love, of passion's silvery laughter,
　　Of lips of woman, and her glances fair :—
Wherever thou canst tread, my foot creeps after ;
　　The tenderest passion issues in despair.

THE MASQUE.

I

THE CHILD.

Before the child the world expands,
And dreams of green or sunny lands
   Float in upon his soul from space.
Each child upon the planet born
Brings back that planet's early morn
   In the sweet sunrise of his face.

The world for each is re-create,
And each may meet and conquer Fate,
   And mould his life to woe or weal.
For each the sea again is blue ;
For each the mountain-summits new ;
   For each the morning bugles peal.

For each God sheds his glory again
On hill and dell and lake and plain :
   To each he brings his flowers anew.
He paints for each the lily white,
And hangs with lamps the dome of night,
   And paints the sky's great ceiling blue.

Aye, through the heart of every child
Flows somewhat of the rapture wild

Which Adam felt, when first aware
At nightfall of the starry deep
From which the Lord God watched the sleep
   Of flowers that bloomed in Eden's air.

In every child the race resumes
Its youth.   Among the garden blooms
   The young child wanders forth.   It sees
With sinless eyes the snowdrop white ;
The cornfield's blaze of golden light ;
   The round-head red anemones.

All is so new, all is so sweet.
The cold is glad, and glad the heat :
   The wintry ice brings pleasant dreams.
What if the winds of winter roar ?
Down to the pond the skaters pour :
   They skate, till out the pale moon gleams.

Nature has lessons for the man :
With other eyes he learns to scan
   The mountains, and the heights of space.
But never colour gleams so fair
As sunset-hues in soft June air
   Upon an upturned boyish face.

From out the air, within the sea,
The radiant sense of joys to be
   Speaks to the boy's heart, or the child's.
The red-eyed roach, the banded perch :
The white trunk of the silver birch :
   The purple heather of the wilds :

The spotted trout, that flashes down
Along the ripples golden-brown
    Of the fern-bordered mountain-stream :
The woods, alive with cawing rooks :
The deep-blue weeded river-nooks
    Where lie the barbel and the bream :

The butterflies, white, yellow, blue,
That haunt the woods, or flutter through
    The clover-fields beside the sea :
The beetles flashing one by one
Across the gravel in the sun :
    The azure sky's infinity :

All gather depth of meaning strange
From the boy's heart.—All shift and change
    Their meaning with the growing years.
The whole of Nature seems to wait
On mankind ; changes with his state,
    And shares his hopes and shares his fears.

From out the air a message speaks
That flushes through the boy's bright cheeks ;
    The gates of wonder never close.
God whispers through the nights of June
Of something lovelier than the moon,
    And something sweeter than the rose.

II

THE YOUTH.

Life thrills me through with all its mighty power :
　　Lord of my darling's heart, I rule the whole.
I reach the golden heart of every flower ;
　　I apprehend the starry night's deep soul.

Love touches all things into sweeter bloom,
　　Transfigures common things, till heavenly light
Gleams from the emerald moss on every tomb
　　And from the smallest blossom pure and white.

I love.　And therefore heaven and God are true :
　　Christ's resurrection was no woman's dream.
Because I love, the sky is ever blue :
　　Because I love, the stars shall alway gleam.

Because I love, I understand the love
　　That led God's heart to suffer for the race.
God died for all, his love for all to prove,
　　As I would die for one belovéd face.

If I thus love, can God love less than I ?
　　The Ruler of the spheres love less than man ?
The God whose breath pervades eternity,
　　Can time-born Satan intercept his plan ?

Nay ! all shall end in joy.   All troubles pass.
 Did not I just now kiss my darling's hand ?
Chirp, merrier cricket, from the tall green grass !
 Break, bluer seas, upon a whiter land !

Sing, happier birds, from leaves more soft and dense !
 O gold-finch, chanting from yon apple-tree,
God's love which made the heaven a nest immense
 For all the stars, made thy small nest for thee !

For thee and for thy love he made the small
 Sweet nest of moss and straw and twigs that holds
Your four eggs safe, as heaven's nest holdeth all
 The gold stars safe within its cloudy folds.

And for my love and me he made the earth,
 And all its azure skies, and all its flowers.
" Love on," he said : " Rejoice with tenderest mirth,
 And seek the fields while I hold back the showers.

" I set upon the hedge the scented may
 That thou might'st pluck it.   And I made some white,
Some red : the red may for your wedding-day,
 The white pure blossom for your wedding-night.

" I made laburnum, yellow, starry, fair,
 That ye might gather this and be content ;
Not craving for star-blossoms of the air,
 But gathering here the golden bloom I sent.

" And I made lilac—purple flowers and white :
 The silvery bloom for her, the deep for thee.
And I sent breakers dark and breakers bright
 To be your coursers over the wide sea.

" All things in double forms I made for you :
  The chestnut-blossoms red, the blossoms pale ;
The crocus sunlike in its fiery hue,
  The crocus white as thy love's wedding-veil.

" I made the golden sun to light your day :
  I made the silver moon's less garish light.
I gave the nightingale his amorous lay,
  And bade him chant it on your bridal night.

" When the first star lay, resting in my hand,
  Poised, ere I hurled it forth upon the deep,
In my far-seeing thought your love I planned
  And chose star-warders for your nuptial sleep.

" Before the first flower blossomed, I ordained
  Within my soul the blossoms she should wear.
Ere time began, within my thought I stained
  Deep-red the poppies for her deep-black hair.

" And, as time onward sped, through rose on rose
  I poured the sweetness and the fragrant bliss
Which, quite perfected now, her lips disclose,
  And culled from flowers the sweetness of her kiss."

*   *

So God said, having us in his regard,
  Us two, and us alone, my love and me ;
As if the whole sublime heaven, golden-starred,
  Were made to light one inlet of the sea.

As if the sun were for a single flower
  Created,—for one blue-bell in a lane :
As if creation's every previous hour
  Were preparation for our final reign.

So ever will we reign, my love and I :
　The one thing deathless is a love like ours.
It gathers depth from the unmeasured sky :
　It gathers sweetness from the whole world's flowers.

My love is mine for ever.　I am hers.
　Nought charms me save the royalty in her look.
At her least touch my being thrills and stirs
　To-day, as at her first long glance it shook.

No love that changes is the love supreme :
　No love that falters is the love divine.
Death would not wake me from my passionate dream :
　No love that tires of love is love like mine.

For sooner could God's hand displace the sun,
　Or hush the drum-roll of the stormy sea,
Or, having made stars countless, leave not one,
　Than quench the unending fire of love in me.

III

THE DAUGHTERS OF EVE, THE TEMPTRESS.

The soul of man is troubled much ;
    Man toils from day to day ;
Yet woman soothes him by a touch,
    And fans his cares away.
If man at morn looks half in scorn
    On woman—let her wait !
All men at night must seek delight
    And pass love's golden gate.

The heart of man is weary indeed,
    Tired out with victories won :
It moulds and unmoulds many a creed;
    It plots beneath the sun.
Let woman wait !   The golden gate
    Of love must open soon.
Man's thoughts by day are grim and grey ;
    They change beneath the moon.

The woman's kingdom from of old
    Has been the kingdom fair
That is not won by sword or gold,
    But by her golden hair.

Man worships gold, yet from of old
  Has worshipped chiefly this—
Her golden hair, and found it fair,
  Though less sweet than her kiss.

Let man pursue his path by day :
  Aye, let him deem he rules
The wide earth with imperial sway,
  And that we are his tools !
Our tool is he : for straightway, see,
  One kiss can change his schemes.
One swift kiss dealt !   Away doth melt
  The fabric of his dreams !—

Man flashes through the battle-smoke
  And mixes in the fray,
While under shade of elm or oak
  We pass the summer day.
Man draws his sword upon some horde
  Of foes, in deadly fight !
For all his strength, he yields at length,
  And seeks our lips at night.

Man worships.   Aye, he worships well,
  And builds cathedrals fair,
And shapes his schemes of heaven and hell,
  Plans who shall enter there.
But all these plans are works of man's :
  God made us to destroy
Man's every scheme by love's wild dream
  And passion's larger joy.

Man prays and vows, and struggles high
   Towards God and heavenly air.
He points his ladder towards the sky,
   And hopes to enter there.
His own wild plan can hoodwink man :
   He dreams of heavenly bliss,
And yet would sell his soul to hell
   For one sweet harlot's kiss.

Man dreams of jewelled gates of heaven
   And rich gold-paven floors :
His heart, he thinks, to God is given ;
   He loves, and he adores :
The shaven saint may nobly paint
   The heaven he deems so grand—
Away it flies at woman's eyes,
   Or thrill of woman's hand !

We are the rulers of the earth :
   Its iron gates give way :
Kings soften at a woman's mirth ;
   Obedient thralls are they.
Our valorous lords can rule with swords
   The lands their prowess took ;
But sword and shield must bend and yield
   Before a woman's look.

God hardly knows our power, or he
   Perhaps had hardly cared
To grant our lips such sovereignty,—
   Perhaps had paused, or feared.

For man may love God's holy Dove
   And smooth the bright bird's breast :
It is but show ; full well we know
   Man loves a woman best.

God's angels ! ah, we know their worth—
   Poor high-souled gold-winged things !
Their song will not be famed on earth
   So long as woman sings.
The angels' helms in heavenly realms
   May glitter, and be fair ;
Man loves to rest on woman's breast,
   And toy with woman's hair.

There's something sweeter to a man
   Than honour, virtue, fame :
A single wave of woman's fan
   Can often mar a name.
The reaper leaves his golden sheaves,
   The pilot wrecks his ship,
And not for much—just once to touch,
   Unchecked, a woman's lip.

The man of science leaves his stars,
   Grows weary of the deep
Of heaven ; his head is vexed by Mars,
   But Venus gives him sleep.
One sweet June-night he slams outright
   The bright heaven's purple door ,
He loves the skies, the stars' bright eyes,
   But—he loves woman more !

Another loves to gather flowers
   On hillside, or by stream :
He's wrapt through sultry summer hours
   Within his floral dream.
And yet, when comes the summer night,
   Away the flower-dream goes !
He finds a woman's neck more white
   Than even his whitest rose.

IV

THE POET AND THE PESSIMIST.

Pessimist.

The world grows dark.—The poet's heart is dreaming;
  But when he wakes from sleep,
Will he not see proud War's red harvest gleaming
  Beneath white moons that weep?

Will he not understand the bitter anguish
  Of all things here below?
Will he not mark the flowers and green leaves languish,
  The sweet loves fade and go?

Will he not learn that God dwells at a distance,
  Far past the reach of prayer?
Will he not teach, and teach with stern insistence,
  That love is light as air?

Poet.

The world grows bright.—The golden crocus praises
  Its great Creator's hand;
The warm sun kisses the small red-tipped daisies;
  The blue sea loves the land.

The brown stream lisps along its aldered edges :
    The flashing trout darts by.
Lo, the snug nests within the hawthorn hedges,
    And eggs blue as the sky !

Not all is sorrow.—Where Death's solemn carriage
    Crawled, yesterday, along,
To-day the flowers and chariot-wheels of marriage
    And young love's fearless song !

Pessimist.

I give love just one month.—Then he'll grow weary ;
    Find sameness in her air ;
Find silvery speeches from the same tongue dreary ;
    And—if his wife be fair—

Long madly for dark eyes and darker tresses :
    Or—if brunette she be—
Prepare to sell his soul for blonde caresses
    And eyes blue as the sea.

Love is desire.   Desire is surely fleeter
    Than cloud or wind or spray.
Duty is very sweet, but pleasure's sweeter,
    And pleasure wins the day.

Poet.

Yet nobler hearts rely not on caresses ;
    They feel, as they grow old,
That true love ever deepens, though the tresses
    Are grey that once were gold.

The man and wife have fought the world together;
  Have faced life's stormy air;
Have struggled through black days and evil weather;
  Challenged, and slain, despair.

The man to-day beholds an angel treading
  Where once the woman trod;
She is content, within the man's eyes reading
  No more the man,—the god.

Pessimist.

And, if she die, how soon she'll be supplanted!
  And, if he die, how soon
(Giving her time to flaunt her crape dress—granted!)
  There'll be a honeymoon.

Man thinks he grieves at death.   Nay, he rejoices!
  There is more room to breathe.
The welcomest voice of all glad welcome voices
  Is the hoarse voice of death.

It says: " Rise up, thou live soul, take thy pleasure;
  No ghosts peer through the gloom.
Buy mistresses with all the dead man's treasure,
  And picnic at his tomb."

Poet.

In Kensal Green there stands a tomb of marble,
  And every day brings there
A loving woman—and the red-breasts warble,
  "Sweet love knows no despair."

Each day she places on the marble cover
  Some blossom fresh and new ;
'Tis meadow-sweet to-day : to-morrow clover,
  Or lilies pearled with dew.

Her husband died. God took, and she resigned him.
  Love chose that they should part ;
Life seems but one short day, at night she'll find him,
  And hold him to her heart.

V

THE ARTIST.

The other day I passed along
The Green Park, brooding o'er a song
    And fitting word to word.
Spring's mantle bright across the trees
Was gaily flung.   Bird sang to breeze,
    And breeze sang back to bird.

And first a ragged girl passed by.
Her eyes were bluer than the sky:
    Her hands looked pinched and cold.
She asked for alms.—"What hair," I thought;
"The sun's self surely has been caught
    Within its coils of gold!

"Her figure has the supple grace
Of women of the Eastern race :
    The spirit of the spring
Has surely sent her forth to-day
To meet a poet on his way
    And teach his heart to sing.

"Strange is the poet's heart," I thought ;
"A thousand eyes had noticed nought
    Of beauty in her mien.

She flashed upon me like a ray
Of sunlight, and she filled the day
　　With splendour of a queen."

Another heart perhaps had heard
The ragged suppliant's pleading word :
　　But was I negligent
In that I only saw the skies
Reflected in her deep-blue eyes,
　　And, seeing, was content ?

If I had dreamed of vulgar pence,
Could I have dreamed the dream intense
　　That filled my heart with light ;
My singing shall immortalize
Her golden hair, her deep-blue eyes,
　　Even if she died that night !

What has a singer's heart to do
With common thoughts ? Her eyes were blue :
　　I saw them, and I dreamed.
Now was not that God's work for me?
To look, and with my soul to see
　　The shades that in them gleamed ?

When Christ bestowed upon the blind
New sight, had he a poet's mind,
　　Dramatic, forceful, keen ?
The blind man had his fitting place :
Fate sent him there, no doubt, to grace
　　The foreground of the scene.

Not active work but song divine,
This is the poet's part. 'Twas mine
    Beneath those azure skies
To meet the girl whom through the spring
God led,—aye, just that I might sing
    The wonder of her eyes.

If Christ redeemed the world, I too
Redeemed from death those eyes of blue
    And gave them to the race.
As surely as he healed the blind,
I loved, and sang, and gave mankind
    Another deathless face.

        *   *

And then there passed a couple gay,
Out, clearly, for a holiday,
    English to tips of toes.
A Paisley shawl of varied sheen
She wore : she wore a bonnet green,
    With ribbons all of rose.

He wore upon his legs and back
Thick English cloth—the eternal black
    That clothes eternally
The manhood of the English race.
A pleasant smile lit up his face,
    That did one good to see.

Oh how he worshipped, right content,
The lovely girl whom heaven had sent
    To be his sweetheart-queen !

    E

He loved her in her Paisley shawl ;
He loved its fringe's graceful fall ;
    He loved her bonnet green.

He loved and worshipped : worshipped too
The flaring gown of brilliant blue
    And ribbons all of rose.
Would he be faithful ? Faithful—aye !
Right faithful, till his dying day,
    To ribbons, and to nose.

What did it matter unto him
That grey eyes were a trifle dim,
    And hardly dim the dress :
The nose ill-shaped, complexion bad ?
He saw, he loved her, and was glad.
    She was a goddess—Yes !

He had the English sense of form.
Her patent-leather boots by storm
    Took this poor tradesman's heart.
Beneath the shining boots, no doubt,
Great bunions strove to struggle out
    And made the stitches start.

That did not matter. Not the least !
The tradesman's simple heart was pleased :
    Not Venus could have given
With shapeliest limbs of snowy white
To his true heart such keen delight,
    And keen delight is heaven.

So this poor girl in brilliant blue,
My grocer friend, brought heaven to you :
    And what brings heaven to me ?
We artists are another race,
English perhaps in form and face,
    But Greek in sympathy.

His strange keen insight into form,
Though eyeless crowds about him swarm,
    Must set the artist's mind
In lonely grandeur quite apart
From those who understand not Art,
    The cattle of mankind.

" The nude " they scoff at.   As if God,
When Eve his radiant daughter trod
    The grass of Paradise,
Sent milliners from Regent Street
To strap her waist, and clenched her feet
    Within a leather vice !

As if he brought to Adam there
A being whose feet—could you but bare
    Those organs, leather-pent—
Would to pale Adam's gaze disclose
A gnarled conglomerate of toes
    Distorted, crumpled, bent.

As if he copied from the life
An English girl, or English wife,
    Stiff, starched, be-collared, prim,

And brought her, booted, blushing red,
To Adam waiting lone, and said
    " Behold thine Eve ! " to him.

      *   *

And then I thought, " How easy indeed
For that poor grocer to succeed
    In winning heavenly bliss !
He will be faithful to his wife,
No doubt, throughout his vulgar life,
    Nor seek another's kiss.

" No yearning, strange and sweet and sad,
Pervades his spirit.   He takes with glad
    Content what God has given.
His wife, with shapeless lips and nose,
Is unto him a very rose
    Gathered in heights of heaven.

" Let God recruit his angels thus !
But as for artists, as for us,
    Another heaven we seek.
The heaven of beauty—that is ours.
We worship colour in the flowers :
    We love form, like the Greek.

" A curve of eyebrow leads astray
Our spirit through a marvelling day.
    We love.   And where's the harm ?
Yes : Joseph lacked the artistic sense,
Else he would not have ta'en offence
    When beauty sought to charm.

" For woman moulds all things anew.
She adds fresh glory to the blue
    Of heaven, and one by one
She shapes the stars. The lily bright
Without her touch were hardly white :
    She recreates the sun.

" Each day the artist turns with scorn
From past loves. Are not flowers new-born
    With dews of every day ?
To him the one sin is fatigue.
This morning last night's dream's a league,
    A league and more, away !

" For, like to God, he can create.
Born every day, through morning's gate
    He passes,—meets the blue
Of each fresh morn with loving eyes,
And woman ever brings surprise,
    And love is ever new.

" A thousand dreams have past away :
The artist is as keen to-day
    As ever in first love's hours.
Each evening, when the stars arise,
He gathers dreams from woman's eyes
    As moths draw sweets from flowers.

" Each evening he can say, ' I love.
By all God's golden stars above
    I never loved before !

I never gazed in eyes like thine :
I feel thy soul is made for mine
    To trust in and adore ! '

" Each summer morning he can swear,
' I love the sunlight in thine hair
    As I loved never yet ! '
What other souls repent of long
Turns in the artist's soul to song,
    But never to regret."

VI

THE POET.

O artist dreaming thus thy life away,
  There is a higher life than thou canst guess.
Art thou a poet? sweet love answers, "nay."
  Was Christ a poet? woman answers, "yes."

The highest poethood is ever this:
  To love as Christ loved, and to save the race.
Not to spend wild years, seeking kiss on kiss,
  But to draw forth the soul in woman's face.

To aid the weary, and to lift the low:
  To show God's pity in the human sphere:
Besought by sorrow, never to say "no":
  To lend the helpless heart a ready ear:

To honour woman, and, if woman slip,
  To stand by ready, with strong outstretched hand,
As God sends starlight to the struggling ship,
  Or the staunch life-boat pulling from the land:

This is true poethood.—Aye, not to love
  The rose the less, but to love virtue more:
Not to love earth less in that, far above,
  The poet sees the stars that sail or soar.

Hast thou God's vision? art thou part of him?
  Can thine eye, steady, mocking at fatigue,
Traverse vast spaces where man's eye grows dim,
  Pursuing phantom star-ships, league on league?

Art thou so near to God thou canst not pray,
  Since prayer is offered to a distant form?
Thy church, heaven's blue dome on a summer day?
  Thy hymns, the staves that thunder through a storm?

Canst thou through throbbing heart and thrilling nerve
  Feel God's life tingle? canst thou, looking up,
Discern God's sculpture in the rainbow curve,
  Or, glancing downward, in the tulip's cup?

Is woman unto thee past measure more
  Than unto fools and grovellers of the race?
God's woman-nature sent us to adore?
  One moment's glimpse of the eternal face?

Canst thou, beholding her, behold God's sense
  Of form in every curve of neck and limb?
God's deep love, insupportably intense,
  In the eyes that follow man and worship him?

Canst thou see what no common eye can see,
  And, penetrating far past space and time,
Be clothed upon with God's eternity—
  And, as he made the ebon night sublime

With countless stars, make generations bright
  With songs that breathe through ages yet to be
The passionate fragrance of one summer night,
  The scent of sea-weed on a mortal sea?

Then, being more than man in thought and frame,
  Be more than man in noble act as well ;
Be poet in thy deeds, not only in name ;
  Flash down song's sunshine to the depths of hell.

Thou wilt not reverence Christ ? Be more than he.
  He is not jealous. He will stand aside.
Thou hardly carest for God ? He cares for thee ;
  And he is greater, having less of pride.

If thou canst light one brief torch, he can light
  The watch-fires glimmering through the camps of space.
One lyric song perchance thine hand can write :
  He writes the Epics of the human race.

And yet he cares for thee.—Be like to him.
  Be God, if yet thou dream'st this thing can be.
Drink deep of God's life, let the cup o'er-brim.
  Deem that thy wine-glass can contain the sea !

Thou wilt not own a Master ? Be thou lord.
  So long as thou doest justice, all is well.
Thou hast to slay wrong with a fiery sword :
  What Christ's tongue left unspoken, thou must tell.

Yet, stars and suns and sunlike songs above,
  Sits the eternal Father, God unseen.
Love is the Father. Be thou perfect love
  And thou shalt be God's Son, as Christ has been.

VII

HUSBAND AND WIFE AT LORD'S.

A MODERN IDYLL.

He speaks, then
  muses :—

> " *Well hit!* "   (Ah, soft and pale she lay
> Upon my breast that summer day !
> But softer yet and yet more white
> Within my arms that summer night)—
> > *Click went the bat, click went the ball !*

She speaks, then
  muses :—

> " *Well bowled !* "   (Ah, very sweet his way
> Was, on that far-off summer day :
> And how his eyes shone fierce and bright
> With passion through that summer night)—
> > *Click went the bat, click went the ball !*

He :—

> " *Well stopped !* "   (My wife's hair shines with gold :
> My love's was black in days of old.
> Gold saddens, black hair maddens, me :
> How black it shone, splashed from the sea !)—
> > *Click went the bat, click went the ball !*

She : —

> " *Well caught !* "   (Will ever strong arms fold
> About me as did John's of old ?)
> " *Look, Harry—they are running three !* "
> (Oh that June night beside the sea !)—
> > *Click went the bat, click went the ball !*

He :—

> " *Now he'll be out !* "   (Out in the wood
> Her mouth met mine, when close we stood,
> And the world faded quite away :
> The next day was my marriage-day)—
> > *Click went the bat, click went the ball !*

She :—

> " *A drive for four !* "   (Beneath my hood
> His face leant round.   Silent we stood.
> His mouth was sweet as bloom of may.
> The morrow was my marriage-day)—
> > *Click went the bat, click went the ball !*

He :—

> " *Well saved !* "   (Ah, lips, how close you clung,
> And how that black-bird guessed and sung !
> My lady's kiss is proud and cold :
> Your kiss was young and warm and bold)—
> > *Click went the bat, click went the ball !*

She :—

> " *One wicket more !* "   (Thy lips were young :
> ' Taste of their sweets !' the brown thrush sung.
> I loved you : till I fell for gold.
> I loved you,—amorous, ardent, bold)—
> > *Click went the bat, click went the ball !*

He :—

>   " *Well fielded !* "   (Ah, the June-wind came
>   Upon us like a burning flame.
>   Thy mouth was close, thy breath was sweet,
>   I felt thy bosom's throbbing beat)—
>   > *Click went the bat, click went the ball !*

She :—

>   " *Well thrown !* "   (Ah, married years of shame
>   Have drowned love in me, dimmed its flame.
>   I wonder, were we now to meet,
>   Would one pulse in my bosom beat ?)—
>   > " *How fast these Eton wickets fall !* "

VIII

THE SCEPTIC.

I.

God made the earth exceeding good.
He clothed the hill, or clothed the wood,
  In verdurous raiment fresh and fair.
He filled the earth with living things :
With flashing of innumerous wings
  He filled the sunlit heights of air.

He filled the hollow sea with life.
Strange sea-flowers in the far depths thrive,
  And wondrous fishes, scarlet-scaled,
Dart like small flying suns along ;
And where the eager tides wax strong
  Rushes the salmon, silver-mailed.

God made the day, and made the night.
He made the sun's engrossing light
  To brighten all the daylight hours :
Then, lest the sun turn tyrant, made
The night to give soft rest and shade
  To man, and solace to the flowers.

He made the stars that shine above
The earth, and speak to man of love,
   And lead love's footsteps with their light :
The sweet and passionate stars that say,
"If man is sovereign of the day,
   Woman is priestess of the night ! "

He made the dawning sense of love
That seems a glory from above,
   A rapture sent from very far.
Upon the lips of man he set
These words " I love you," and he let
   Those words be woman's guiding-star.

Upon the woman's lips he placed
A sweetness pure, a sweetness chaste,
   A royal beauty, and a bloom
That never flower will quite attain.
He said to woman, " Love and reign.
   For love there is not any tomb."

One kingly right he gave to man ;
His right it is since time began ;
   The right of passionate address.
" I die of love.   Wilt thou not save ? "
And then the Lord to woman gave
   The right to smile, and answer " Yes."

And then God gave the lips the right
To meet, and sent the dark-winged night
   Angelic, to bring sleep and rest.
He bade the deepening twilight close
The secret whiteness of the rose,
   But ope the flower of woman's breast.

II.

Then, having made all things so fair,
God breathed upon the whole despair :
   Winter was in his bitter breath.
Where God set Love among the flowers
To make more sweet the sweetest bowers,
   He now disposed the form of Death.

Disease, and death, and misery came.
God started with a mighty aim
   But failed to carry out his plan.
With insufficient care he worked:
Or else some desperate evil lurked
   Within the clay that moulded man.

All turned out evil.   Discontent
With pain and sin and grief was blent.
   Man's whole life's effort has been this—
To ward off death.   His effort fails.
He hammers in the coffin-nails
   Upon the morrow of a kiss.

From ancient pre-historic hours,
When unrecorded hands flung flowers
   On granite cairn or flint-cut tomb ;
From days remote past speech to these,
Mankind has fiercely sought to seize
   Life's ghost retreating through the gloom.

And once man deemed his hand had caught
The skirts of Life.   Christ rose, man thought,
   And shortly would return to reign.

And still his faithful Churches say
There surely soon will come a day
   When Jesus shall be seen again.

III.

The world heeds not.   Two thousand years
Will soon have passed.   A million fears
   And hopes are dying every day.
Bright sunlight gilds the hours of noon :
At night in heaven God lights the moon :
   But Christ's step never comes our way.

It never *will* come.—When the race
Ceases to hope that Christ's same face
   Will shine, when every hope has passed,
Man's mightiest effort will have failed.
The ladder grand that should have scaled
   The heaven, will topple down at last.

This was man's Epic thought sublime.
He could not of his own force climb
   To heaven, so Christ should climb instead.
Himself could never burst the tomb,
So Christ should issue from the gloom
   Alive—the Jesus who was dead.

And when this Epic thought of man
Has wholly passed (for it began
   In dreamland, and will thither go)
What hope will then be left on earth ?
What Mary bring a Christ to birth ?
   What Peter strike a second blow ?

No Christ will help us then, my friends.—
When once a fairy story ends,
　　There is no sequel to the tale.
No second Christ will ever rise :
Nor will ye seek, if ye be wise,
　　To peer too far behind the veil.

Christ, if he opened once the tomb
And passed beyond its sombre gloom
　　Into the sunlit after-air,
Will never ope its portals twice.
It grips as in an iron vice
　　Each corpse we fling it, white and bare.

It was man's hatred, vast, supreme,
Of death which started first the dream
　　That in the struggle life might win.
Now that our loveliest dream must pass,
We are more sad and lost alas !
　　Than if the dream had never been.

IX

THE WIDOWER.

I.

Why God should take so sweet a thing
   I know not.   Sorrow drives me wild.
Why should the Lord unsheath his sword
       And point it at a child?

Why should the Lord distinguish me
   From others,—crown me with his hate?
Now she is gone, I am alone:
       Alone, I have to wait.

Now all things seem alone as well,
   Though all things seemed so different then.
The cowslip seems to have sad dreams,
       Aye, sad as those of men.

The purple foxglove seems alone:
   The yellow-hammer on the hedge
Is widower too.   The speedwell blue
       Grieves at the water's edge.

All things are sad that once were sweet :
   I never knew how much she gave.
The larch and fir lament for her :
        Laments the blue sea-wave.

The sea-beach misses now her tread :
   The ships' sails seem less silvery white.
She used to raise the sea-weed strays
        And hold them to the light.

She used to hold them in her hand
   Against the rich sky's sunset-gold.
The setting sun touched every one
        To glory manifold.

But now the sea-strays seem quite changed ;
   Poor brown, or green, or crimson leaves.
Yon white sea-bird has not one word
        Of hope for him who grieves.

There is no hope in all the world.
   My love has left me.   She is dead.
I knew till now so little how
        I loved her bright gold head.

*   *

She was a child in many things,
   And these child-women are so sweet.
Can it be like a God to strike
        A mere child off her feet ?

She sought so little, God, of thee ?
   Just to be with her husband here.
She sought not much—To feel my touch ;
        To know that I was near :

To walk with me through golden corn
   And gather poppies by the way
In summer-time.   Was that a crime?
       Didst thou for that sin slay?

For stealing poppies from thy fields,
   With here and there an ear of corn—
Is that, Lord, why she had to die?
       Could not that theft be borne?

And then, Lord God, to hurt her so!
   Was not that cruel, evil, base?
I see the young hands clenched and wrung!
       I see the sad white face!·

To hurt a child.   Is that, Lord God,
   The way to win man's love indeed?
Beside her bed, when she lay dead,
       I cursed the Christian creed.

A vast grim wanton baseless lie
   To say that "God is love" it seemed.
For she lay there; so pale and fair,
       Looking as though she dreamed.

And yet I knew that she was dead,
   And that her life had passed away
—The cruelty!—in bringing me
       A living son that day.

*   *

To think that God had thus combined
   With sons of men to treat her so!
The surgeon's knife assailed her life:
       God let that sweet life go.

You say he sent the son instead.
　　The son instead?　Curse him, I say!
His mother's life fled on the knife
　　　　　That bore him to the day.

God sent the son?　God curse the child!
　　He rent his mother's life in twain.
Beyond demur he murdered her.
　　　　　Speak not of him again.

Let me forget the living son.
　　I would not curse him, for her sake
. . . Yet, when I sleep, my curse rings deep,
　　　　　And deeper when I wake.

II.

You say she waits for me in heaven?
　　O cold poor comfort!　Fifty years
Here I may wait before heaven's gate
　　　　　Opens to prayers and tears.

To prayers and tears?　The worst of all
　　Is this,—that all man's longings cease.
In fifty years the prayers and tears
　　　　　Will yield to painless peace.

That is the worst.　She will forget
　　In heaven, and I on earth shall feel
Love steal away, slow, day by day,
　　　　　Past prayer's reach or appeal.

For love depends on sight and touch,
  And in the end all memories die.
The aging brain forgets love's pain,
      Forgets love's ecstasy.

This the deepest pang of all :
  To know that what I feel to-day
I shall not feel when long years steal
      The power of pain away

We may not meet for fifty years :
  By then, to-day will be forgot.
My eightieth year ! I shall not care
      Whether we meet or not.

            *   *

Yes, welcome even to-day's wild pang
  Beside the thought of pangless days.
Ah ! when God likes, how hard he strikes
      The shields our faint hands raise.

Through shield and corslet clean he strikes :
  No armour can withstand his sword.
Man's heart he breaks : man's joys he takes,
      With his " Thus saith the Lord ! '

And then—the cruellest thing of all,
  As far as man's dim eyes can see—
He makes the brain forget its pain :
      That waits in front of me.

That waits in front.—I shall look back,
  When thirty years have passed away :
In hues how faint will memory paint
      The feelings of to-day !

This is God's double murder. First
    He slays my darling suddenly :
Then, sure and slow, still more must go ;
        Her image next must flee.

The woman first—her picture next,
    Painted within my deepest brain.
Time blots and blurs that home of hers,
        And slays her there again.

The woman first—and then the brain
    Deep into which her image grew.
If I, being strong, survive her long,
        I shall be wrought anew.

New summers will impress their flowers
    On this recipient thought of mine.
" Thou diest not yet : Live and forget "
        Thunders the voice divine.

I hold her picture in my brain :
    I cling to it ; I hold it fast.
But God can break the frame, and shake
        The picture out at last.

God even can create afresh
    The spirit of love, and comfort me :
Make me untrue ; create anew
        Love's former ecstasy.

My darling's hair was golden-bright ;
    But God can send dark locks to charm :
Around a waist, young, slender, chaste,
        Can fold my traitor's arm.

He is the traitor.   I despair,
  And struggle to despair for aye.
If through the night God flashes light,
      Is that my fault, I say ?

It is most bitter—worst of all,
  Or so to-day it seems to me—
That, when I long to hush all song,
      The thrush chants in the tree :

That, when I long that love should die
  With my white darling in her grave,
God dares to say, " Perhaps one day
      Love may uplift and save."

God wantons with our brains and hearts :
  We may not even love the dead.
He interferes.   He stops our ears ;
      " Love these," he says, " instead.

" Love these live beings.   Care for these.
  Pink blossoms flush the apple-spray.
The waves are blue.   The birds renew   ,
      Each year their wedding-day.

" Thou carest for the dead alone :
  Yet live soft glances seek for thee.
Love while thou mayest.   Be kissed, embraced,
      But leave the dead to me.

" In my embrace I clasp the dead :
  My solemn arms about them fold.
Thy wife is dead.   Seek for thy bed
      A warm breast, not a cold."
            *   *

Most horrible !   If thou must take
  The darling of my life away ;
If my small star, seen from so far,
          Offends thy great sun's ray ;

If my one lily small and sweet
  Makes envious all the flowers that bloom
In Paradise before thine eyes,
          So that they claim her doom ;

If thou must slay the one sweet thing
  That made a sad life sometimes fair ;
Yet leave me this—my dead wife's kiss,
          And my profound despair.

X.

THE YOUNG GENIUS.

I.

God recreates the earth and air,
And makes the vast blue waters fair,
    And makes the earth's wide meadows green
For every genius therein born;
For each regards the past with scorn
        As if it had not been!

Each genius, by his birthright grand,
Inherits sea and sky and land;
    For each God clothes all stars anew
In fiery splendour.—Shakespeare's dead!
But still the sun is golden-red,
        And still the waves are blue.

The first white snowdrop is as fair
To genius, when Spring's soft hands bear
    Her gentle early gifts to him,
As if no snowdrops ever leaped
Before above the mould, or peeped
        Into the crocus-rim.

The first white butterfly he sees,
That dances edgelong on the breeze,
   Is white as that which Adam saw.
The azure kingfisher who flies
Athwart the reeds creates surprise,
   And even a sense of awe.

And unto genius most of all
Is woman ever new. Eve's fall
   Made her perhaps less strangely fair
To Adam. But though Adam grieve,
His Eden holds an unfallen Eve
   And genius finds her there.

Yes ; ever to the genius-eyes
The tender light of Paradise
   Beams forth from woman's perfect look.
Her lips are fragrant as the flowers
That in life's morning's golden hours
   From Eden's banks she took.

As butterfly is white and new
For genius, sea-waves spotless blue,
   And every star new-robed in sheen
Triumphant,—so for genius stands
Woman, new-wrought with virgin hands
   And splendour of a queen.

God, that he might forget her fall,
Created genius most of all,
   And set within the genius-brain
The power of worship passionate ;
That woman he might reinstate,
   And honour her again.

That God might constantly repeat
His own deep sense of wonder sweet,
    The passionate awe, the joy sublime,
Which first he felt creating Eve,
He made the genius-heart achieve
    The same work through all time.

Subordinate to his alone
He set the kingly genius-throne,
    And bade his poet-souls receive
His thought anew ; that every age
Might so repeat the Eden stage,
    And shape its perfect Eve.

II.

So genius, finding all things new,
Must recreate its kingdom too
    And pay no homage to the past.
" Lo ! God is in these hills and streams.
With miracle the present teems :
    With wonder sweet and vast."

But no man listens to his tale.
He seeks to draw aside the veil
    That hides the solemn stars of space :
He seeks to represent to man
God undivulged since time began
    Save through some human face :

But no, mankind will nought of him.
His own friends say, " How strange a whim
    We knew that poets lived of old ;
We knew that prophets spake of God ;
But this man do the same ?   How odd !
    His heart is overbold.

" For Revelation came and went
When Jesus Christ from God was sent
   To carry out God's mighty plan.
God's pity shone in Jesus' face,
And he redeemed the human race ;
   He lived and died for man.

" Poets have lived. The whole world sang
When Shelley's wondrous live harp rang,
   And thrilled the height and thrilled the deep.
All Nature in her joyous hours
For Keats' brow wove her fairest flowers ;
   Aye, lulled him soon to sleep.

" The whole of history spake indeed
Through Hugo. What soul can succeed
   In adding aught to things once said ?
Yea, God himself who made the sun
Was satisfied—he made but one.
   Darkness ! if that were dead."

Darkness ? O fools, the solemn night
Brims over with perennial light ;
   A hundred million suns in space
Flame round about the Eternal's throne,
And each sun guards and herds its own
   Planets that wheel and race.

So with mankind. Whatever things
Poets have sung, each poet sings
   New truths, new aspects of the old.
Yes, even Christ did not exhaust
God's fulness.—At his death life paused
   Then on life's bright wave rolled.

But ever, genius must renew
The same old struggle, wrestle through
　　The same old thickets of dismay ;
Be dubbed Beelzebub, when most
Inspired by that strong Holy Ghost
　　Who lives and speaks to-day.

Still must the son of God, the bard,
Find life's long battle bitter hard,
　　Meet envy, hatred, wrath and scorn ;
Still will he, struggling hard to lift
Mankind, receive mankind's one gift—
　　Christ's battered crown of thorn.

III.

Moreover, genius never feels
Save in extremes.—Its whole brain reels
　　With wild delight, or rocks with woe.
From one extreme it plunges on
To other heights and depths that none
　　Save genius' self may know.

It worships God, it worships long
Within his house with prayer and song ;
　　Then lo ! his Temple's gold gates close :
The poet sallies forth, and finds
Lovely upon the summer winds
　　The soft breath of the rose.

Then all his heart is seized and bound.
What cares he for the hallowed ground,
　　The Temple's walls and solemn panes ?
He loves the rose, he loves the flowers :
He wanders for wild happy hours
　　Along the balmy lanes.

He is a Greek.   He meets the eyes
Of woman, and his whole heart lies
   A willing captive at her feet.
" Praise Venus !" now his whole heart sings.
The heart that once was Christ's he flings
     Before her altar sweet.

Unstable?   Yes, but even so
The thoughts and songs of genius grow,
   And eddy along their destined course.
All is extreme.   All is superb
And strong and reinless ; without curb ;
     Unfettered, full of force.

God speaks not only in one hour,
Not through the beauty of one flower,
   But through the flowers of endless time.
When genius and the Lord collogue,
They speak not in the vulgar brogue
     But in a tongue sublime.

The commonplace well-balanced fool
Who speaks by rote and lives by rule,
   What shall he of God's glories see ?
What shall he know of woman's heart ?
Or of the mountain-range of Art,
     Or of Art's ecstasy ?

But genius, wild, extreme, perverse,
With lips that bless, or lips that curse,
   Brow-bound with thorns, with sorrow shod,
However man's heart may despise
The deep love-yearning in its eyes,
     Is strangely close to God.

XI

THE UNLOVED WIFE.

Am I a wife, I wonder, if I feel
   Hardly one link between his heart and mine?
Is it my fault if I must kneel
   And worship at an alien shrine?

Duty? Yes, duty. Was it not God's part,
   When he planned out my being, to provide
A husband for my woman's heart
   And for some manly heart a bride?

When God first made me—when he made the girl,
   And made her love bright flowers and all things fair;
The grand green sea-wave's crested curl;
   The kestrel's swoop across the air;

When he so made me—made my soul a part
   Of living Nature, made me Nature's bride,
Was it to sacrifice my heart
   And couch me at an old man's side?

Old man? If he were faithful, well and good!
   My whole heart longs to worship and adore.
But this god—wrought of rotten wood!
   This tree—worm-eaten to the core!

Is this a staff that I can lean upon ?
  Can I twine ivy round this ancient stem ?
Can ever God in heaven atone
  For shattering so my diadem ?

My early diadem of dreams was sweet :
  Dreaming of love, I woke to life-long shame.
A slave I am at lust's fierce feet ;
  A woman only in the name.

I know it now. He wanted me for this—
  For this, this only. He was tired of all
Old loves. He sought a virgin kiss ;
  He sought a new white-bosomed thrall.

He wanted health and beauty ; wanted me,
  To add new zest to appetites perverse.
I was to bring my purity,
  And play the part of wifely nurse.

I was to poultice with my living frame
  His frame, worn-out, half ready to depart !
He gave me title and a name,
  And I gave him—a young girl's heart !

Yes : for I thought I loved him. Even so.
  There is no limit to a young girl's faith.
She is so fresh from heaven, you know !
  Too full of life to dream of death.

She thinks that God, who made the sweet spring flowers
  And dropped heaven's gold among the daffodils,
Reigns over all earth's days and hours
  And swayeth all things as he wills.

G

She thinks that God who made the **heaven so** fair
  With countless stars, made also love's delight.
She craves nought else, if love is there,
  For love makes every moment bright.

*   *

I thought he loved me.   I had noble hope.
  Though he was old, I could have loved him well.
In woman's heart is endless scope :
  Both heights of heaven, and depths of hell.

I would have tended him, and loved him too.
  I did not yearn for younger hearts and eyes.
Young reckless wild hearts sought to woo :
  I could have been so strong and wise !

If he had helped me !   If he had but seen
  I needed help !   If he had cared one straw !
Why then to-day I might have been
  Spotless, my faith without a flaw.

But he—he sought my downfall, so I think.
  I see it now.   I see the whole at last
At lovers' schemes he chose to wink,
  Till many amorous hours were past.

And then he let me know of his own deeds
  (That was to tempt me into lower shame).
Oh, in this world the wrong succeeds !
  A single match can light hell-flame !

He knew I loved him—when we first were one.
  To punish me for that surpassing crime,
He made me aware of evil done
  In my own house ; aye, many a time.

He made me aware of his own lowest sins,
  And took a fiend's own trouble to explain
How delicately sin begins
  And that it does not end in pain !

That was his pleasure, scientific, sage :
  To mar my mind by contact with his own ;
To pour the poison of his age
  Into a rosebud but half-blown.

To ruin his own wife, this was his scheme.
  There was a something *piquant* in the thought.
It had the freshness of a dream :
  It was a wrong as yet unwrought.

To ruin others—that was old and stale !
  To ruin me, his wife ; to see me sink,
Sin, till I passed the social pale,
  Till he could see my sisters shrink,

Shrink at the contact with the faithless wife :
  This was a novel rapture, wholly sweet !
A worthy ending of his life !
  Satan's success, and God's defeat !

And this he set himself to. This he sought.
  He roused my jealousy by many a plan :
Fever within my frame he wrought :
  Then brought the occasion and the man.

He roused my passion, and he took good care
  That some one should be ready (Yes, I see !)
—" He thought I needed change of air :
  Would Robert bear me company ? "

Then, when the whole was done, love's fierce hours spent,
  He smiled a cynic smile and said just this :
" What puzzles me is why you went
  So long without young lips to kiss ! "

*   *

To-morrow is the Divorce Court.   But to-night
  Is still my own.   This flask will settle all.
I drink. . . .   Ah ! how my chest grows tight.
  My head reels round so.   I shall fall !

XII

THE CYNIC.

The snow-white bloom upon the hawthorn hedges
   Offends my weary restless eye
Again this year.   Again with silver edges
   The clouds plunge through a deep-blue sky.

Spring follows spring.   But each its predecessor
   Pursues along the self-same track.
A blue-leaved tree would be a strange transgressor,
   And so would be a grass-blade black.

I weary of the sameness of creation :
   Its endless repetition palls.
Each race pursues each flying previous nation ;
   One rises, when another falls.

In London still the Jewish dark eyes glitter :
   They have not changed their warm brown hue.
In green dense leaves the brown-winged linnets twitter :
   The thrush sings as it used to do.

If nations spring up, eager to dismantle
   Their rival nations' casemates grey,
Their instruments of rugged war they handle
   Like nations who have passed away.

The madding hosts who on the plain of Brussels
  Flattened the corn with leaden rain
Have met again. War's sanguine grim ghost rustles
  For ever through perennial grain.

The sea hurls up its sea-weed from the abysses:
  The same strange red and purple-green
Still dyes its fronds,—and still the blue wave kisses
  The chalk. All is as it has been.

The frowning battlements and crags of Dover,
  The turrets black and bastions grim,
Watch the wide fields of corn and crimson clover:
  The silver sea-gulls swoop and swim.

No flower has changed its tint, no cloud its colour,
  Since conquering Cæsar sought our shores.
The leaping waves are not one slight shade duller
  Since they resented Roman oars.

The same old weary round without cessation!
  The same bright wheels for ever spin!
The Greek soul wanes. Rises the Roman nation.
  Then English deeds, and crimes, begin.

The same old weary hackneyed road historic!
  The dusty same old path of fame!
Flashes, and hues, and splendours meteoric—
  Sorrow, and base decay, and shame!

And so with love. Not even love can alter
  The course of things, or travel far.
Love lasts an hour, and then love's sweet wings falter:
  And so it is in every star.

In English glades, in English woodlands spacious,
  The rose is white and sweet to-day :
Our English women's lips are very gracious ;
  And yet their gold hair turns to grey.

The blue-black hair still thrills the soul and maddens,—
  The hair that mocks the sheeny rook :
And still a woman's glance redeems or saddens, —
  But Eve's eyes had the self-same look.

In London parks we hear the same love-laughter,
  Changed not at all in note or ring,
That sounded, and the Greek youth followed after
  Through meadows golden with life's spring.

Along the white-housed streets of modern Paris
  Love walks, and sorrow steps as well.
Still, still, the world's supreme redemption tarries :
  Heaven still shakes daily hands with hell.

Regard the skies.   Ponder their weary sameness!
  Stars still, and stars without a change !—
The sun is large,—and yet how full of tameness.
  How narrow is creation's range !

Could we behold the surfaces all glistening
  Of stars beyond the vision's reach,
Could we approach, we should find our ears listening,
  Perhaps, to vulgar human speech.

The furthest star would reproduce emotion,
  Perhaps, that we watch round us here.
Blue waves again of an incessant ocean
  Would meet our eye, and haunt our ear.

Green leaves and snow-white buds and bloom redundant
   Would edge the farthest planet's rim.
In Mars war's foaming tides would fill the abundant
   Red wine-press to the frothing brim.

In Venus golden hair would tease and weary,
   And green-grey eyes would lead us wrong :
And still our hearts would shiver at the dreary
   Old sound of Summer's languid song.

Star beyond star would tell the self-same story :
   Perhaps the fairest planet planned,
Could we but reach and analyse its glory,
   Was moulded by our maker's hand.

Perhaps the wide creation's lord and swayer
   In the most lovely-seeming star
That floats islelike upon soft layer on layer
   Of clouds, in regions dim and far— .

Perhaps in this fair star he has built a city
   Like London, in as wild a land,
And set therein—he, knowing not love nor pity—
   A street as hellish as our Strand.

XIII.

THE ANARCHIST.

I.

Another deluge must be sent
  To purge the earth of sin ;
To make an end of discontent
  And let new life begin ;
That so, oppression's soul being slain,
Man's soul may live, man's soul may reign.

Another deluge must descend
  Upon the earth, and save :
All kingly tyranny must end,
  All priests must dig their grave.
A fiery deluge must make clean
The earth, destroying what has been.

There is no other road but this
  To peace, and heaven on earth.
There is no other path to bliss :
  Nor is there aught else worth
A man's considering—save the plan
How to redeem the race of man.

It cannot be redeemed by love:
    It can by fire and sword.
Christ brought sweet pity from above,
    And men's hearts called him Lord:
What was the end of pity? see;
The teeming earth's vast agony!

The whole must be destroyed, and then
    Remoulded, built anew:
Shaped by our saviour-hands again;
    The bright skies painted blue;
The earth's fair meadows painted green,
And blossoms robed in golden sheen.

Another Genesis we'll write,
    And grander than the old!
From gloom more deep than primal night
    A dawn of lovelier gold
Shall flash upon the world's last hours,
And gladden the faint-hearted flowers.

Where God has failed, when man's hour comes
    Man, conquering, will succeed.
He'll build an earth with brighter homes:
    The hungry he will feed.
No poverty will mar the plan
Of the regenerate world of man.

Aristocrats! rich brainless fools
    Who revel, so long fed
By serfs, and priests—your servile tools,
    Who steal the poor man's bread,
Tremble! the dawn is coming fast
That, having dawned, will be your last.

Your palaces and parks are ours ;
  Your gardens, rich with bloom ;
Your hot-houses of tropic flowers :
  Your wealth we shall resume.
We lent you at the world's day-break
What now our mastering hands will take.

We lent you all that you possess ;
  We lent it for a time.
Man with his multitudinous " yes,"
  His franchised voice sublime,
Bids us resume the wealth we lent
And end the toilers' discontent.

Yes ; you have spent our savings well.
  Things are not all amiss.
Your houses, after rooms in hell,
  Will be abodes of bliss.
Your stately couches will provide
The needed rest, so long denied.

Your couches, soft and finely wrought,
  Whereon your women lay,
Will serve an end ye never thought,
  In this, man's latter day.
We'll take them, and bring you instead
The poor man's straw, and truckle-bed.

Our daughters ye have taken oft,
  And treated them as slaves,
And kissed their young lips pure and soft
  Hard by their fathers' graves :
But now the end has come indeed
Of all your lust and all your greed.

          *   *

What justice did we ever get
    From your proud God, or you?
We slept upon the heather wet,
    Agued with rain and dew:
You slept in feather-bedded hives,
Warmed—by the bosom of our wives.

You were the landlords, we the slaves:
    You had the power with you.
The Christian says, "God loves and saves:"
    Curse him! it is not true.
Truer to say, "God damns and hates,
And closes on the poor heaven's gates."

Our daughters sold themselves for bread:
    On that you counted—yes.
God would not let our wives be fed
    Without their lords' caress.
If they were comely, then they throve;
By selling noblemen their "love."

" A woman never starves," you say:
    " Why should she?" why indeed?
She's always worthy of her pay,
    And always can succeed
(Unless her husband interferes)
In winning some kind rich man's ears.

And *if* the husband interferes,
    He does it at his cost.
What matter foolish sighs and tears?
    Resist, the farm is lost!
The landlord has so sure a plan:
He can coerce both wife and man.

And then you bid us look to God,
  Rely upon his care,
Bend dutifully to his rod,
  Or seek his house of prayer.
The true God curse—if God there be—
You and your false God's sophistry!

Your priests are evil as yourselves :
  They sell their faith for gold.
The life of Christ is on their shelves :
  They study parchments old :
They sip port at a snug fireside,
Forgetting how their Master died.

They preach a God of justice, while
  The poor man surely sees,
With bitter curse or bitterer smile,
  That such creeds only please
The fancy of the rich unjust
Man-devil, who lives on wrong and lust,

Those who adore the "God of love"
  And seek his gaudy fanes
Are those who in rich circles move :
  The Lord so quickly gains
Believers, when he feeds them well ;
Their faith grows as their bellies swell.

II.

Therefore we, seeing that all that is
  Is past redemption marred
And that your proud philosophies
  Serve only to retard
The people's reign, declare indeed
Wild war on king and priest and creed,

On every creed : for hope dies out
    As the world older grows,
And there will come a day no doubt
    When man's mind will repose—
Will cease to pry into God's plan,
And only busy itself with man.

Then on the earth a happier day
    Will dawn. When heaven has passed
Completely from man's dreams away,
    And when the foolish last
Sermon has mumbled at St. Paul's,
Man will hear wisdom's voice that calls.

He then will concentrate his gaze
    On earth, and earth alone :
On blue waves bounding through the bays,
    Not on God's golden throne.
Of all mad dreams, the maddest was
That dream of ruby and chrysoprase !

The faith that somewhere in the sky,
    High raised with airy beams,
God's palace shone resplendently
    And flashed on prophets' dreams
From jewel-facets rays sublime,
And put to shame the world of time.

Ezekiel saw its golden doors :
    Isaiah dreamed he knew
The patterns of its emerald floors :
    It flamed upon the view
Of John of Patmos. Even Christ's eye
Saw many mansions in the sky.

But now we see no golden towers,
  No turrets tall and fair :
We see a few white wilding flowers ;
  We feel the fresh sea-air ;
We know our earth can be restored,
Saved from the thraldom of the Lord.

We know that when the selfish dream
  Of heaven has passed away,
Then first the stars will nobly gleam
  With free unhindered ray ;
Then first our hearts will say, " How sweet
Is sunlight over golden wheat ! "

Then first our hearts will say, " How bright
  This red geranium glows !
How blue this larkspur is ! how white
  This jonquil, or this rose ! "
The waves will sound upon the shore
With music never heard of yore.

The sweet world had no power to charm
  When all man's heart was set
On heaven with hope, or with alarm
  (That has not died out yet !)
On making good his wild escape
From Satan's ever-following shape.

Then heaven o'ershadowed things of earth.
  But all is changed to-day :
Who thinks of angels' grief or mirth
  Within our London grey ?
London has grown, as heaven grew less,
And swallows up God's littleness.

There is no room, there is no p'ace,
  For God and heaven and hell.
The growing wisdom of the race
  Serves amply to dispel
Old dreams.   The towers of Zion fade,
And heaven's far vistas, glade by glade.

The New Jerusalem is gone.
  The City from on high
Departs, and leaves us here alone
  Beneath our foggy sky.
Our angels at the Horse Guards wait :
Spurred, booted, cuirassed, belted, great !

This life is ours.   Be it ours to make
  This life, as best we can,
Devoid of suffering, pain, heart-ache,
  A present heaven for man :
To bring the sacred pleasures nigh
That were located in the sky.

That end to gain, all that we see
  Must wholly be destroyed :
A social vast catastrophe
  Must make the whole earth void
Of kings and rulers, who to-day
Stand in the advancing ocean's way.

When Revolution's thunderous surge
  Has swept the whole earth clean,
A higher planet shall emerge :
  Life nobler than has been
Shall bear fruit on the earth Christ trod,
And, God being dead, man shall be God.

XIV

THE PANTHEIST.

God oftenest frowns in anger—then he shakes
The seas to wild wrath; but his sweetness makes
   An orange lily, or a damask rose.

When the green downs are bright with golden rays,
And when the blue waves ripple in the bays,
   It is that God's soul takes its deep repose.

But when earth's battle-fields run red with gore,
Or when the white waves thunder on the shore,
   It is that God in a sublime unrest

Needs outlet for his inward force. His heart
Revels as ships' torn planks asunder part,
   And through the midmost battle flames his crest.

His mood of savage anger wrecks the ship :
His tender moment curves the maiden's lip :
   Before he sleeps, he spreads the sable night

Above him for a canopy sublime :
His passionate heart inspires the poet's rhyme,
   And fills the poet's eyes with rapturous light,

H

His fiercer moods command the sins of man :
The blood-stained sword-point in the battle's van
   Is God's,—and by his will the cannons roar.

In one great wondrous stormy moment he
Created at a stroke the stormy sea,
   And bade its breakers surge for evermore.

In love-sweet moments he designed the white
Fair form of woman,—and he set the light
   Of his eternity within her eyes :

Yea, for her sake he made the waters blue
And painted in imperishable hue
   The fervent length and breadth of summer skies.

It was while, quiet, he observed her face
That he designed the starry heights of space,
   Just as a palace wherein she might dwell :

It was while thinking how man would betray
That God planned out in fiery wrath one day
   The dungeons of interminable hell.

So all things represent the diverse moods
Of God : the lakes, the forests, and the woods ;
   The strong, the weak ; the hideous and the fair ;

The leper, white and horrible and foul ;
The sweet-tongued linnet, or the shrieking owl ;
   The wren's round nest ; the lion's blood-splashed lair.

But man and woman chiefliest represent
God's nature.   Woman is God's calm content
  In quiet loveliness and pure sweet things :

Man learns from God his passionate unrest,
His strength, his ardour.   O'er the wild sea's breast
  He roams, while woman by the brookside sings.

XV

THE MAN OF SCIENCE.

Help us, O giant Force !   We know not of thy glory :
    Unknowable thou art, and wilt be to the end.
Helpless we are, from youth until the head grows hoary:
    Canst thou lend life and aid?   Canst thou be God and Friend

Amid the seething stars, the measureless world-forces,
    We struggle and are tost, blind Nature's easy prey :
The stars glide on their road, the suns fulfil their courses ;
    These all in soulless calm thine urgent word obey.

But what of flesh and blood ? the human spirit moving
    Along the path of Fate, and groaning as he grows :
Deep in the earth's green breast his track of progress grooving :
    Is he to thee more dear than harebell or than rose?

" Never a sparrow falls "—so said the great Redeemer—
    " Without the Father's will."   Ah ! is the grand thought true ?
Or was the Christ, for all his might, but one more dreamer,
    The greatest dreamer our sad worn world ever knew ?

" The hairs of all your heads are numbered "—so he told us—
    " Ye do believe in God : believe besides in me."
If he but spake the truth, God's love doth ever hold us:
    It shines in heaven's blue, it ripples in the sea.

Yet, when we look around, we see our race devoured
  By Nature's restless fangs, and rent from day to day :
Man's spirit racked with grief, and woman's soul deflowered ;
  Pleasure immersed in tears, and summers sprent with spray.

The stormy sea destroys ; the fierce suns beat and blind us ;
  Within the foul morass the deadly serpents lurk :
There is not one tall hill where sickness may not find us ;
  The summer breeze conspires with Nature's treacherous work.

Our cities teem with sin : our streets are like the alleys
  Of hell : our armies wallow in each other's gore.
Disease invades the bowers of gentlest moon-kissed valleys :
  The more we learn and know, we do but sin the more.

And if Christ never oped the grave's dark lowering portal ;
  Ne'er trod triumphant forth,—deceiving and deceived ;
If ne'er his armour rang on far sweet heights immortal,
  How is the human race then widowed and bereaved !

But through the awful voiceless dark, great unseen Spirit,—
  With or without the Christ,—our spirits shall not fail.
His faith in deathless Love the dying years inherit :
  New Christs arise beyond his senile Church's pale.

Whether the earth be chilled by bitter age and frozen,
  Or whether it be hurled amid the sun's red deeps,
Still are we thine elect, thy sons though later chosen :
  Still past the furthest spheres the soul's clear whisper leaps.

Oh, 'mid the *melée* of stars and mystery of forces
  That seethe and whirl and spin, and toss their golden spray,
Still will we trust the soul's unchanged deep hidden sources,
  And wordless though we be, amid that tumult, pray !

If haply o'er the clash of solar systems meeting,
  Convolving into flame, and hurtling through the air,
God's ear (acute) may catch the sound of our entreating ;
  If haply through the void may rise some spirit's prayer.

If haply through the void God's answer swift-descending,
  In spite of rage of stars, may reach the human ear,
And with the human soul its sympathetic blending
  Enact,—though battling suns crash sphere on white-hot sphere.

If haply, though the air be full of desolation,
  And though the corpse of Christ lie stretched across the way
God may be living still, and guiding every nation,
  And eagle-winged to help the wingless souls that pray !

XVI.

THE LOVERS.

The danger makes the joy so much the sweeter.
   What flower delights like that the mountains hold?
   Who wins most boons from Love?   The arm most bold.
When rapture's easy, rapture's wing is fleeter;
   But ever peril's wing is freaked with gold.

O lover holding in thine arms thy treasure,
   What matters it to thee if daggers smite
   And hurl thy soul to sudden death to-night?
Thou enteredst heaven and knewest immortal pleasure
   When she, once, shone before thy mouth, quite white.

True; guards are near.   That makes the kiss so tender. —
   True; danger looms.   That makes her limbs so white.—
   True; the night flies.   That makes her eyes so bright.—
True; 'tis but once.   So take thou all her splendour.
   Soon 'twill be o'er.   So multiply delight!

          *   *

Doth even now the sound of their dull sleeping
   Mix with her tremulous laughter all subdued
   And madden passion into fiercer mood?
Wild is love's harvest, when revenge is reaping!
   That last kiss settles the old life-long feud.

How strange her eyes look, through the darkness gleaming !
　　And oh her lips, how close and warm they press !
　　And oh the infinite heaven-sweet caress !
" Are we alone, love ?　Are we dead, or dreaming ?
　　Close to God's throne the rapture would be less."

" Nay, not in heaven we meet.　*His* slaves watch near us.
　　It is not heaven.　Within the midnight's keep,
　　Guarded by Love, for one safe hour we sleep.
Never again the morning sun shall cheer us.
　　To-morrow's midnight darkness will be deep !"

　　　　　　　　　*　　　　*

A cry !　The doors are beaten in and broken—
　　Trampling upon the stairs of many feet—
　　A struggle : and the short June-night so sweet
Mingles with blood-red dawn.　Few words are spoken
　　When swords and hearts more keen than sword-blades meet.

They both are dead.　What matter ?　Is our living
　　Measured by hours that on the earth we stay ?
　　May not one night like this for centuries weigh ?
Woman takes time in her sweet hands, when giving
　　Delight that makes eternal one brief day.

XVII

FOUR WAYS OF REGARDING THE COMET.

In 1897 a comet will appear, and will fall into the sun, this being the first instance during human history of any such catastrophe. It seems probable that the heat thereby generated will be so great that the whole solar system will almost instantaneously be consumed.

Papers of the year 1882.

Scientist.

In fifteen years the fiery rain will fall
And shroud creation in a blazing pall.
　　No soul shall then escape.　And yet how grand !

Man of Business.

In fifteen years !　Just when my firs commence
Their stately growth (they'll form a noble fence).
　　How it will lower the value of my land !

Theologian.

Repent, and turn ye from your evil way,
Now, while there yet is time, and yet 'tis day,
　　Or God will 'whelm you in the fiery sea.

Artist.

What, only fifteen years, and then no more
To watch the blue waves break upon the shore !
　　No woman's lips through all eternity !

Scientist.

Grand beyond words !   Predictions will come true.
Across the midnight skies of purple-blue
　　The great torpedo comet-boat will glide.

Man of Business.

And I shall just have won position then ;
Wealth and renown, the high esteem of men ;
　　One comet-flash will shatter all my pride !

Theologian.

Christ will renew the earth, with new desire.
His enemies within the comet-fire
　　Will perish, in that great Day of the Lord !

Artist.

Beauty will perish.   Can God make that new ?
The old sweet earth will die, thrust through and through
　　By the fierce comet's red malignant sword.

Scientist.

How all who mocked at us will tremble then !
Loud have we spoken ; often and again ;
　　Yet never would the people lend an ear.

Man of Business.

Where had I better bank my savings now ?
What use is it to labour and to plough,
　　If such a harvest-moon will soon be here ?

Theologian.

Most merciful is God! He gives man time.
Then lo! his fiery rage on sin and crime
    Will swift descend. The comet is his slave.

Artist.

The comet is God's servant? Oh, to-day
I kissed the lids of eyes of lovely grey :
    Can cruel God close such eyes in the grave ?

Scientist.

Steady and certain is vast Nature's plan.
She pauses not for woman or for man :
    With calm deliberate stride her steps advance.

Man of Business.

But cannot something adequate be done?
Cannot your Science drive into the sun
    This comet threatening us with torrid lance?

Theologian.

What, thwart God's scheme of vengeance? Never, sir !
Entirely in God's method I concur.
    I'd rather die than see the bad escape !

Artist.

And my one sorrow is just simply this ;
That I shall burn to cinders, and so miss
    The comet's colour and imposing shape !

XVIII.

GROWING OLD.

There is a holy joy in growing old,
  If but the soul grows as the strength declines.
Life's winter need not freeze with flowerless cold,
  Though spring's brave golden sun no longer shines.

Though passion's blossoms wither, are the stars
  Not nearer, as our ripe souls yearn through space?
Heaven's far-lit windows gleam devoid of bars,
  Wide open, on the upturned aging face.

We are more near to death, but nearer too
  To countless loved ones who have gone before;
Who watched death's grey waves quickening into blue,
  As sunlight reached them from the further shore.

This brings content,—aye, rapture.   Perfect peace
  Of spirit should be the sweet lot of the old :
A large trust that God's bounty cannot cease ;
  Hope that life's fairy-tale is not half told !

Hope that the Power which made so passing fair
  Our earthly springs, made green leaves interlace,
Can bring with grand result its force to bear
  On higher spheres—that hold some higher race ?

*   *

Strive so to live that, when you come to die,
  Sweet thoughts may follow you from all your land :
Thoughts that shall shine like stars within the sky
  Of death, and make the sombre prospect grand.

Thoughts both of man and woman.—Let men say,
  " He changed our souls to fire, to slay all wrong : "
Let women think, " He lifted sorrow away,
  And made us stronger, being himself so strong.

" No woman was the worse—the better, all,
  For loving help and helpful love he gave.
He lured no trusting weak one to her fall.
  Our blessing reaches him beyond the grave."

*   *

On one side clamour of our winds and waves ;
  Babble of voices ; golden stars that burn ;
Birds singing in the elm-trees over graves ;
  White tombstones couched amid the cluster'ng fern :

White tombstones—yes ! But bright life over all :
  Above the graveyard skies of ceaseless blue :
The starlit heavens for canopy and pall :
  This on one side. But, dead man, what of you ?

Can your eyes now behold the summer skies ?
  Can your ears hear the summer birds that sing ?
—Or is the silence where the dead man lies
  Perhaps the noblest gift that death can bring ?

For through that supreme silence that no voice
  Of mortal penetrates, that starless gloom,
God's voice may sound ; and it may say, " Rejoice,"
  In accents thrilling through the fast-closed tomb.

" Rejoice : thy work is over. Take thy rest.
    Of sweet peace drink thy fill. Thy strife is o'er.
Pillow thine head on the Eternal's breast.
    Suffered thou hast? Thou shalt not suffer more.

" Are there no stars to light thee? Is it gloom
    Within the grave? I am thy star, thy light.
Though death to every sun and star spake doom,
    The Lord thy God is stronger than the night.

" There is no death, if thou art part of me :
    No night, for I will be thy mid-day sun ;
Pour at thy feet a new-created sea ;
    Before thy gaze make silver rivers run.

" I am the Lord thy God. The world is mine,
    And thou hast helped that world along life's way :
Fear not, though never glow-worm star should shine ;
    The God who made the stars is more than they."

*   *

This I regret—this grieves me, growing old—
    That, though maybe to heavenly fields I pass
I never more shall see the cowslip's gold
    Sprinkle with glittering gems the green spring grass.

I never more shall see—whatever waits
    Of glory and beauty far beyond the tomb—
One earthly sunset open crimson gates,
    Or one wild crimson clover-field in bloom.

Moreover all the valiant deeds to come,
    Great deeds in which my nation will take part—
Shall I behold them from some heavenly home,
    And will they thrill to fire my heavenly heart?

The next great war!   When Europe shakes again
   Beneath opposing millions' battle-tread,
When Belgium is once more a battle-plain
   Or the Swiss mountain-meadows reek with dead,

Shall I behold?   Shall I be closed off quite
   From all the stirring clash of things to come?
When England next arises in her might,
   Shall I be barred behind the eyeless tomb?

When England treats, upon some future sea,
   The giant-armoured fleets men now prepare,
Will not her trumpet-voice reach even me?
   Shall I not long, long madly, to be there?

When France and Russia force us, it may be,
   To test our iron-plated darkling horde
Of monstrous vessels, churning up the sea
   With Titan screw or fierce torpedo-sword;

Or when the red line, where far Indus flows,
   Wrestles for India, on one mighty day,
Shall I be heedless how the battle goes,—
   Silent for ever, wholly past away?

*   *

My eyes will soon be dimmed.—God will behold
   All stars for ever, and all suns of space.
In fiery rank on rank of glittering gold
   Their hosts will charge and wheel before his face.

I shall not see the flowers: but God will see
   The flowers of endless springs, through endless days.
He'll share the rose's own eternity,
   And wander through the sealed years' hidden ways.

I shall not hear the thunder, or the roar
  Of ocean.—God will hear the thunders roll,
And hear the huge waves plunge upon the shore,
  And guide the flashing lightnings to their goal.

New moons will silver placid wastes of sea ;
  New suns will blaze above the golden sand :
New lovers—yes, to all eternity—
  Will gaze in eyes that love and understand.

God will behold.—The glorious dark-brown hair
  Of maid on maid he will caress and stroke.
Through spring on spring his palette will prepare
  New soft green colours for each budding oak.

He will array each kingfisher in blue,
  And robe the goldfinch—touch its cheek with red :
Crumble to dust the stars,—then make all new ;
  I shall be gone, but God will not be dead.

O living mighty Lord, into thine hand
  I give myself, and all I may not see :
The green robes of the cliffs, the corn-clad land,
  The thyme-tufts shaken by the summer bee.

Thou ever hast the past before thy gaze :
  The present and the future are but one
To thee.   We see all life through clouds and haze ;
  But thine eyes front and blench not at the sun.

YOUNG GIRL'S SONG.

Golden dawn is breaking
　　Over land and sea :
All the birds are waking :
　　Does my love love me ?

See, the morning's sweetness
　　At the window-pane !
Summer's full completeness
　　Has returned again.

In my heart all flowers
　　Seem to blossom now:
Bloom of woodbine-bowers ;
　　Buds of apple-bough.

Hardly can I fancy
　　What is most in bloom,—
Jasmine, purple pansy,
　　Rosebuds in the room,

Or my own young gladness
　　Bidding sorrow flee,
Sorrow, pain, and sadness,
　　Over leagues of sea ;

1

Bidding sorrow leave me
  For the good God says
Nothing ought to grieve me
  In these summer days ;

Nothing ought to sadden
  Mine, a young girl's heart ;
All hours ought to gladden ;
  All pangs to depart.

There are wars and troubles
  In the world, I know
—There are white foam-bubbles
  On the stream below :

Fierce and strong and rapid
  Does its current gleam,
While the poplars vapid
  Watch it in a dream.

But I see the blossoms
  At the water's edge :
Lilies' golden bosoms,
  Feathery bloom of sedge.

When the sun amazes
  All the banks so green,
Then I count the daisies,
  Tipped with crimson sheen.

Gold-crest, wren, and linnet,
  These I watch and love :
God sends every minute
  Music from above.

In the morning early,
　Singing in the sky
'Mid the cloud-wreaths pearly,
　Chants the lark on high.

When the warm sun blanches
　Mid-day with its heat,
In the beech-tree branches
　Sings the throstle sweet.

Then the blackbird whistles
　From the holly-tree :
Tom-tits from the thistles
　Chirp, and call to me.

On the river-border
　Red-breasts cut a dash ;
Stout knights of the Order
　Of the crimson sash.

Then the singer rarer,
　While the moon-rays gleam,
Makes the world a sharer
　In her deathless dream.

So God sends me singers ;
　Till night's darkness deep
On the river lingers,
　And the bird-choirs sleep.

II.

Yet far sweeter fancies
　Fill my heart at times ;
Sweeter than romances
　Of far Eastern climes.

Yes, I have a lover !
    Does my love love me ?
He's a sailor-rover,
    Married to the sea.

Yet I know he's faithful :
    Though the waters blue
(Fierce perhaps, and wrathful ?)
    Bore him from my view.

Wheresoe'er he wanders,
    Nigh what alien shores,
Sure am I he ponders
    On me, and adores.

Hourly from his pocket
    Sure am I he takes
That small golden locket,
    Clasped by silver snakes.

Sure am I he gazes,
    Wheresoe'er he be,
On three small dried daisies
    In it . . . and on me !

III.

God has given me gladness :
    I must pass it on.
I must banish sadness,
    Not be glad alone.

See the sun, how proudly
    He bends down to bless :
Calls the daisy loudly
    To his strong caress !

All on God dependent
  Pass his blessings on.
Is the sun resplendent?
  He creates the moon.

I must give my pleasure
  To the world again.
Glad beyond all measure,
  I must lessen pain.

Hear me, Father, hear me!
  Thou hast bent to bless:
Sent the sun to cheer me;
  Sent the air's caress;

Sent the rose-buds trailing
  At the window-pane;
Sent these petals hailing,
  Gold laburnum-rain;

Sent the fragrant breathing
  Of the fields in May,
Blossoms interwreathing,
  Lilac-branch and spray;

Sent the dark-green laurel,
  Sentry at the gate;
Birds that chirp and quarrel
  Lest they be too late,

To my window flying
  For the bread-crumbs there—
Titmouse pert and prying,
  Chaffinch debonair!

—Let me give the gladness
   Thou hast given to me
To some soul in sadness,—
   Change to ecstasy

Sorrow of some laden
   Weary heart and brain :
I, a laughing maiden,
   I would solace pain.

With my touch caressing
   I would soothe the sad ;
Fill man's life with blessing,
   Make the whole world glad !

THE OLD MAID.

She gave her life to love. She never knew
　What other women give their all to gain.
Others were fickle. She was passing true.
　She gave pure love, and faith without a stain.

She never married. Suitors came and went :
　The dark eyes flashed their love on one alone.
Her life was passed in quiet and content.
　The old love reigned. No rival shared the throne.

Think you her life was wasted? Vale and hill
　Blossomed in summer, and white winter came :
The blue ice stiffened on the silenced rill :
　All times and seasons found her still the same.

Her heart was full of sweetness till the end.
　What once she gave, she never took away.
Through all her youth she loved one faithful friend :
　She loves him now her hair is growing grey.

THE BLIND POET.

Within a humble London room
   A poet lived and wrought :
He saw the sweet spring-blossoms bloom,
   But only in his thought.

His eyes were darkened.   But his soul
   Had power to see the skies :
Of Nature's lore he read the whole
   With his heart's loving eyes.

A thousand spirits walk the earth,
   Yet have no power to see :
They miss its sorrow, miss its mirth,
   Its beauty.   Not so he !

For him the sun was full of light,
   And blue the bright sea-wave ;
The wind-tost woods returned delight
   For music that he gave.

The rosebud in his song was red ;
   The sun-kissed hills were green :
The daisy to his door was led,
   As proud as any queen !

For to each flower he gave a life
   Beyond the life of time,
And by his music made the strife
   Of wrestling storms sublime.

*   *

Aye, all hearts loved him.   But the dead,
   They loved him best, it seems.
They hovered round about his bed,
   And drew him through his dreams.

They drew his spirit towards the land
   Where all who love shall see.
They took the blind man by the hand :
   He followed fearlessly.

They led him from this land of ours,
   And promised him a boon :
"Thine eyes shall feast on heavenly flowers,
   On heavenly sun and moon ;

"Thou shalt see heavenly stars," they said ;
   "Thou shalt breathe heavenly air ;
Thou shalt know rapture 'mid the dead,
   Who, living, knewest despair :

"Follow."—He listened to the voice,
   And left us here in gloom.
Yet has he made the wiser choice :
   He has left his darkened room.

He saw on earth pale ghosts of stars ;
   But that dim life is done :
Death bursts his darkness' prison-bars ;
   To-day he sees the sun.

FOUR BALLADS.

I.

A SOUTHERN VENGEANCE.

Under the bright room where they lay,
Deep in the stonework gaunt and grey,
    I will build a dungeon grim.
She and her lover (I stabbed him dead,
And his blood-drops splashed her breast with red)
    Shall rest in the darkness dim.
Under the bright room where they lay
They shall wait in the dark till the Judgment Day
    Flames out upon her and him.

(How it goes ring, ringing, through my brain,
That foolish light old swift refrain
She was singing when we met in Spain ;
" I love you, I love you—" again and again !)

    My hands may tremble. I will not shrink.
    Clink goes the trowel. Clink ! clink ! clink !
        Clink ! clink ! clink !

Under the bright room where they slept
Till up from the sea the gold sun leapt,
    In sunless darkness deep

They shall rest till the solemn trump of doom
Shakes the walls of their wedding-room
    And summons their souls from sleep.
White by his couch her form shall stand,
And her lips shall struggle to kiss his hand
    And her eyes shall strive to weep.

(How I remember the tinkling stream
And the night that passed in a maddening dream—
The room where we slept, and the pale moon-beam,
And her eyes with their wonderful passionate gleam !)

    Death's cup is ready.   Her lips shall drink.
    Clink goes the trowel.   Clink ! clink ! clink !
                    Clink ! clink ! clink !

Under the bright room where they lay
I will build a dungeon, and no day
    Shall ever enter there.
I will take her, stately and lovely—so
That the heart of a god might madden and glow
    With love of her thick black hair :
Then, brick by brick and stone by stone,
I will build her up in the vault, alone
    With the man her eyes found fair.

(Darling—" the gnat has stung the white
Of your beautiful arm," so I said in the night :
" Lay your arm in the moon's soft light ;
Let me suck the poison out —my right !")

    I will not pause to remember or think.
    Clink goes the trowel.   Clink ! clink ! clink !
                    Clink ! clink ! clink !

Under the bright room where they lay,
The room that looks on the sunny bay,
          I have built a sunless tomb.
There my darling and he shall be wed.
I stabbed him—curse him! He lies there dead,
          Stark on a couch in the gloom.
Down in the dark she shall live with him:
They shall kiss in the dark, till their eyes grow dim
          And their lustful limbs consume.

(I loved her so.   Oh, my raven hair
And the beautiful throat I found so fair!
I loved you—a girl with shoulders bare—
And I love you still.   That means despair.)

          I work.   I sever the past's last link.
          Clink goes the trowel.   Clink! clink! clink!
                    Clink! clink! clink!

Under their bright room, far below,
Where the grass spreads rank and the mosses grow,
          She shall stand and feast her eyes
On the corpse of the man she loved so well,
Till she starves to a corpse in the vault's dim hell
          And, grasping her dead man, dies.
Outside, the butterflies white will race,
And the girls will pass to the market-place,
          Singing under the sunny skies.
Step into the tomb, my lady fair.
Your death-cold lover is waiting there
With a brave true kiss for the thick black hair,
Such a brave true kiss for the thick black hair.
                    (Clink! clink! clink!)

II.

"YO HO! YO HO!"

Over the blue waves leaping
　The eager vessel flies ;
It laughs at the green isles sleeping,
　And it smiles at the sunny skies.
But the pilot's song is of sadness,
　For he knows in the midnight deep
That the white waves rise to madness,
　And he knows where the drowned men sleep.
But "Yo ho! Yo ho!" sing the men below ;
" We care not a fig what wind may blow,
　　　　　Yo ho! Yo ho!"

The ships that are passing hail them,
　Loud echoes the sailors' shout ;
Did ever their bold hearts fail them,
　While the flagons of wine held out ?
The pilot dreams of the haven,
　And the woman he loves ashore :
Black hair like the wing of the raven—
　Will he never see it more ?
But "Yo ho! Yo ho!" sing the men below ;
" Give us wine, and the ship to the bottom may go !
　　　　　Yo ho! Yo ho!"

The pilot thinks of his darling
    By her grey-haired mother's side—
("Yelp!" go the hoarse waves, snarling)
    His beauty, his heart's own pride.
He thinks of the Church so quiet
    On the side of the old green hill
(The wind is beginning to riot,
    And the ropes are never still).
"Yo ho! Yo ho!" sing the men below;
"Shall the wind's chirp frighten us? No, no, no,
                  Yo ho! Yo ho!"

The evening saddens and darkens,
    And the roaring surges swell;
The pilot sighs, as he hearkens
    To the sounds he knows so well.
Yet in spite of the sea-waves' warning,
    There is hope in his song to-night,
For England's cliffs in the morning
    May flash on the seamen's sight.
But "Yo ho! Yo ho!" sing the men below;
"When the bottle goes round, the fun will grow,
                  Yo ho! Yo ho!"

But the ship from her course is swerving;
    On the sharp reefs howl the waves
With ponderous white crests curving,
    And the green gulfs yawn like graves.
And the song of the pilot changes,
    As he stands at the helm—still there—
While his eye o'er the black night ranges,
    To the wild song of despair.
Still "Yo ho! Yo ho!" sang the men below,
For death can be drowned in the bowl, we know,
             "Yo ho! Yo ho!"

III.

THE BLACK FLAG.

Would you know the life that is fair and free ?
Climb the downs, and gaze o'er the open sea.
See you the schooner at anchor there,
And the black flag, strange in the sunny air ?
That is the bark of the pirate king,
And this is the song the pirates sing :
" We scuttle a galleon every day,
And the blue sea washes the stains away ;
   Can drowned men rise from sleep ? "

Yesterday morning, rank on rank
They stood, while a doomed man walked the plank.
Soon only a bubble marked the spot,
But the light-heart pirates heeded not ;
They danced on deck, and they laughed and sang
Till the ship's old timbers echoed and rang—
" Though the deck run red with the signs of the fray,
The sea can wash all stains away,
   And we are the lords of the deep.

" Men think they love, on the dull stale shore ;
We love, where the billows plunge and roar.
We take our pick of the captured girls;
Some like black tresses, some love gold curls ;

We take our pick, and the rest we drown,
And they tumble after their sweethearts down
To the blue clear depths of the Indian bay,
And the tide will carry them right away
         While their sisters wail and weep.

" Then under the trees, if ever we land,
Close to the waves on the golden sand,
We spread for ourselves a royal feast ;
The wine shall flow for a night at least !
And there by the firelight on the shore
Our jolly old chorus loud we roar,
' Will the waves betray us ?   Nay, nay, nay !
For the sea can wash all stains away,
         Though the prisoners die in a heap.'

" One of the captured girls we crown —
The one with the eyes of lovely brown.
She sorrowed at first.   She is reconciled,
And there is'nt a pirate-heart more wild.
Bride she shall be of the pirate king,
And her bright red laughing lips shall sing
' When the sea-king speaks the waves obey,
And they wash the blood of his foes away,
         And their bones the green depths keep.' "

That is the life that is fair and free—
So the pirates think—on the fair blue sea.
But if ever a king's ship spies them out
They must sharpen their cutlas-blades, no doubt,
For the king's stout sailors will harry them then
And their one last chance is to die like men,
Die in a frenzy, fierce and gay,
And the sea will wash their blood away,
         And the waves will over them leap.

IV.

THE FAIRY BELLS.

Of old at night, when the woods were bright
   And the air was warm with the warmth of June,
The bells of the fairies tinkled light
   And their eyes flashed under the summer moon.
Yes, then you might hear, when the moon shone clear
   Through the woods, or over the purple fells,
Sometimes distant and sometimes near,
   The sound of the beautiful fairy bells,
               The beautiful fairy bells.

Alas ! men's hearts waxed selfish and hard,
   And they only cared for gold and gain ;
The ears of the fairies grew quite jarred
   By the puff, puff, puff of the rattling train.
To deep dark forests the fairies fled,
   And we all are sorry—though no one tells —
That the innocent sweet old days are dead
   When we all could hear the fairy bells,
               The beautiful fairy bells.

But still when lovers are fond and true,
   If they listen within the woods of June
When the stars shine through deep skies of blue
   And the white clouds kiss the shy-faced moon,

K

They may hear, they may hear, soft, sweet and clear,
  A sound that rises, a sound that swells,
Sometimes distant and sometimes near—
  The sound of the beautiful fairy bells,
            The beautiful fairy bells.

A POET'S GETHSEMANE.

A POET'S GETHSEMANE.

PART I.

THE AGONY OF YOUTH.

I.

IN LONDON.

I hold her letter in my hand.
 . . . Which is it who so sorely lies?
The girl?   That's hard to understand.
 God?   Baser falsehood that implies.
But one, or both, have lied—that's clear.
I hold truth's plain death-warrant here.

" I love you not," her letter says :
 " You even insult me by the thought."
Insult her ! . . . . I who had given my days
 My heart, my life, to please in aught
The woman who now writes to me
With a girl's perfect cruelty.

" My love is given to him whose wife
 In some short weeks I am to be."
Then why, in God's name, did she strive
 To win my pure first love from me?
She found, no doubt, a light fierce joy,
Experimenting on a boy.

A boy's heart! Yes, she thought, no doubt,
   That I could take the thing in jest :
Could serve her, follow her about,
   And give some love,—yet not my best.
My love was sweet in summer-time.
It lasts till winter—that's a crime !

It pleased her in those summer hours :
   The passionate worship that I brought
Was new to her.—We gathered flowers ;
   Her swift eyes searched for mine, unsought.
Her hand pressed mine. Its velvet touch
Thrilled through my palm,—and that was much.

It seems half lovely, as I look
   With burning wild gaze back to-day
--The meadow-sweet beside the brook ;
   The broad sea-spaces, silver-grey ;
The walks beneath the moon at night ;
The boats' sails, brown or snowy white ;

The stream that gurgled past the mill ;
   The arbour at the garden's end ;
Our quarrel on the corn-clad hill ;
   Her laughing anger with her friend ;
Her knife—with which (with skill sublime !)
I carved our names, to mock at time ;

The very robin, perching near
   In the wide low-branched apple tree
And craving largess without fear
   Of bread-crumbs as we sat at tea
Within the bower beside the stream ;
These things flash on me as I dream !

*   *

And yet I hold her letter—Yes,
  It proves the former things were lies ;
Her soft hand's touch,—like a caress !
  Her glance,—like God's glance from the skies !
My castle of bright dreams must fall :
She never cared for me at all.

And yet she *did* care—There's the pang,
  The viewless horror. That's the spear
That rends my heart with iron fang,—
  The crowning shattering maddening fear
That, after all, the woman's heart
Is, always, of my own a part.

That is the terror. When a girl
  So leads a youth's wild heart astray
God does not let her lightly curl
  Herself to sleep for many a day
Within the bosom, or the bed,
Of him she now has chosen to wed.

No, God sends anguish. There's the fear :
  She yet may rise and come to me ;
Fierce passion yet may win her ear
  And, murmuring therein constantly,
May make her hate the man for whom
She now consigns love to its tomb.

For, when her eyes met mine, I know
  There was a something in their gaze
Which, though long years may come and go
  And many an autumn strew the ways
With wild leaves shivering at the rain,
Will never flash through them again.

Never.   He cannot draw her eyes
    To his, as yesterday I drew
Their glance, and saw the tear-drops rise,
    And laughed as through my soul I knew
That she who once those far shores trod
With me was given to me by God.

When once the soul has seen the soul,
    The man and woman cannot part :
Another lover may control
    The woman's body,—not her heart.
Of all things sad, I think that this
Sad thing by far the saddest is.

And this is ever a poet's fate !
    To know the woman his indeed,
And then to know she knows too late :
    To know that God's will has decreed
That she shall learn what love implies
By murdering love before his eyes.

A poet by his subtle force
    Of soul and being can discern
The woman's nature still in course
    Of being created ; he can burn
With passion for the soul half born—
The soul her " husband's " soul will scorn.

The poet sees what she can see
    Hardly at all—her nature true :
He feels this linked eternally
    In sweet communion ever-new
To his true nature ; feels her wife ;
Rooted in him : his breath ; his life.

And then he sees the woman swerve
  And, knowing not her counterpart,
Give touch of body, shock of nerve
  (Never the shock of heart and heart!)
To some man who can only see
What's evident externally.

This man becomes her "husband": though
  The poet feels with sweet divine
Strange agony, "Though this be so,
  In God's sight still the woman's mine.
Aye, though he hold her, hold her fast,
Her soul will fly to mine at last."

*   *

And then the Vision!   Who sent that?
  Was that some lying spirit's design?
—As in my lonely room I sat
  (Her hand that day had thrilled through mine)
There came, one night, a sudden sense
Superb, engrossing, clear, intense,

A sudden sense that she was there,
  Close by me in that very room;
Herself, proud, queenly.   While the air
  Grew fragrant as with summer's bloom,
Through this sweet air the woman came
And touched my lips with lips of flame.

Then, through the long miraculous night
  I lay awake, yet slept it seemed
A slumber broken by delight,
  And through my soul her strange eyes gleamed.
I clasped her in our marriage-bed:
"How beautiful you are!" I said.

And then her body, wondrous, white,
  Pure, full of maiden strength and calm,
Seemed to transfuse me with its light :
  Glad mouth to mouth, warm palm to palm,
Quite till the crimson dawn of day
Wrapt in our marriage-bliss we lay.

And night by night the woman came :
  For some six nights the glory gleamed
For some six nights all heaven aflame
  All earth aflower and fervent seemed
Aye, night by night I seemed to rest
Triumphant on her very breast.

I closed my eyes each night,—and then
  Unclosed my eyes, and she was there ;
Ever the same : each night again
  She seemed to watch me, noble, fair,
Pure-wifely ; and she laid her head
Beside mine in my lonely bed.

*   *

That was the Vision.—I believed
  The living God had sent it me :
With joyous full heart I received
  Its message of great ecstasy.
She was my wife. So God had said,
Who sent her angel to my bed.

And, now that God had done this thing,
  Could any hold that God would lie ?
That he would steal my wife, and fling
  Deep into hell irrevocably
The soul who had believed his word ?
Could God deny himself ? Absurd !

Could God now prostitute my bride
  By placing in another's bed,
Warm from the pressure of my side,
  The form to mine but lately wed?
Could God thus rend her limb from limb?
Give soul to me—body to him?

Nay, never! For my Vision stood
  Superb and strong, emphatic, clear.
If any dream of old held good,
  If God once spake in Abraham's ear,
If he with Moses held discourse,
He had spoken to me with no less force.

In modern London just as clear
  The Lord had spoken out to me
As where the heights of Sinai sheer
  Rose in their grim austerity.
To me the Lord had spoken who spake
To fishers on the Eastern lake.

There were not visions two or three,
  Gods two or three, but only one.
God spake to Christ : God spake to me :
  And what he promised would be done.
God lied to me? He lied to all.
By this his truth must stand or fall.

So, full of faith, I went to her,
  Believing that the Lord who sent
The sacred Vision could not err
  And that his sovereign justice meant
That she should mar her mother's scheme
And bring fulfilment to my dream.

For, "surely now I see," I said,
   "She does not love him.   She is mine.
Her white ghost slept within my bed :
   Her ghost-arms round my neck did twine
The woman's self must now fulfil
The high God's undisputed will."

     *   *

She would not see me.   But instead
   She wrote the pencil scrap I hold.
I read it,—and my heart fell dead :
   I, who had been so strong and bold,
So full of faith—that this should be
The end of all God's pageantry !

"Leave me," she said, " and be a man :
   Yes, leave me and all thought of me.
I do not change : I never can.
   To him whose wife I am to be
My love is given,—aye, all my heart.
For ever you and I must part."

This on the Vision's very top !
   This flung in God's face as reply !
My heart came to a sudden stop :
   I did not reason, or ask why
So strange, so mad, an answer came,
Befouling her and God with shame.

I simply seemed turned quite to stone.
   I left the house—I know not how—
Without a sigh, without a groan :
   (I wonder at my calmness now)—
Crushed utterly ; completely slain;
Too throughly stricken almost for pain.

II.

AT OXFORD. SIX WEEKS LATER.

Six weeks ago! How long it seems
 Since through the quiet London Square
I walked, bereft of hopes and dreams,
 And felt my whole life leafless, bare,
Barren for ever. Now to-day
The earth is gladdened. It is May.

I walk beside the river's marge ;
 I see the grey old Oxford towers ;
Watch flashing skiff, and glittering barge,
 And, on the banks, the same old flowers.
Town, river, fields—all are the same :
My only sameness is my name.

I feel as if I bore within
 My frame a corpse. With living eyes
I see the quick foam-bubbles spin
 Adown the weir ; I see the skies ;
I see the flowers ; I see the oars
Sweep by the old thyme-scented shores.

And yet I know that I am dead
 And that the horror of despair
Grips all my heart. . . . . They must be wed
 By now—and does he find her fair ?
And does he twine with tender hands
The sweet long loosened brown hair bands ?

Was last night—yes?—their wedding night,
    Or will it be to-night?   Will he
Win from her lips unknown delight
    And find her sweet exceedingly?
So soft to touch? so good to kiss?
And was my darling born for this?

And was I born to watch the oars
    Flash by the thyme-sweet Isis' banks,
To pace these green sun-lighted shores,
    To watch the tall reeds' dark-green ranks,
While, underneath the May-stars bright,
Such horror may take place to-night?

If I am mad, God madden me
    Completely!   Then I shall not know
The limitless eternity,
    The unplumbed dark depth, of my woe.
I shall not always see them then,
Nor hate the very thought of men.

I shall not always—as at night
    Without fail now—with hot eyes see
A bride with tearful glance and bright,
    A man in love's proximity.
I shall not watch within the gloom
Of their half-lighted bridal room.

I shall not count their every kiss,
    As now I count—as now I say,
" A hundred for her lips ! and this
    He lets from mouth to forehead stray.
I know last night he found her fair ;
So many times he kissed her hair."

If I were mad, that were a boon !
   I am not mad ; and so I see
—Beneath these very stars and moon
   That through my window mock at me—
My wife, whom God in vision gave,
His wedded wife,—his wedded slave !

           *   *

The days pass on. I hate this place :
   I hate the country green and fair ;
I hate the bright swift boats that race ;
   I hate the pure sweet-smelling air ;
I hate the river broad and blue ;
I hate these trees the sun gleams through.

I'll back to London ! There, at least
   I shall feel nearer to the past :
The distance will have then decreased
   Between me and where I saw her last.
I shall be happier near the spot
Where she so loved, yet loved me not.

London ! I died in town in March,
   And I'll revisit town in May.
The flower-beds near the Marble Arch,
   With hyacinths or tulips gay,
Are fairer than these country meads
Wherethrough the blue old Isis speeds.

I shall be near the house wherein
   I saw her last ; saw those strange eyes,
In which I fancied love had been,—
   In which I saw the tear-drops rise.
I'll turn once more that old sad page
Of life, and make my pilgrimage.

Yet, cre I go—to leave in doubt
   The issue longer—is that wise ?
I'll search the papers, ferret out
   The truth, and with unflinching eyes
Gaze at the names,—if so it be :
Their date of marriage I must see.

Here are the papers.   Let me search
   The file ; last month it must have been :
I think that I can guess the church—
   (I wonder, *did* the devil win
The game ?   I even now believe
That God might send my heart reprieve.

Yes, even now I will not hold
   That God could lie—so basely too :
She has not married—is not sold :
   God and my darling still are true)
Ah—in the *Times*—their names– great heaven!
Married. . . on April twenty-seven.

III.

LONDON. IN JUNE AND JULY.

I saw her face again at Lord's.
   Her eyes met mine. She grew quite pale.
Her eyes' expression ill accords
   With happiness. The same old tale
I think it is. The mothers sell
Their daughters, and so people hell.

I think she loves me.—Oh, her heart
   Was sweet and grand and full of power!
She loved and worshipped all true Art :
   She should have helped me tend to flower
The bud of poesy that she
Discerned and nurtured first in me.

In this strange age, when all is new,
   When Thought arises from the tomb,
There was such glorious work to do—
   But she shrinks back into the gloom : `
What dulls for her Time's golden dawn ?
The sunset o'er a Rectory lawn !

She might have held a poet's heart,
   Held it for ever. She and I,
Wedded in love and love of Art,
   Married most sympathetically,
Might nobly have helped the world along,
She by brave thought, and I by song.

The chance is over.—Though her eyes
   Met mine at Lord's the other day,
They soon will meet the calm blue skies
   In the green country, far away
From London smoke and London noise,
And far from action's rarest joys.

High thought will quit her heart and brain :
   Aye, gradually the thought of me,
At first a pang, a passionate pain,
   Will change to a faint memory.
Then the dull prose of daily life
Will make her—just a parson's wife.

L

She will read Keble on the lawn,
   And talk of Keble to his friends :
Our hearts will far apart be drawn ;
   We shall be seeking different ends ;
Her husband-priest will weigh her down,
And scatter to the winds her crown.

I loved her so ! I would have died
   To help her thought,—to lift it on.
Upon the forehead of my bride
   Thought's fairest circlet should have shone.
I loved in early days to see
Her young thought's budding potency.

Now it is over.   Day by day
   Her thought must grow more dull and hard :
Winter will blight the blossoming spray ;
   The Church's keen frost will retard
The growth of blossom-thoughts and deeds
That would have widened past old creeds.

Yes, she is his.   His—evermore.
   Not only body, lovely face,
Sweet lips a god's heart might adore,'
   Shoulders a god's arms might embrace,
Not only this—the mind as well
Is prostituted.   That is hell.

The mind and body both must go :
   The head, the heart, the young pure soul :
All will be, by a process slow
   But sure, diverted to a goal
Far other than our young hearts dreamed
When at our feet the bright waves gleamed.

The waves must all lament with me !
   The flowers and sprays we gathered there ;
The stars that shone above our sea ;
   · The ferns I twisted in her hair ;
How all must grieve, how all must weep,
That her young soul has fallen asleep !

It will not wake now. Day by day
   The bond—such as it is—will grow
Closer, that binds to common clay
   White marble. Absolutely I know
The full result. I am not blind,
Or mad. (Could I be, God were kind !)

I am not mad or blind. I see
   With clear convincing piteous gaze,
With horrible grim certainty,
   The straight procession of her days.
I see them follow, one by one :
Storm, winter, summer—rain or sun.

Children will come. Yes, even so.
   When God works horror, let it be
Done throughly. Let the man's heart know
   Pain's most complete ascendency !
While I'm in hell, let me explore,
God, thy domain from door to door !

There will be children. These will draw
   Her heart to his,—make her forget
All dreams we dreamed, all sights we saw.
   They'll make the union closer yet
Between the mother and the man
Who makes her mother—Nature's plan !

Yes: I shall know that she who came
   In that strange Vision in the night
Is carrying out the carnal aim
   Of man, and that God thinks this right;
That God first let her sleep with me,
Then wrenched her from me suddenly—

Wrenched her away, and set her down
   Far in the North, and made her there
This country rector's pride and crown,
   And bade her with sore travail bear
Children on children to his bed:
God did this—did not strike her dead.

No—best completest.—Let them live:
   Let this be quite the end of all.
But take ye warning, all who strive
   For God, lest your dream-temple fall:
Lest worse than woman's lips that lie
Be God, who prompts them from the sky.

Lest having done what Christ, I say,
   Could hardly have had the strength to do,
Were he alive in this our day—
   Having believed that God is true,
And woman, you should find that each
Is traitorous past all human speech.

Lest, having fought a fight supreme,
   You should at that fight's ending find
Your faith in God a hollow dream,
   In woman, moonshine of the mind;
Find that to struggle hard with sin
Means to lose all man cares to win.

For I staked all upon the Lord,
　And on the woman.　I have lost
All.　He and she have broken their word.
　—I battled, heedless of the cost,
Fought unto death's point.　Then God lied.
Aye, God, not man, seduced my bride.

PART II.

THE AGONY OF MANHOOD.

I.

SUNLIGHT.

Thirteen long years have passed away
    Since through those autumn woods we went :
It was a bright September day,
    And I was full of sweet content ;
So happy by her side to be—
In heaven, if she but looked at me.

The leaves were turning golden-red ;
    The swift stream splashed along the dale ;
In the far distance, blue, outspread,
    Boundless, with here and there a sail,
The sunlit sea gleamed, saying, "To-night
Reseek my green cliff's moonlit height."

We were so happy, she and I !
    There was no place for black despair
In all the world ! clear was the sky,
    The autumn flowers were sweet, the air
Was crisp and pure. In that green wood
It seemed to me God must be good.

I know she loved me then.   Her eyes
   Sought mine so constantly,—yet fell,
As if with maidenly surprise,
   As if afraid their tale to tell,
When mine searched in their depths to see
If yet she was in love with me.

Ah ! thirteen years.   To-day in town
   My head reels with the strangest sense
That that, my first love's long-lost crown,
   May yet by God's omnipotence
Be quite restored, returned to me,
In all its pristine purity.

I am in love.   I feel it now :
   I feel the sweet sense through each vein.
I am in love : I know not how ;
   And yet I am in love again.
I am in love.   Yes, ten times more
Even than I ever loved before.

I loved—those thirteen years ago—
   With tenderest love.   My love was slain.
I married, and I seemed to know
   Some slight sweet respite from my pain.
I was beloved with passion wild,
And I,—I loved the gold-haired child.

But still through all my married life
   The old fierce former dream prevailed,
And, though I loved my loving wife,
   My heart was ceaselessly assailed
By memories strong.   I loved ; and yet
I could not stifle mad regret.

The old hands drew me, and the eyes
　　Still drew me,—and I seemed to see
Ever the pale-blue Northern skies
　　And heard the wild wind's revelry
Along the Northern shores, and dreamed
That as of old the white moon gleamed.

But now to-day I am in love,
　　In love again,—and now I know
(For this new fact has served to prove
　　Beyond dispute that this is so)
That never, since those early hours,
Has my heart loved with all its powers.

Strong manhood adds a newer force
　　To love to-day.　I love at last
Once more with passion; gain of course
　　An added strength from all my past.
Past loves, like rivers, with their might
Swell the sea-passion of last night.

It seemed so strange—the girlish trust
　　Of her who met me, quite alone.
The wild Strand, thronged with painted lust,
　　Seemed heaven-like when I heard her tone.
She met me, trusted me.　Quite pure
She was.　Her first look made me sure.

And then I loved her.　That, you see,
　　Was just God's mystery—very sweet.
Her simple girlish purity
　　Brought the worn poet to her feet.
In a wild world of wrath and crime
She seemed half sweet, and half sublime.

Then, at the play, I watched her face :
  It seemed so strange--there, quite alone
With this girl full of girlish grace
    And tenderest beauty, flower half-blown.
Alone,—no friend or guardian near ;
And yet she seemed to have no fear.

I think that changed me.   That drew out
  Life's poison from my veins in part.
She was a pure girl, not a doubt,
    With loving eyes and loving heart,
And yet she sat there by the side
Of one in whom all faith had died.

She sat there, knowing nought of me,
  Yet trusting.--Then my whole heart grew
Softer : I loved her purity ;
  I felt it thrill me through and through.
I left her at her mother's door ;
In love with her, for evermore.

*   *

The days are passing swiftly on ;
  Some happiness returns to me :
I feel as if some light had shone
    From out the deep obscurity.
It may be God has watched my pain,
And will restore my love again.

How if God has led up to this ?
  If from the first he thus designed,
And robbed me of my first love's kiss
    To pay me back in higher kind ?
I love this girl ; and can it be
That God may let her love—even me ?

Even me—sad, care-worn, ill at ease,
   At war with self, the world, and him ;
Harassed by wild perplexities ;
   Weary with strife and suffering grim ;
Can she— this young bright girl—be brought
To give my love one passing thought ?

I am so old and weary.   She
   Is young, fatigueless.   Death, it seems,
Were far more fitting bride for me
   Than this young girl, whose dark glance dreams
Sweet dreams of spring, and spring's flowers fair,
While I dream only of despair.

Yet if it could be so ? my prayer
   Would then be answered, and I might
(I think I never saw such hair—
   Coal-black : and then the brown eyes' light !)
—I might, perhaps, again believe
In God.   The sun might shine at eve.

I think God lets me love her too.
   Perhaps God brought me to her side
With a distinct great work to do,
   A true man's work, before I died.
It may be so.   She's on the stage,
So round her all the man-wolves rage.

Curse them ! I know them.   Just because
   She's unprotected, poor and weak,
They'll glance around, and leer, and pause,
   And think their game is safe, and seek
With one accord to steal this pearl.
They'll do their best to ruin the girl.

My dark-eyed darling ! no, please God,
   They shall not ruin you. I say, "No."
Your feet across my path have trod,
   And you have made my tired heart glow :
Would any injure you, of these ?
Across my body if you please !

I stand, and God stands, in the way.
   All London seems against you—yes ?
They say you *shall* sink. But I say
   That you shall *not* sink : nothing less.
I'll fight for you for endless time,
And make the battle-field sublime.

All London on one side, and this
   The low and bad side ? let it be.
Men proffering diamonds for your kiss ?
   Well, let them proffer. Trust in me.
Bribed managers may swear to wrong :
I'll save you,—and crown you with my song.

These men are devils. Day by day
   They struggle to seduce anew
Poor foolish girls, their easy prey.
   They make, themselves a hellish crew,
The stage a hell. They can't afford
To scorn the offer of a lord.

He wants a chorus-girl ? My lord
   May pick and choose. The manager
(Tipped by the youngling) will accord
   His lordship leave without demur
To pass behind the scenes, and try
Girl-fishing with the golden fly.

Money's the question, that is all.
    Just money—money.   Can he pay?
He can?   How soon the girl will fall!
    How Satan hates enforced delay!
A bouquet—bracelet—supper—kiss—
And Miss S. is no longer " Miss."

She has learned the secret ; still a child,
    It may be ; ignorant indeed :
Yet ruined, lost, betrayed, beguiled,
    And just to gratify the greed
Of managers, and lust of men
Who ornament the " Upper Ten."

Not so in your case.   I will step
    Between you and the men who rove
Destroying.   *You* a demirep?
    You sell your beauty, and your love ?
Never !   I swear your soul shall be
Pure to the very end, and free.

At last I see a poet's work
    Before me, worthy of the man,
And, please God, I will never shirk
    The task, but carry out God's plan.
Some hound would fain destroy ?   Not he !
Unless his sword slips first through me.

       *   *

Her beauty brings my youth again.
    A girl's pure freshness can create
Spring's gladness in the heart and brain
    And smooth the forehead grooved with Fate.
The young sweet brilliance of her eyes
Has changed life's sunset to sunrise.

Her magnetism is so good,
  So pure, so sinless. When she came,
Up to my very waist I stood
  Plunged in hell's waters, hot as flame :
But now I think that there may be
Perhaps a God,—yes, even for me.

I dare not dream it. Yet I hope ;
  I struggle with the old despair ;
Drowning, I cling to this frail rope ;
  I worship her dark eyes and hair.
I long to die for her. I long
To make her deathless in my song.

" O thou who cam'st so late in life
  Across my path," so I would say—
" My more than friend, my more than wife,
  Thou who didst turn my night to day,
At least bid not my love depart,
But let me tarry where thou art."

II.

TWILIGHT.

How strong my passionate love has grown
  How strange and sad and hard to-day
What once seemed easy seems ! My own
  She is, and yet I may grow grey
And she may never quite be mine :
Can such a method be divine ?

Old doubt returns.   Can God do this?
  Fill all my heart with love of thee ;
Put thy mouth to my own to kiss,
  And let me feel its purity ;
Make me each day discern thee fair,
And worship more thine eyes and hair ;

Can he do this—did he inspire
  When thou wast (as thou art not now)
In danger, my protective fire
  Of passion— listen to my vow
That, come what would, thou shouldst be safe,
However heart and flesh might chafe ;

O sweetheart, did God do this thing,
  Send me to save thee—and can he,
The just great God, the mighty King,
  Now ravish all thy soul from me ?
Will some new hand approach, and reap
The corn I sowed in agony deep ?

Aye, wilt thou marry?   Shall I stand
  And see the glory fade away
From this our own enchanted land ?
  Will darkness be too strong for day ?
Is this what God demands at last ?
More pain—I thought the worst was past.

Must I, who by those Northern streams
  Saw autumn shed upon the air
Red leaves, and change the flowers of dreams
  To flowerless wastes of real despair—
Must I, who saw my youth's sun set,
In manhood meet a worse thing yet ?

Must I, who, married, feel my heart
　Unmarried, utterly unwed,
Love thee, then see my dream depart,
　Aye, never kiss thy black dear head
Again, though all I asked was this—
A brother's place, a brother's kiss?

If so, I have been born in vain,
　Except to show that truly indeed
God relishes inflicting pain,
　And that the only quite true creed
Is this—that Satan rules the sky,
The sole God from eternity.

*　　*

And then she loves me. Yes, I know :
　For, when I kiss her darling head,
It rises, ever so gently—so—
　And meets my lips. No word is said,
And yet by that one simple sign
I know the girl's pure heart is mine.

Perhaps . . . and have I not the right?
　What man has better right than I?
I've guarded her by day and night,
　Been sunlight in her mid-day sky,
Starlight and moonlight through her sleep ;
I sowed the corn. May I not reap

I think I *could* reap, if I chose ;
　For I have made her life so fair :
Her every happiness she owes
　To me,—each breath of summer air
That she respires, pure, sinless, free,
She owes, and knows she owes, **to me.**

Shall I not take her ?   Shall I stand
  Doubting, reluctant?   Though I'm bound
And wedded, would a God command
  That I should never quite be crowned
By perfect love ?   This virgin's mine !
I feel it : and the gift's divine.

I've won her—surely?   What can man
  Do more than I have done indeed ?
She needed succour.   Lo !   I ran
  To succour,—saved her at her need.
Andromeda was rightly wed
To Perseus, when her foe lay dead.

I who the many-headed foe
  Of London selfishness have slain,
Shall I in turn not surely know
  Reward for all my love and pain ?
Andromeda shall I not take,
And on her lips my long thirst slake ?

A single monster Perseus slew :
  But I have toiled from day to day,
Have fought beneath bright skies of blue,
  Have battled through the fog-wreaths grey,
Have won for her wild countless fights
And overthrown a thousand knights.

Is she not mine beyond dispute ?
  Mine : and my dear one knows it too.
I kissed her fiercely ; she was mute.
  So little now remains to do—
To press my victory to the end,
  Become a lover, not a friend.

Not friend! . . . Ah, would it be to lose
  The deep sweet friendship? Would it be
To stain her pure mind, and confuse
  Her simple trusting thoughts of me?
I cannot marry her. Would less
Be wronging her beyond redress?

Have I fought through a thousand fights,
  Unhorsed black-armoured foe on foe,
Yet is there out of all the knights
  One knight still left me to lay low?
Does one still bar me from the goal?
The lower side of my own soul.

Is, after all, myself the worst
  Of all my enemies?—Have I slain
Thousands, and left their bodies cursed
  And sword-split helmets on the plain:
Have I, with heart ready to break,
Fought London for the woman's sake?

And must I, having saved her now,
  And standing face to face alone
With her, take on me a harder vow?
  Must love's fruits to the winds be thrown?
Must I now with a stronger knight
—Myself—wage this last deadliest fight?

—

BOOK III

CHRIST IN THE HEART.

SONGS OF THE SEASONS.

SONGS OF THE SEASONS.

I.

SONG OF SPRING.

Very bright and very pure and very tender
  Is the golden sunlight on the laughing leaves :
Very lovely is the early morning's splendour ;
  Sweet the lilacs smell beneath the cottage-eaves.
All things wake renewed to vigour and to passion.
  Lo ! the daisies paint their pink tips, one by one :
And the daffodils in their old shameless fashion
  Dip their robes in colour stolen from the sun.

Lovers pass beneath the fragrance of the hedges,
  And they pause, half wild with wonder and with bliss—
(While the river whispers, "See them !" to the sedges)
  And their lips seem soft as velvet, as they kiss.
Blue the sky is, clear of cloud and free of sorrow.
  Such a noble height of rapture has been won
That to-day's delight can dream not of to-morrow :
  All things worship at the altar of the sun.

Yet the sweetness of the season gaineth sweetness
  From the thought of loving Jesus in the sky.
Passion wins its utmost rapture and completeness,
  Realizing that a loving heart is nigh.
What is spring without the feeling that a Father
  Watches, blesses, every noble action done ?
—Sends the flowers of woman's love for man to gather !
  Sends the daisies to be gathered by the sun !

SONGS OF THE SEASONS.

II.

SONG OF SUMMER.

Grand and glorious is the season of the roses.
    Spring has passed, but stronger sunlight gilds the corn.
On the silver stream the lily's head reposes,
    And the ripple lifts it tenderly at morn.
Love has deepened, with the deepening of the season.
    Love has strengthened, with the passing of the hours.
Love has grown beyond the fear of change or treason.
    Love has stolen the glow and glory of the flowers.

Man and woman understand and love each other.
    Through the silent leafy summer lanes they wend,
Hand in hand.   The blue sky smiles down like a mother,
    And the gentle breeze of summer seems a friend.
For in spring the heart of man was full of gladness,
    But in summer rapture gathers all its powers.
Who can dream of sorrow, who can think on sadness,
    While the sky is full of stars, the fields of flowers?

Yet the summer and its glory overflowing,
    Sun and moon and starlit height of purple sky,
Silver stream and forest deep and blossoms blowing,
    All will pass.   Yes, even roses have to die!
But the sweetness of the Christ grows ever dearer
    As life's autumn strips the greenery of the bowers :
And the beauty of another land seems nearer
    As the beauty of the summer quits the flowers.

SONGS OF THE SEASONS.

III.

SONG OF AUTUMN.

When the leaves are whirling through the forest olden,
  Grey and green and brown and crimson dying leaves,
Sodden leaves that only yesterday were golden,
  While the autumn wind-swept foliage sways and heaves,
There are ghosts of lovers through the forest questing,
  Seeking vainly as their weary footsteps stray,
Haunts they loved when all around the birds were nesting
  And the air was sweet with fragrance of the may.

Weary ghosts they are of former happy lovers.
  Now they find no mossy carpet for their feet
Spread within the oaken glades and hazel covers :
  Pale and tearful, in the forest-depths they meet.
" Here was once a yellow primrose-bank," they mutter.
  " Here we built a golden cowslip-throne," they say.
" From yon thicket, with a chirrup and a flutter,
  Dashed the brown thrush thro' the white and crimson may."

Is there any peace of mind for those who ponder
  In the autumn on the summer's vanished bloom,
Save in hope that every blossom-spirit, yonder
  Far in heaven, exults triumphant o'er the tomb ?
Is there hope for human spirits, pale and breathless
  With the struggle and the strife of every day ?
Just the hope that love's true flowers in heaven are deathless,
  Though death withers all the sweetness of the may.

SONGS OF THE SEASONS.

IV.

SONG OF WINTER.

Dreary snows are all around us in the gardens,
   And the starlit frosty sky is chilly blue.
On the silent stream the stifling cold ice hardens :
   The moon shivers at the air it travels through.
Yet the sweetest of the seasons is the winter :
   Winter well may smile at summer's ardent scorn.
When the air was keen with many an icy splinter,
   Love with summer at the heart of him was born.

Love hath summer in his spirit never-dying.
   Does it matter if the wild wind through the sprays
Dashes, leaving all the tossing branches sighing ?
   Does it matter if the snow-drifts pile the ways ?
For in winter through a humble heart and lowly
   God revealed himself to man.   On Christmas morn
Jesus Christ the pure of soul, the Saviour holy,
   Heedless of the bitter winter wind, was born.

And the winter of the spirit—bitter sorrow—
   Who can banish, who can temper, if not he ?
Who but Jesus can remind us that to-morrow
   Shall be sunshine, though murk night is on the sea ?
For in winter, in the season when the berry
   Gleams, bright scarlet on the holly and the thorn,
Men may feast, the saddest spirits may make merry.
   In the winter night the Prince of light was born.

CHRIST IN THE HEART.

CHRIST, AND THE POET.

Satan.

O poet, in whose brain and heart the sweetness
    Of summer reigns and glows,
What bars thy life from rounding to completeness ?
    Where findest thou thy foes ?

Thy foes are surely in the heavens above thee ;
    God gazes down with scorn :—
The golden stars and golden blossoms love thee,
    And the bright clouds of morn.

Upon thy side thou hast the sunset-glory ;
    The clouds in fiery mail.
Each snowdrop whispers thee its pet love-story ;
    Each crocus brings its tale.

Thou wanderest singing by the river-edges,
    And lo ! the ripples pause,
And hush their love-song to the sighing sedges,
    To learn thy music's laws.

Thou hast a power of endless loving-kindness,
    A love of all things born.
But thee God hates. He'll close thine eyes with blindness
    He'll pierce thy brows with thorn !

The love of violets in the mossy hollows—
    This, poet, thou shalt win :
The suffrages of the swift-wingéd swallows ;
    The worship of the linn.

The pure-souled snow-white lilies shall adore thee ;
    The autumnal forest-glade
Shall pour its gorgeous crimson foliage o'er thee ;
    The summer boughs shall shade.

Its rarest pearls the amorous sea shall fling thee,
    Pearls gathered from its breast.
Strange priceless gems the humming-birds shall bring thee,
    Trinkets of throat or crest.

The purple heather in the moorland regions
    Shall nestle round thy feet.
The whole world's songsters, in their countless legions,
    Shall own thy song more sweet.

And yet, thou poet, whatsoe'er thou doest,
    Thy toil shall end in gloom :
When summer skies above thee beam their bluest,
    Prepare thou for the tomb !

Poet.

    I love the bright blue heights of air,
        The sunlight in the morn :
    I love to watch that diamond rare,
        The dewdrop on a thorn.
    I love the white clouds in the skies,
        The blue waves by the land :
    But bluer yet are woman's eyes,
        And whiter is her hand.

Satan.

The morning's light shall pass away,
  It shall be dark at noon :
And night shall lack the golden ray
  Of friendly star or moon.
Thou lovest woman ?   She shall prove
  Thy direst bitterest woe.
She loves thee ?   Yes : and she can love
  Thy neighbour even so !

Poet.

My song shall reach the frail and weak :
  The sad lost soul shall find
That Christ's sweet pity still can speak
  To erring hearts and blind.
Of all the crowns that I can win,
  This is the highest indeed—
To save one woman's soul from sin ;
  To guard her at her need.

Satan.

And having raised her quite from sin,
  Watch how the affair will end.
The girl you spent your soul to win,
  Your fortune to befriend,
Will—for a diamond brooch maybe,
  Or for much less than this—
Barter the mouth your modesty
  Did not presume to kiss.

Poet.

I'll win, please God, a noble name,
  Do noble work indeed ;

Speak words of thunder, words of flame,
    Shake many a rotten creed.
My words shall ring from land to land,
    And many a throne shall quake ;
The sword shall flash from many a hand
    For my strong singing's sake.

Satan.

Dream on, thou fool.   The song wins less,
    The nobler that it be,
The people's homage.   Their caress
    Is won quite easily.
Write folly, with a tinge of dirt :
    You surely will succeed.
Bilge-water, through a penny squirt,—
    That is the chrism they need !

Poet.

I'll write high poems.   I will pour
    Along my throbbing strain
The wild winds' wail, the thunder's roar,
    The music of the main.
Though many a bard has lived and died,
    Still golden sunrise gleams :
The stars shine through night's palace wide,
    And fill my soul with dreams.

Satan.

A dream—that is the poet's life.
    But every dream shall end.
The sweetheart changes to a wife
    (And then the stars descend !)

The wife developes to a scold,
  The songs in which you trust
Will mix with cabbages and mould,
  With cinders and with dust.

CHRIST.

O poet-heart, despair not.—Know
  That every song of thine
Has made some angel's spirit glow ;
  Yes : every noble line.
All earthly joys thou hast to miss?
  Earth's hopes and passions end ?
Yet is it not sufficient bliss
  That Jesus calls thee " friend ? "

II

CHRIST, AND THE LOVER.

Satan.

Lovelier is she than a poet's dreaming?
Brighter are her eyes than starlight gleaming?
   Is the sun less golden than her hair?
Did thy youth pass greyly and in sorrow?
Weary, didst thou sleep—and on the morrow
   Didst thou wake, and find a goddess there?

Lover.

Lo! my soul was lost. Alone I wandered.
By the deadly river-waves I pondered,
   Gazing in their dark and bitter flow.
But my heart was changed, for true love found me:
Took my weary life in hand, and crowned me:
   Spread across the heavens a sunset-glow.

Satan.

Sweet she is; but time's track never changes;
Over all the golden fields he ranges,
   Flower-destroying—Shall he spare thy bliss?
Pleasant are her lips; but time will chill them,
Not for ever will the old sweetness fill them,
   Thou wilt tire before the thousandth kiss!

Lover.

I was lost and sad, and very weary.
Through the gloom of life, the darkness dreary,
  Came the vision of a perfect thing.
Autumn was it.   Through the forest-arches,
Underneath the October-yellowed larches,
  Came a presence fairer than of Spring.

Satan.

And again, when thou dost wax quite olden,
Underneath the autumn foliage golden
  Thou shalt wander—wander quite alone.
Death may love the lips thou lovest dearly ;
Death's grim bugle-call may ring out clearly,
  And her lips may answer with a moan.

Lover.

Surely God, who made this perfect creature,
Set the stamp of heaven in every feature,
  Having given, will take her not away ?
Can God steal from heaven the stars that glitter
Slay the golden sun ?   Oh, that were bitter !
  Can he pour wild darkness over day ?

Satan.

Even if she lives, thou wilt not know her
When another fifty years shall show her
  Changed and gaunt and wrinkled to thy gaze.
Hardly then thy changed heart shall remember
Her who made the dark woods one September
  Sweeter than the woods of sunniest Mays.

Lover.

Darling ! As the long years fleet and perish,
With a tenderer sweet love will I cherish,
    Guard, protect, and tend, and worship thee.
Never will my strong love change one tittle !
Though the waves may eat away the brittle
    Rocks that seemed so stalwart round the sea !

Satan.

Long before one iron-bound cliff has faltered,
Will thy love be changed in form and altered ;
    While the stern cliffs still resist the wave,
Every gleam of passion will have vanished.
Slowly next thy love-thoughts will be banished,
    Till at last they are ghosts around a grave.

Lover.

When we wandered in the golden morning
Through the fields, we watched the flowers adorning
    Leaf and stalk and petal, every one.
" See," we said, " the blossoms' hearts are jealous !
Each to outstrip her rival bloom is zealous,
    Each desires her sovereign lord, the sun."

Satan.

And at night-time over field and garden
Fall the moon-rays, and the blossoms harden
    Heart and leaf and petal in the cold.
When the sun arises in his splendour
Dead are all those blossoms over-tender,
    Though he kissed them with his mouth of gold.

Lover.

Once I doubted all things, all things human ;
Railed at God, and scoffed at man and woman ;
   Now I find a never dreamt-of bliss.
God has sent me blessing for my curses,
In his undeserved and priceless mercies
   Given me heaven in one pure woman's kiss.

CHRIST.

Lover : hold thy noble faith unshaken !
Love her purely.   If thy love be taken,
   Know that she is safe with God and me.
Know that past the heavens, with angel sweetness
In her face, she waits thy soul's completeness ;
   Past the stars, the thunder, and the sea.

III.

CHRIST, AND THE WIFE.

Wife.

Godlike is he, full of noble passion,
And I love him in a wild sweet fashion :
  All my heart has worshipped and adored.

Satan.

Wait, and test him.   Though thou hast a poet
For thine husband, faithful time will show it—
  All the sinful weakness of thy lord.

Wife.

Long I loved him, yet I feared to shame him :
Hardly dares my loving wifehood claim him :
  O my poet ! O my lord and king !

Satan.

Just because his spirit worships beauty,
He will break the bonds of love and duty :
  In wild regions will his spirit sing.

Wife.

By his power of sweet idealization
He can work a giant transformation,
  Change the fog-gloom into summer's sheen.

Satan

Aye : and by his morbid genius-fancies
Crowd the London pavement with romances,
    Change the tawdry street-girl to a queen.

Wife.

Not what *is*, he sees. The wild waste hedges
He can clothe with may-bloom, tip the sedges
    By the river with soft feathery bloom.

Satan.

Aye : and he can fancy that a fairy
Greets him—poor red-handed black-nailed Mary !—
    In a London work-girl's stuffy room.

Wife.

But I trust him. He, my lord and master,
Will not plunge our twin life in disaster :
    Forth his sweet songs ripple like a wave.

Satan.

Forth his false words flutter. Swift and burning,
They can fill a woman's soul with yearning,
    But they lead to darkness and the grave.

Wife.

Christ himself was not more godlike surely.
Lo ! his song so tenderly and purely
    Sounds forth. Can this king of men love me ?

Satan.

—And a dozen others ! Nay, a million.
In his dreams he counts wives by the billion :
    Can his waking be content with thee ?

Wife.

All the world of women-hearts must love him !
All the mighty stars that shine above him
    Hardly form a fit crown for his head !

Satan.

Yet to-night, as in some yielding billow,
Deep his wondrous brow sinks in the pillow
    Of a woman's rosy-curtained bed.

Wife.

I can help him in his daily labour :
Polish clean and bright his song's swift sabre,
    By the which he slayeth sin and guile.

Satan.

Yet he needs some change and recreation.
Not in raising a down-trodden nation
    Will he find it, but in woman's smile.

Wife.

In his song the blossoms full of sweetness
Bloom.   He gives the sunshine its completeness.
    God is gladder, when a poet's born !

Satan.

Yes : the world will crown his brows with laurel.
He will love the world, and only quarrel
    With the wife whose brows he crowns with thorn.

Wife.

Woman's love can save him, if he stumbles.
When doubt's far-off thunder groans and rumbles,
    Faith shall change to blueness all the sky.

Satan.

Faith *is* needful.   If he sings supremely,
He can do a deed or two unseemly
    When not followed by thy loving eye.

Wife.

After long laborious hours are over,
Through the fields of corn, the fields of clover,
    We will wander, taking noble rest.

Satan.

Yet methinks he sometimes finds a sweeter
Rest, and for his tired-out spirit meeter,
    At St. John's Wood, on a wanton's breast.

Wife.

Other women envy me.   No wonder !
To the world his genius spake in thunder.
    Ah ! how gently spake it unto me.

Satan.

Just as gently, at its first beginning,
While it thinks the blue wave worth the winning,
    Speaks the tempest to the trembling sea.

CHRIST.

He will grow to what thy love requireth.
God will give thee what thy heart desireth,
    Loving woman.   Love him to the end.
Let him find in thee not wifehood merely,
But a ready brain that counsels clearly,
    And the wise heart of an helpful friend

IV

CHRIST, AND THE MAN OF GENIUS.

Man.

In youth I thought the world was bright ;
The starry fields were full of light :
   The grassy fields were full of bloom :
But oh, how surely brightness goes !
Full of high hopes, my life arose :
   Hopeless, it travelleth to the tomb.

Satan.

That is the end of all—to seek
God's love, to burn to unfold and speak
   God's gospel to the human race,
And then to hear death through the air
Thunder his gospel of despair,
   Or lose all for a woman's face !

Man.

Of all the curses God can shower
The heaviest surely is the dower
   Of genius, burthening heart and brain :
To feel an ever-intenser woe
Than others, or a rapturous glow
   So fierce it deepens into pain !

Satan.

That is your lot.   For ever thus
To teach immortal truths to us,
    Yet lonely through life's waves to steer.
That is the glory of the thing :
To carve, or write, or paint, or sing,
    Yet never find an audience here.

Man.

If God be true, I can endure,
Struggle to be unselfish, pure :
    Yet fear I, judging by the past,
Lest, like the brain of Talleyrand,
The noblest genius in the land
    May mix with sewage at the last.

Satan.

That is the beauty of the thing !
To think that mighty brains, which sing
    Of passionate joys and passionate pain
And flowers and stars and sunlit skies,
May serve, when once their owner dies,
    To choke a gutter or a drain.

Man.

To love more deeply, hour by hour,
The simple beauty of a flower,
    The stars God's conjuring hand forthshook,
And yet to feel that all one's might
Can add no one star to the night
    Nor one white lily to the brook !

Satan.

That is your helpless genius-dower.
Man's song cannot create one flower:
   The mightiest sculptor time may send
To mould the marble, cannot flush
The white stone with the bright blood's blush;
   Cold marble is it to the end.

Man.

To know so much! to feel the right
Far past the rampires of the night
   To penetrate to God's high throne!
And yet to feel thought sinking back,
Defeated, on the same old track,
   And to be left once more alone!

Satan.

Again the dower of genius, this.
To madden for Jehovah's kiss;
   Right through the starlit rooms of space
To hunt his shadow, endless task;
To see God's eyes flash through his mask,
   But never to discern his face.

Man.

Prisoned to be by time and space!
To long to have gazed on Jesus' face
   And seen the royal kindness there!
The Churches tell us he arose.
But when or how? what preacher knows?
   Their gods are ghosts, their words are air.

Satan.

You'll never know.   And, when you die
And think a passage through the sky
    Will open (as it oped for him !)
You will be shoved i' the ground instead,
And beetles round about your head
    Will gather for their gambols grim.

Man.

To know what noble souls have died,
And what sweet women ! to be tied
    For ever to an English blonde.
Never to know the exact rich bliss
Which pulsed through Cleopatra's kiss !
    This makes a passionate soul despond.

Satan.

Aye, God will let thy spirit dream :
But when it comes to facts, I deem
    He'll not send beauty to thy bed.
Her whom thy lust would stretch out there
He'll marry to a green-grocer,
    And send thee an ill-breath'd bride instead.

Man.

To yearn across death's solemn night
So thunder-dark, yet see no light
    Of one dead well-loved starry face
Flash out for all one's yearning ! this
Last sadness lurks within each kiss ;
    This coldness thrills through each embrace.

Satan.

Yes: when thy mother dies, thy friend,
Thy wife, thy sweetheart, that's the end,
    The end of all—be sure of this.
Kiss while thou canst.   Within the tomb
No widower wins a young girl's bloom.
    Death proffers not a second kiss.

Man.

To peer between life's prison-bars
And watch those golden ships, the stars ;
    Yet never in life, or death maybe,
To board a single star-ship ! no.
For ever through heaven's deeps we go,
    Yet hail no consort on the sea.

Satan.

The same with life.   The human soul
Is like your earth-ship.   Though its goal
    May lie beyond eternity,
Alone for ever it must steer
And never through all ages hear
    One true voice hail across the sea.

CHRIST.

O genius-heart, be brave and strong.
When thou despairest, suffering long,
    Think on my life, remember me.
Thy soul soars on, all stars of space
Sail on, before my Father's face,
    And harbourage lies beyond the sea.

V

CHRIST, AND THE POOR MAN.

Satan.

All thou seest of splendour and of sweetness,
  Gulf and river, rock and wood and wave,
All that wealth can bring life of completeness,
  If thou wilt but trust me, thou shalt have.

Man.

I am happy in my humble garden,
  Happy 'mid the red geraniums there:
Happy, when the good God breathes his pardon
  And his blessing down the starlit air.

Satan.

Pardon ! not of God need'st thou crave pardon :
  Rather let him pardon ask of thee.
Why should thine hands change to horn and harden,
  While another lives in luxury ?

Man.

Yet the unequal lot is God's appointing.
  Happier am I in my humble sphere
Than the Pope, for all his proud anointing,
  Or the king with courtiers at his ear.

Satan.

King thou art by right.   The rich man's slumbers
  One day shall thy legions rudely break.
True, the wealth is his.   But thou hast numbers.
  Strike ! for thy seduced sad daughters' sake.

Man.

That thought maddens.   That, and that thought only
  Drives the avenging blood to heart and head—
That the rich man leaves his wife's couch lonely
  While he wantons in a work-girl's bed.

Satan.

King thou art,—the sole true monarch, doubtless.
  Had the myriads of the northern Czar
Seen this sooner, his red hand were knoutless,
  And their hands had snapped each prison-bar.

Man.

Dreams of fierce and blood-stained revolution,
  These are born of darkness and of thee.
We retain, through Europe's wild confusion,
  Hearts made clear by sunshine and the sea.

Satan.

Yes : the sea is free.   Its waves would cheer you
  Onward to the final grim attack.
Think what boundless wealth is ever near you !
  What a city London were to sack !

Man.

Yet the Thames, with its strong eddying waters
  Curling downward to the sea's blue plain,
Seems to plead for English wives and daughters.
  Shall we make it blood-red like the Seine ?

Satan.

Wives and daughters! when did ever wealthy
  Strong man, covetous of girl or bride,
Hesitate by violent means or stealthy
  To abduct your weak one from your side?

Man.

Yet I look for days of equal measures,
  Work for all men, healthy homes for each:
Laws to guard the poor man's best loved treasure —
  Daughter, wife, and liberty of speech.

Satan.

These are going, unless you bestir you.
  Sword and bayonet, truncheon, gag, and chain;
Workhouse-prisons wherein to inter you
  Living; these the gifts are ye will gain.

Man.

If the end be this, not ever thunder
  Through the midnight with such fury rolled
As will wild revolt, while weak fools wonder,
  Through the long streets where they hide their gold.

Satan.

Grand! let every continental nation,
  Awe-struck at the English workmen's might,
Watch the multitudinous devastation
  And the balefires flashing through the night.

Man.

If it ever comes to such an issue,
  Deadly, desperate, will the mad fight be.
Down will crumble walls like paper tissue,
  When hoarse riot charges like the sea.

Satan.

Famous! I will head the workmen rallying
   Through the Parks and Squares with banners red.
When the Life-Guards through their gates come sallying,
   Whitehall shall be choked with cuirassed dead!

Man.

Never Paris saw so fierce a battle
   Through its long and sanguine-tinted days.
When the Guards' drums through the dense fog rattle,
   We'll reply by our revolvers' blaze.

Satan.

Princely! that will be a noble sample
   To the nations round, and yet to be.
English artizans shall set the example.
   Let the surging red flags follow me!

Man.

Then the rich man's foot within his garden
   In his brother's blood perchance shall slip.
Stately duchesses shall sue for pardon,
   Kneeling 'mid our ranks with ashen lip.

Satan.

Glorious! when the captured girls are waiting,
   While their fathers' hot blood licks the sewers,
Splashing red down gutter and through grating,
   I will whisper, "What of girls of *yours?*"

Man.

This is certain—If that day of thunder
   Ever breaks on London, those who see
Will behold hell's barriers burst asunder,
   Fiends unchained, and raging devils free.

CHRIST.

Satan, when the hell-gates leap asunder,
  Dreading lest some flippant sword-edge scar,
Fearful lest some heedless bullet blunder,
  Safe will lurk, observing from afar !

VI

CHRIST, AND THE SOCIAL REFORMER.

Reformer.

The world is perfect as God made
Its heights of sunlight, depths of shade :
   ·God's image in it we restore.

Satan.

Your pupils daub the world with mud :
Or else will send a sea of blood
   Circling along from shore to shore.

Reformer.

The world was perfect.   Leaf and flower,
Starlight and moonlight, sun and shower,
   Fulfil the high God's perfect will.

Satan.

And ye will add a starlight new
When, torch in hand, ye issue through
   The portals, to consume and kill.

Reformer.

What lessons for the race are there—
In the heavenly depth of starlit air.
   What truths the star-land has to teach !

Satan.

The proletariate little cares
About the lessons of the stars :
    It has its dirty shirts to bleach.

Reformer.

Astronomy.   What nobler lore ?
Or from the sea-weeds on the shore
    To educe the laws of life and growth.

Satan.

Nay ! stuff your pockets full of sweets.
The children gathered from the streets
    Like bull's eyes best, I'll take my oath.

Reformer.

Such small things teach, if man would learn—
The heather's bell, a tuft of fern :
    God's signs are seen in every spot.

Satan.

The people's sign-boards point the way
To where, at foggy close of day,
    The fieriest brandy can be got.

Reformer.

Ah ! in the future we shall bring
To bear the lessons of the spring,
    The teaching of the summer rose.

Satan.

And find that those you would uplift
Would rather you would let them drift
    Straight to damnation, in repose.

Reformer.

A genius grand is in the poor.
Behold, we open Music's door
    And let the poor man enter in.

Satan.

Try them with Beethoven, Mozart.
But don't be angry, do not start,
    If Vance and short-skirt ballets win.

Reformer.

The picture-galleries we will ope
On Sundays.   There, our leaders hope,
    The working-man will take his wife.

Satan.

On Sundays, as a general rule,
The workman thumps her with a stool,
    Or jobs her with the carving-knife.

Reformer.

The noblest singing they shall hear.
We'll train their fancy, train their ear,
    The grandest thoughts to comprehend.

Satan.

And find that they—yes, one and all—
Would rather see at a Music Hall
    The white-eyed Kaffir.   Yes, my friend.

Reformer.

Christ was the first who understood
The people,—saw the undreamed-of good
    Latent in heart and hand and head.

Satan.

And therefore on the cross he died,
And all the fickle people cried,
   "Give us Barabbas in his stead!"

Reformer

The whole world lies before us. Wide
Its wonders stretch on every side.
   Vast are the truths life has to teach!

Satan.

The people you would lift so high
Would much prefer—though you may sigh—
   To crack their nuts on Brighton beach.

Reformer.

The children shall make holiday
Among the flowers and fragrant hay,
   And love the beauty of the flowers.

Satan.

They love the gutters and the mud.
I've seen a dead rat's skin and blood
   Amuse a blue-eyed child for hours.

Reformer.

They'll leave the stifling town at morn,
And watch the sunshine on the corn
   And butterflies with wings snow-white.

Satan

Children pull off flies' wings, you know.
I've often watched them doing so,
   And revelled in the dainty sight.

Reformer.

A long day by the sea's white foam !
They shall sing hymns, returning home,
    And ever love the blue-waved sea.

Satan.

Sing hymns !   Through Lambeth when I walk
The tiny children's filthy talk
    Is really shocking, even to me !

Reformer.

If only we can educate
The shop-girls ; force the sluggish State
    To educate them, one and all.

Satan.

Men train them in such different ways :
Opinions differ in these days :
    I think they're sweetest, when they fall.

Reformer.

Once educate—then all is well.
Love can redeem the lost from hell,
    And shield the soul sin would destroy.

Satan.

Sin ?   That is such an ugly name.
A sealskin jacket means the same,
    And sounds more delicate, my boy !

Reformer.

Work hard ; keep sober ; rule your tongue ;
Love truly, chastely ; marry young.
    Domestic joys are joys which last.

Satan.

My work-girls dread domestic bliss.
Why sell your freedom, when you kiss?
Marriage is dying out quite fast.

Reformer.

I see the good in every one.
You count the spots upon the sun,
And in the fairest find a sin.

Satan.

My eyes are microscopic. Yes.
I stand by when the girls undress,
And count the blotches on their skin.

Reformer.

Is all life's labours then in vain?
Long effort, struggle, bitter pain.
Must evil still outbalance good?

Satan.

The great Reformer, Jesus, died
With ruffian-robbers at each side,
Nailed on a common cross of wood.

Reformer.

That seemed like failure—dismal, vast,
The bright stars must have gazed aghast,
When loving Jesus had to die.

Satan.

It was the death-blow of his dream.
The soldiers saw the blood-drops stream,
And laughed to see them. So did I.

CHRIST.

On every Church in Christian lands
To-day my cross as symbol stands
  Of mine eternal victory.

VII

CHRIST, AND THE KING,

King.

Leagues and leagues of rolling upland, leagues and leagues of
  mountain ground,
Leagues and leagues of stormy waters where the giant surges
  sound,
These are mine, and mine for ever.   Through the farthest East I
  reign,
And the rivers wait my mandate ere they plunge into the main.

Satan.

Lord thou art of all things clearly, lord of day and lord of night.
In the morn the sun thy servant pays thee homage, brings thee
  light.
At the eve the stars thy servants cast their crowns before thy feet,
And thy women do thee service even softer and more sweet.

King.

Are there lands yet left to conquer?   I am weary, though I reign
Over mountain, mead, and valley—over river, rock, and plain.
Are there hearts yet left to conquer?   Are there women more
  divine
Than the girls whose golden tresses at my palace windows shine?

Satan.

Wealth and kingship last for ever, and all pleasures can be brought
To thy feet, O mighty Ruler!　Thou need'st stint thyself in
　　nought.
Plunge from pleasure into pleasure, as a bather in the sea
Leaps from breaker into breaker.　Trust thy future unto me.

King.

Yet I dread the far-off future—sometimes wake up in my bed,
Pause from dallying with the glory of a woman's golden head,
Pause half frightened, with the sweetness of her kiss upon my
　　mouth,
Hearkening as the thunder summons its loud legions from the
　　South.

Satan.

Dream not of the far-off thunder.　Death and thunder are so far.
Lo! to-night my slaves shall bring thee, when the evening's lonely
　　star
Through the silence of the heavens drives its chariot wrought of
　　pearl,
An untouched and trembling maiden.　Take thy pleasure with
　　the girl.

King.

Yet an end will come of pleasure.　Through the desert monsters
　　moan,
And the ghosts of those I've vanquished haunt the stairway of my
　　throne.
Deep in blood my feet have waded.　Must I wade for evermore
Through red waters?　Must my footsteps in my palace slip in
　　gore?

Satan.

Kings have need to stifle scruple. Kings must sweep their foes
   away,
As the current sweeps the sea-weed round the circle of the bay.
Lo ! thou art a mighty monarch. Thou hast taken to thy bed
Wives of foemen without number, and hast laid their husbands
   dead.

King.

Star by star the high heaven opens, full of wonder is the night.
I am ruler in my palace. Here a million lamps are bright :
Here a thousand women wait me.--God is mightier, mightier far !
Lord he is of heaven's blue regions, far beyond the faintest star.

Satan.

Art thou envious of Jehovah ? Canst thou never be content ?
Lo! the whole wide earth I give thee—sea, and isle, and continent.
Thou hast served me, served me truly. Lord thou art of earth
   and hell.
Must thou lust for powers beyond thee, crave for God's high
   heaven as well ?

King

Nay, I drive the fancy from me. Bring me women, bring me
   wine !
Let the girls dance wanton measures till their smooth limbs seem
   divine !
Let the captives suffer torture ! Let the tigers crowd the ring !
I will watch them tear the prisoners. I will live and die a king.

Satan.

That is better, that is braver. That is speech I love to hear.
The proud vaunting of a monarch rings like music in my ear ;
And I love to see the captives drag their entrails in the dust,
For the sight of blood is pleasant, and it whets a monarch's lust.

King.

Yes, when all the sports are over and the fierce arena clears,
I feel joyous and feel tender.   Then I weary of the spears
And the bleeding and the fighting, and I long for sleep and rest,
And to kiss the pale-pink nipple on a maiden's balmy breast.

Satan.

True : the glory of a monarch is to slay the husband first,
To watch anguish do his bidding, to see torture do its worst ;
Then at night-time, past the turmoil and the throbbing of the strife,
To let passion do its utmost on the body of the wife.

King.

Bid the people throng together.   They shall own me king and
lord.
God may rule by loving-kindness.   I will sway men by the sword.
I will light red fires of torment that shall leap between the bars
Of the prisons, and extinguish God's pale candle-light, the stars.

Satan.

Canst thou not devise a torment newer than the fires' old blaze ?
Write in blood a noble poem that shall ring through endless days?
Mothers hast thou ripped in sunder, wrenched the babes from out
their womb,
Tossed the infants on thy spear-points, closed the living in the
tomb- --

King.

There are fifteen hundred prisoners in the dungeons of the town :
There are fifteen hundred diamonds wanted for my royal crown.
Let the diamonds wait a little.   I can scent a rarer prize.
There are fifteen hundred prisoners.   Bring me fifteen hundred
eyes.

Satan.

That is glorious, that is kingly. That is past expression grand.
Ruled there ever such a monarch o'er so fortunate a land?
His right eye each prisoner loses, but the left eye still remains.
See how mercy kisses judgment! See how just a monarch reigns!

King.

There are half a thousand captives in the fortress, prisoned deep.
They shall writhe amid their life-blood, twining in a tangled heap.
Break their legs, and hurl them living in the ditch beside the
  tower.
All who pass shall see them rotting, for a token of my power.

Satan.

Better still, aye even better! That is past all language fine,
And the genius that devised it in its greatness matches mine.
Judgment once more kisses mercy, and with tenderness is blent.
Break their legs, don't kill them outright. Give them five days to
  repent.

King.

Bid the people throng together. I will make a royal feast.
Let the lamps at night be lighted. I am king on earth at least.
If vast angel-hosts in heaven wait Jehovah's stern command,
Round about me fifty thousand of the desert's spearmen stand.

Satan.

Who shall wait thee in thy palace, when the feasting all is done?
When the lamps before the moon fly, as she flies before the sun.
When thy head with merry feasting and with laughter reels and
  whirls,
Who shall wait thee of thy smooth-limbed satin-bosomed supple
  girls?

King.

Let the girl to-night be ready, who last night upon my bed
Lay so snow-like on the velvet (Let the tigers wait unfed).
In the afternoon the circus, and the blood-stained combat's charms :
But at night the king's the captive, prisoned in a woman's arms !

CHRIST.

King, to-night when solemn darkness closes down on land and sea
Thou shalt meet the only Ruler who hath kingship over thee.
Thou hast made the pale stars tremble on their thrones within the
    sky ;
But to-night thy soul shall tremble, for to-night thou hast to die.

VIII.

CHRIST, AND THE PHILOSOPHER

Philosopher.

Hardly can I ever utter the amusement that I feel
 When I hear the preachers prating of their ever-loving King !
God exults in all the evil, as a glutton in his meal.
 God creates the murderous Winter, not alone the soft-eyed Spring.

Satan.

Yes, if only God were conscious, one would say his sense of Art
 Were the deepest thing within him.   While the people strive to
 stay
Evil's chariot, God will never let that Juggernaut depart
 —Puts his shoulder to the chariot, lifts the wheels upon their
 way.

Philosopher.

Could the good without the evil ever hold out for an hour ?
 Never !—Every lady strutting in her grand silk down the street,
Full of pureness like an angel, full of beauty like a flower,
 Were it not for the poor harlot would be never half so sweet.

Satan.

True, the Force that moulded all things is dramatic at the core ;
 Has its due sense of proportion; sets the good beside the base ;
Flings the millionaire his nuggets ; plants the beggar at his door ;
 Shapes the cripple as a contrast to the young girl full of grace,

P

Philosopher.

Often, very very often, do I chuckle to myself,
    Watching how the good souls struggle, thinking God is on their
      side.
God is far too good an artist to put evil on the shelf:
    God's superbest Rembrandt-picture was when Christ was crucified.

Satan.

Yes, I watched with keenest pleasure that strange scene upon the
    hill.
    Deeply would you have enjoyed it, could you only have been
      there.
Judas played his part divinely.   Pontius backed him with a will.
    Mary "made up" to perfection, purple robe and golden hair.

Philosopher.

Were God fool enough to further all the pious aims of man,
    Were he weak enough to combat sin and folly, I'm afraid
Art would perish.   Was there ever since the earliest rhyme began
    One great poem without terror?   Light implies its foil of shade.

Satan.

Were God such as Christians teach you, not one poet would there be!
    Never Æschylus had moved you, never Sophocles had sung!
Never Dante could have led you by the Inferno's fiery sea!
    Never Homer could have chanted, when the battling world was
      young!

Philosopher.

Vast the loss would be, tremendous.   Not a novel, not a play,
    Not a poem, could be written save for Satan's ready aid.
Crime it is that lends the colour to a world that tends to grey.
    God puts on the golden pigments.   His son Satan adds the
      shade,

Satan.

Thanks. I value the distinction.—When the tragic poets fail,
  Finding dearth of crimson colour in the world the Christians make,
Then they come to me imploring, and I drive another nail
  Into Jesus, and his blood-drops mix to admirable lake.

Philosopher.

People rail at crime and murder. Yet the pleasure these imply !
  Christians sitting at their breakfast o'er their sausage and their
    toast,
Reading in the morning paper that a murderer is to die,
  Feel a thrill of keen excitement. Murders have a charm 'or most.

Satan.

Strange it would be if Jehovah whom the people worship here
  Should be like a Spanish maiden at a bull-fight, in her place.
As she needs its wild excitement, so he needs perhaps to peer
  From the windows of his palace on the death-pangs of the race.

Philosopher.

Crimes have sprung from many causes—from the love of wealth
    and power,
  From the lust of man for woman ; yet beyond conception odd
Is it that the Inquisition, of iniquities the flower,
  Sprang from lust of man for heaven, and from love of man for God.

Satan.

Therefore is there need most urgent that a newer creed be taught :
  That the gospel of pure reason should be preached, with all it
    brings :
That mankind should be instructed that God only lives in
    thought
  And that he himself is sovereign, the sole living king of kings.

Philosopher.

Day by day to feel more self-poised, day by day to grow more
    grand ;
  Day by day to learn new secrets of the silent starry lore ;
To feel ever the brain strengthening in its power to understand ;
  That is worth the pain of living, though the pain of life be sore!

Satan.

All the skies are sundered for thee, all the secrets of the deep
  Blue tremendous heaven are opened to thy keen and searching
    look.
Thou canst count the murky portals, whence the fiery thunders
    leap.
  Thou canst enter the wild comets, name by name, within thy
    book.

Philosopher.

This is life's end, this is rapture. This is man's sufficient goal.
  Far away in bygone ages the great Roman poet saw
That the secret of true godship is within the human soul,
  And that all the worlds together move by never-changing law.

Satan.

Yes. Lucretius, whom I aided in his godlike labour, knew
  That man's dreams of God were baseless—that the only God
    indeed,
Strong, eternal, self-sufficient, deathless, vast, triumphant, true,
  Is the soul of man transcending every form of every creed.

Philosopher.

Prayer has ever been a weakness. Self-sufficient life is grand.
  When the soul of man is strengthened, when the soul of man is
    free,
He will grow by law eternal, like the blossoms of the land ;
  He will move by changeless impulse, like the tides within the sea.

Satan.

Through the ages I have wrestled with the dreamers of each
  race,
  With the poets, with the thinkers, with the lords of prose and
  rhyme ;
Teaching that the glory of manhood is for ever thus to pace,
  Prayerless, faithless, creedless, godless, on the foam-swept
  shores of time.

Philosopher.

Once I prayed: but that is over.   Once I hoped: but that is past.
  It was but a moment's weakness.   Now my inmost soul is
  strong.
I have won the perfect endless philosophic calm at last.
  I have conquered in the struggle, though the strife was fierce
  and long.

Satan.

Teach the people thy strong secret.   Teach the uselessness of
  prayer.
  Teach that man's sufficient godship in his own soul he must find.
Teach that faith in God is harmful; both a weakness and a snare.
  To the doubting bring assurance, and bring light unto the blind.

Philosopher.

I can see—my reason shows me—that of all the faiths of man,
  Faith in God is most degrading !   The soul shivers at the
  thought.
What ! an Eye has followed history since our history first began.
  What ! no deed in noble silence and in darkness has been
  wrought.

Satan.

If an Eye eternal follows, through the sunlight and the shade,
  Ye are like the prisoners followed by the warder's sleepless eye.
Night and day your God observes you through the peep-holes he
    has made
  In the heavens, flashing on you his star-lanterns from the sky.

Philosopher.

Yes: the thought is most degrading.   If we marry, even then
  Not a moment free from spying, though the darkness may be
    deep !
Every kiss by God is counted—fifty, twenty, thirty, ten—
  For the Eye eternal watches man and woman when they sleep.

Satan.

Not one deed is wrought in private, if the Christian creed be true.
  Not a man can kiss in private, not a young girl can be got.
For the Eye eternal pierces all the cloudland, flashes through ;
  And it fathoms every secret, and it searches every spot.

Philosopher.

Oh far nobler is the silence, as Lucretius felt and saw,
  Of the boundless starlit heavens, and the silence of the sea,
And the silent sure progression of unalterable law.
  Let the Christians crown their Jesus.   Give the godless void
    to me !

Satan.

Yes, for free from wrath and tumult may the soul of man abide
  Where no gods can ever harass, where no gods can ever slay.
Unobserved save of the starlight then a man may hold his bride.
  Followed only by the sunlight may a man pursue his way.

Philosopher.

Then the soul in its completeness stands for evermore alone.
  Could it steer its thought-ship boldly to the farthest shores of
    space,
Never would its keel encounter one rock-fragment of God's
    throne :
  Never would the darkness open and reveal the Eternal's face.

Satan.

That is strength ; to steer right onward, seeking nothing from on
    high—
  Neither guidance, love, nor counsel.   Do the star-ships, when
    they steer
Never failing, never foundering, through the storm-shoals of the sky,
  Say "God help us !" or "God guide us !"   If they said so,
    would God hear ?

Philosopher.

No : they sail their course eternal through the darkness of the
    night,
  And they strike not one another, though no helmsman's hand
    there be !
Twilight draweth back for darkness, darkness giveth place to
    light,
  Morning brings its golden sunshine, yet no wrecks are on the
    sea !

Satan.

Ever o'er the airy waters will the star-ships sail secure,
  For the force that leads them onward is but matter's restless
    hand.
If a living God convoyed them, could their pathway be more sure ?
  If a conscious helmsman guided, could their course be better
    planned ?

Philosopher.

Worse it would be, worse in all ways. For the conscious God
    might sleep.
Constellations might be kindled! starry clusters might consume !
If he left the helm a moment, half a million suns might leap
    Down the breathless airy cliff-sides and plunge ages into gloom!

Satan.

Rest in peace. Believe and doubt not, for the truth I tell to thee.
    Godless was the primal darkness, and the first waves felt no hand
Rein them when they charged with rapture o'er the green floor of
    the sea,
    Nor was God within the sunlight when it first caressed the land.

Philosopher.

That is all I crave for—freedom from the oppressive sense of One
    Ever gazing through the myriads of the stars that gem the sky,
Ever speaking in the sea-waves, ever shining in the sun ;
    Just to handle my own soul's helm, and to feel that I am I.

Christ.

Not in all the pride of reason can my Father take delight ;
    Not in genius does he glory, not in stubborn force of will ;
But he hears the sad soul praying through the silence of the night,
    And he speaks in solemn sweetness to the child-like spirit still.

IX

CHRIST, AND THE ROUÉ.

Roué.

The old delights have lost their charm,
  Love's rapture is no longer keen.
To lift a girl's sleeve, kiss her arm,
  Is not the joy it once has been.

Satan.

A few days' rest, and you will be
  The same good fellow as of old;
Ready to win love gallantly,
  Or buy a night's delight for gold.

Roué.

All pleasures certainly are one
  Woman—still woman.   She is bliss.
Yet, ever, fresh desire's begun
  Before the ending of a kiss.

Satan.

And fresh desire shall find its goal.
  Can I who roused it, not supply?
Can I not feed the hungry soul,
  As God with bright stars feeds the sky?

Roué.

Ah, would that I were as the sky,
  And every star a mouth most sweet!
Each night through all eternity
  A new star-goddess at my feet!

Satan.

Stars! I can better do than this:
  Can vary every night your fare;
Can change the method of a kiss,
  And make the pander's self despair.

Roué.

I was not always what I am:
  I loved the ferns in country lanes;
The shallows where the swift trout swam;
  The fox-glove with its purple stains.

Satan.

And now you love—yes, thanks to me!—
  A night of pleasure better far
Than in old days you loved the sea,
  Or sight of flower, or sight of star.

Roué.

True: every pleasure now has grown
  Into one pleasure,—into this—
All day, all night, all day, to moan
  For some new woman's mouth to kiss.

Satan.

But I can bring you new delights:
  A married woman; next a girl.

You shall spend soft Italian nights
　　Where at your feet blue waters curl.

Roué.

I cease to argue.　I have sold
　　My soul to you.　Let that suffice.
—The last you brought had lovely gold
　　Thick hair,—but what a heart of ice !

Satan.

I'll bring you next a heart as warm
　　And gentle as a summer day,
And you shall seize that heart by storm
　　—Worth winning—just to throw away.

Roué.

Can you find nothing new to kiss ?
　　No unattempted cliff of crime
To scale ?　No wild undreamed-of bliss,
　　At once Satanic and sublime ?

Satan.

I'll try.—I'm training now a nun
　　Expressly for you.　You will find,
When all she has learnt has been undone,
　　The girl exactly to your mind.

Roué.

I see.—You teach her to believe
　　In heaven and God,—in love and prayer.
I am to teach her to deceive,
　　To lie, to wanton, to despair ?

Satan.

You'll find it spicy. That, I think,
    Is the best use of God, indeed
The only use. A girl will sink
    The sooner, weighted with a creed.

Roué.

I like the notion. Teach her well.
    Let her believe in heaven and hope.
I'll teach her to believe in hell
    And find God through a microscope.

Satan.

Yes, you will teach her. In a year
    She will be fit, with all your lore,
To open in our London here
    What we may call a brothel-store.

Roué.

Or else to leap—poor girl—one night
    Into the river's ice-cold tomb.
I never liked that ending quite :
    It has a certain air of gloom.

Satan.

Why so ? There are so many more.
    One takes the foolish headlong leap ?
Another waits upon the shore
    And asks you to her room, to sleep.

Roué.

True. Sorrow and remorse soon die
    Within a new girl's loving arms.

Who cares for sin and death? Not I!
  I only care for woman's charms.

Satan.

That's manlier tone. Away with shame!
  Now stoop your ear (the wind blows rough);
I think the parson's wife is game
  At—you know where. A hint's enough.

Roué.

I know! She has the loveliest hair
  In all the world—the real blue-black.
My friend the parson, have a care!
  I'll cuckold you behind your back.

Satan.

Go in and win. I'll bear the blame.
  It is the easiest thing in life.
And—as I said—a fig for shame!
  A fig-leaf for the parson's wife!

Roué.

At any rate this much I know,
  That though my life may end in gloom,
I've lived it out with glitter and glow.
  Write "Rare old sinner" on my tomb!

Satan.

Yes. Gathering women-flowers most fair
  In all the streets and all the ways
Is the best mode to banish care
  In the chill evening of one's days.

Roué.

They never fail one.   Day and night
  They wait, desiring to be wronged.
Two-thirds of London girls are light ;
  Was ever yet the Strand so thronged ?

Satan.

The evening papers back me well.
  Now, if a girl is shy or slow,
They point out that the road to hell
  Was sweet for Lady "So and So !"

Roué.

Some seek the Senate, seek the Bar :
  The poet's laurel others claim.
But woman always was my star !
  I loved her more than wealth or fame.

Satan.

Each to his taste.   The scientist
  May travel through the stars by night ;
You always wanted to be kissed
  As soon as God put out the light.

Roué.

God poured the dark across the skies
  That man might know how brightly gleam
(At seventeen) a woman's eyes ;
  God sent us sleep, that love might dream.

Satan.

Yes—never mind the poetry ;
  You never thought so much of that.

You hurried her so much that she
  Dabbed down the candle-wick quite flat.

Roué.

Old fellow-sinner !   Satan, friend,
  Faithful so long, and proved so true,
Through life, through death, I still will wend,
  Staunch to the last, along with you.

Satan.

Enough !   And put remorse away
  (Some symptoms I have lately seen).
It ill befits your hair of grey ;
  It suits the girl of seventeen.

Roué.

Ah, seventeen !   How sweet an age !
  The soft young breast—the ripe red lips,
Balmier than apple or greengage—
  The marble throat—the slender hips—

Satan.

You make my old mouth water quite !
  Besides, there's want of modesty
In daylight chat.   Just wait till night,
  And we shall see what we shall see.

Roué.

Eyes made for love !   Lips made for man !
  Youth made to lighten age's gloom !
The only magic thing that can
  Make roses in mid-winter bloom !

Satan.

God made a young girl's lips for this,
  That to the agéd they might bring
New life—as once a maiden's kiss
  Worked wonders for a Jewish king.

Roué.

I am as David !   I desire
  The sweetness of a young girl's form.
Her young limbs cheer me more than fire ;
  Her close-pressed body keeps me warm.

CHRIST.

In hell thou shalt cry out for one
  Who loved thee truly—cry in vain.
When the brief body's joy is done
  Begins the eternal spirit's pain.

X

CHRIST, AND THE LOST WOMAN

Woman.

Of old the river-banks were sweet.—
The waves played round my girlish feet,
 As in the brook I gathered cress.
I stooped. Then, quicker than a thought,
The wicked ripples laughed and caught
 The bright skirt of my Sunday dress.

Satan.

And who came through the wood that day,
With face so handsome, step so gay,
 And eyes in which no evil seemed?
And who, found standing in the brook,
Blushed child-like at his laughing look
 And then went home, and cried, and dreamed?

Woman.

It was a dream, and nothing more.—
I see him standing on the shore:
 I see the blossoms by the stream:
I hear my mother ask me why
That night I seemed so strange and shy,
 Pacing the house as in a dream.

Q

Satan.

Was it a dream that followed—town;
Long rows of houses, smoky brown;
   And then one night a dainty bed
In the grand house he took you to;
Wild kisses all the long night through,
   Till morning flamed out rosy-red?

Woman.

A dream, a wicked sinful dream!
My mother's stern words ghost-like seem,
   Which warned me when I fled away:
His kisses on my lips are ghosts:
Grey phantoms are that bed's tall posts,
   And spectral is that dawn of day.

Satan.

And was the blue-eyed child a dream
Who, like a moment's sunny beam,
   Flashed o'er your life one golden spark?
You loved the father in the child,
And half with fate were reconciled.
   God stole your darling. All was dark!

Woman.

God took the baby. Better so.
He had his father's glance, I know.
   I would not that my womb should bear
A child who, in the days to come,
Might lure the heedless to their doom
   And goad some girl's heart to despair.

Satan.

Nay, had the child become a man
And ended what his sire began,
  That would have been dramatic, great.
He might have seen some other girl
At play where the blue waters curl
  Beside your mother's cottage gate !

Woman.

Thank God, he died ! The poor thin child —
I loved it with a passion wild,
  The only love-power left in me.
And yet I hardly cared to groan
When I was wholly left alone,
  A wreck upon life's tossing sea.

Satan.

And yet he would have spared you gold,
Had you but written. But you sold
  Your honour, sank so foully low.
What can a man of character
(The best-intentioned) do for her
  Who fancies profligacy so ?

Woman.

Love once and lose, then all is lost
For woman. Man can love a host
  Of women, so he fancies—yes.
Our love is agony or bliss.
We give one man an angel's kiss :
  We give the rest a whore's caress.

Satan.

An over-subtle **point to** me
That seems, and quite a travesty
   Of amorous joys and love-delight.
No : on the whole, I hold with man
That every girl's the same who can
   Be sweet companion for a night.

Woman.

A man can love a thousand girls.
Smooth black soft tresses, yellow curls,
   Blue eyes, fierce dark eyes,—all are one.
Man finds a thousand faces fair ;
Loves all the stars that fill the air.
   Woman is faithful to the sun.

Satan.

Woman loves once, and that's the end !
Then, when her lover, or her " friend,"
   Forsakes her, what is left to seek ?
The river.--Which makes clear to me
The folly of her theory,
   And proves her reasoning false and weak.

Woman.

The river ? Yes. It flows along :
Not as of old with sweet soft song
   Near Oxford, past my mother's door.
There is no may-bloom on its banks ;
No tall green reeds in rustling ranks ;
   This moonlight gilds a flowerless shore.

Satan.

Plunge in, and get it over.—You
Keep dreaming of the old waves of blue
  That once you watched with girlhood's eyes.
The moon that parts yon cloudy rack
Peers down from heaven on wavelets black
  To-night.   You are in town.   Arise !

Woman.

My life is dark as is the stream.
It once was bright with flash and gleam
  Of love's own sunlight, like the wave.
But now the stream and I are one :
We have bade farewell to the sun :
  The moon shall light us to our grave.

Satan.

Man cares not.   God ?   He does not care.
One moment's flash of golden hair
  Upon the surface of the stream,
Then all is over.   You make way
For a new suicide next day,
  And pass from man's sight like a dream.

Woman.

I wonder, is the water cold ?   '
Drowning is pleasant, I've been told.
  The morning sun is far-off yet.
I wonder, is it hard to die ?
Others have drowned—and so can I.
  One plunge—and then I shall forget !

Satan.

Not one soul loves you.   Quick, my girl!
How pleasantly the waters curl:
　　The moon is shining nicely, too.
My spirits are leading from the Strand
Another young girl by the hand:
　　Hurry—or she may jostle you!

Woman.

Just let me fold this poor old shawl
And lay it down behind the wall,
　　And hat and gloves and necktie.   There . . . .
The water looks so cool and deep—
If I can pluck up heart to leap,
　　There will be no more pain to bear!

CHRIST.

Pause: for thou art not quite alone.
Far-off in heaven I heard thee moan,
　　And through the starlit silent sky
I hastened, as of old, to save.
My love is stronger than the grave,
　　And mightier than man's enmity.

XI

CHRIST, AND THE SPIRITUAL LOVER.

Lover.

I love my lady with a love beyond
  The love of this world,—far more deep.
My love is potent, like a fairy's wand,
  To ope the gates of magic sleep.
She came to me, and loved me in a dream
  More sweet than aught that earth can bring.
A pure soul-passion gives the earth a gleam
  Of changeless May, perpetual spring.

Satan.

Hold to the earth, for it will serve you best.
  These old green fields, so full of flowers,
Are fairer than yon heavenly mountain-crest
  Where Jesus sits, alone for hours.
Not all the music of the seraphs' lyres
  Is worth a young girl's laughing tone.
No dream-kiss, trust me, woman's mouth desires!
  Kiss live lips.   Leave the ghosts alone.

Lover.

Beyond the ephemeral loves of every day
  There is a strong love, far more grand.
My lady's sweetness drives low thoughts away :
  I am content to kiss her hand.

If never here on earth we may be one,
   Beyond the stars, beyond the sea,
Beyond the moonlight and beyond the sun,
   We shall be one, eternally.

Satan.

Beyond the moonlight and beyond the sun
   It will be very dark indeed!
I hardly think a woman can be won
   By such a cold and cheerless creed.
Beyond the starlight and beyond the skies?
   There are no loving women there.
There is no passion in an angel's eyes,
   Nor lustre in an angel's hair.

Lover

Yet in a wondrous dream my love and I
   Were wedded, and our joy was deep.
The holy stars, like warders in the sky,
   Watched over our enchanted sleep.
No earthly passion is as pure as this:
   We won a glimpse of what shall be.
There was eternal rapture in our kiss,
   And passionate immortality.

Satan.

Woman believes in nothing of the kind,
   While you are dreaming, she will act.
She'll marry some one else, you'll surely find:
   Some common-place rich fool, in fact.
While you are dreaming with your foolish head
   And communing with stars and sky,
She will be snug with somebody in bed,
   And bear twelve children by and bye.

Lover.

The only way to understand earth's flowers
  Is to believe in flowers more fair.
Fruits far more gorgeous gleam in heavenly bowers
  Than any that earth's forests bear.
The very fragrance of earth's choicest rose
  Suggests a fragrance more supreme :
The wind that from the sweet furze-bushes blows
  Of something sweeter makes us dream.

Satan.

If there is anything in heaven as sweet
  As furze and roses, or as fair
As woman, I will hie with eager feet
  And take my lordly pleasure there.
But no, my friend, you are deluded quite ;
  Far out—yes, very very far.
Your heaven will culminate in cloudy night,
  Devoid of woman, flower, or star.

Lover.

Great souls have loved, and they have gone before.
  They call us from beyond the tomb.
They tell of sunlight on a stormless shore,
  And blossoms in unfading bloom.
One day, if we are true, my love and I,
  And follow Christ with fearless feet,
We shall be risen angels in the sky,
  Or seraphs near God's mercy-seat.

Satan.

The best-positioned angel in the sky,
  As far as my experience goes,
Would rather kiss a milkmaid on the sly
  On earth, or pick a fresh moss-rose,

Or fish for red-eyed roach within the pond,
  Or bearded gudgeon in the brook,
Than strut through heaven with robes and silver wand
  Or watch the thunder in God's look.

Lover.

The older that I grow, the more I see
  That earthly love must fade and fall :
But spirit-love endures eternally
  And laughs at death's hoarse bugle-call.
God was a strong God, when he made the sun
  And set the stars like lamps in space :
But never was his grand work fully done
  Till his love smiled through woman's face.

Satan.

And will it smile through fleshless skin and bone ?
  Can God or man delight to see
A woman's corpse ? Will you call that " my own,"—
  That wretched white love-travesty ?
Love in this life ! For in the dreary tomb
  Nought grows of woman, save her hair.
Her form rots slowly in the wet cold gloom,
  And wet cold red worms revel there.

Lover.

My love walked with me through the golden corn.
  How bright the scarlet poppies glowed !
Cloudless was all the summer sky that morn.
  The skylarks sang above our road.
But fairer days await us, when we die.
  God raised up Jesus from the dead,
And we shall follow him, my love and I.
  In our behalf the Saviour bled.

Satan.

Had Jesus been content to trust to me,
  He never would have perished so.
I warned him, far away in Galilee.
  But he would never listen—no.
Mark the result. At thirty-three he died,
  Unmarried, and a failure quite.
Like you he dreamed. But he was crucified,
  And passed into eternal night.

Lover.

Into eternal morning. Lo! to-day
  In England, far from Syrian skies,
His cross points upward through the fog-mists grey
  And every Easter sees him rise.
He understood the heart of woman quite,
  And loved her—not for golden hair,
Or flashing eyes, or shapely limbs and white.
  He taught her that her soul was fair.

Satan.

Love, while it is to-day. Love, while the sun
  Glitters upon the bright blue wave.
In this warm world a woman can be won,
  But what lips meet within the grave?
Love Cleopatra, while the occasion serves.
  Love Helen, ere the red worms creep
Across the bosom on whose perfect curves
  Enamoured Paris sank to sleep.   .

Lover.

The life of Dante gives the lie to you.
  Through many a year of pain and gloom
He waited, knowing that his soul-love true
  Tarried for him beyond the tomb.

Her earthly marriage faded quite away,
　　Like mists of night before the sun.
Who doubts that Dante and his love to-day
　　Are wholly wedded, past all changing one?

Satan.

And yet, when everything is said and done,
　　The victory's in the first embrace !
Dante dreamed finely, but the husband won,
　　And kissed the eyes and kissed the face.
Another stole her while the poet slept
　　(Dreams take the most majestic shapes !)
Into love's greenhouse lo ! another crept
　　While Dante dreamed, and ate the grapes.

Lover.

I care not whether on the earth I win
　　My lady's lips.　Her soul is mine.
Our holy marriage-rapture will begin
　　When earthly marriage-joys decline.
The joys of earth flash like a star's faint light :
　　They glitter, then fade into gloom.
But as the sunshine is the spirit's might :
　　It mocks at darkness and the tomb.

Christ.

The earth is good.—My Father made it fair.
　　I love the rivers and the sea :
I love the thyme-scent on the summer air,
　　And slumbrous singing of the bee.
Though this world is not heaven, it leads man back
　　To heaven.　Tread in the paths I trod.
The golden stars ye see illumed my track
　　Far past those golden stars to God.

XII.

CHRIST, AND THE ORTHODOX CHRISTIAN.

Satan.

Forsake thy father, and forsake thy mother,
  Unless in Christ's safe fold they be !
Hardly the earth's green hillocks hide or smother
  The fierce waves of hell's fiery sea.

There are the blue-eyed babes upon the billows
  Leaping, whom God condemns to this :
Writhing and twisting on their red-hot pillows,
  And shrieking at the fire's keen kiss.

There are their mothers wringing hands and groaning
  (And some plunge in the red-hot wave).
Above the saints are singing and intoning,
  And praising Christ—who could not save.

O Christian choose the safe path, choose it early,
  And enter at the narrow gate.
Make for the golden doors, the pillars pearly.
  To-morrow it may be too late !

Right through man's heart of hearts God's sword-arm lungeth :
  Nor age nor sex shall flee from him.
Through human serried ranks his lightning plungeth :
  In their own blood his foes shall swim.

The sinner, though he fled by star-paths longer
  Than all the starlit tracks of space,
Would find the Avenger's foot more fleet and stronger ;
  At the last star would meet God's face.

Christ is the Lord of all. Believe and follow.
  Believe : or thou shalt surely die.
The songs and psalms of earth ring faint and hollow ;
  But thunder-pæans shake the sky.

Renounce the loves of earth,—the hands that beckon,
  Woman's alluring subtle smile.
Who yields his soul to love shall surely reckon
  With judgment in a little while.

Christ is the Son of God. Believe, or perish.
  His arm is stretched out from on high.
The flower-lipped loves your fleshly frail hearts cherish
  Along with you shall surely die.

Nought hath avail, save one thing—to deliver
  By faith your souls from flames of hell.—
Pause not to gaze at silver lake or river,
  Or sunset o'er the purple fell :

Pause not to dream by rippling ocean-marges ;
  Pause not for lure of laugh or kiss ;
Young girls' white bosoms oftenest are the targes
  Wherethrough hell's fiery arrows hiss :

Pause not.   Seek Christ's ineffable redemption.
Put all things else away, aside.
If ye will haste, ye yet may win exemption
From struggle with hell's lava-tide.

The songs of birds within the leafy arches;
The songs of girls beside the stream ;
The glades wherethrough the stately red deer marches ;
The boughs wherethrough the blue jays gleam :

The morning sun that through the foliage glistens,
Changing green leaves to magic light ;
The stars' strong song whereto the wild sea listens,
Checking its frantic coursers white :

The whispered words of lovers, as they murmur
" O love, how sweet this life can be ! "
The sunshine on the white cliffs, standing firmer
For shocks of all the unquiet sea :

The peace upon the green downs, soft and grassy ;
The mountains, in whose dark arms sleep
The storms, till, rattling thunder-harness massy,
Swift from their mountains' arms they leap :

These things are nought—mere phantom-visions steering
Their course along a ghostly stream.
Hell shakes the doors !   God's judgment day is nearing,
And all ye see is but a dream.

Christian.

Through storm and strife and anguish keen,
The sword of goodness in my hand,
With faith for staff whereon to lean
And Christ for Rock whereon to stand,

With helmet of salvation strong
   And heavenly sandals on my feet,
I march along, with holy song,
     All evil's hosts to meet.

Satan.

And thou shalt win unending bliss,
   If thou wilt quite renounce the glee
Of earth, and seek the Bridegroom's kiss
   That waiteth in eternity.
For round the holy and spotless King,
   The Son of God, the world's desire,
Bright hosts of risen angels sing,
     And thou shalt join their choir.

Christian.

My joy is in the Lord of hosts.
   The flowers of earth may fade away,
The sun wax dim, the stars like ghosts
   Diminish : Jesus shines alway.
But one thing troubles me—to think
   That I from heavenly heights may peer,
And see some shrink upon the brink
     Of hell, whom I loved here.

Satan.

God hath the sovereign right to save :
   God hath the sovereign right to slay.
He raised up Jesus from the grave :
   But Judas' soul he tossed away.
Grieve not for wife or friends who fail
   To win thine heaven along with thee ;
If thou wert strong, and they were frail,
     Praise God,—and grateful be.

Christian.

If only I could win my wife
   For Jesus; lure her heart to hear
The message of eternal life;
   Inspire a salutary fear!
But this world holds her. O my love,
   Can my torn heart contented be,
If I must move through heavens above
        While hell's depth swallows thee?

Satan.

Leave all to God; for he can make
   Thy soul content and glad on high.
Thy heart's deep thirst his love can slake:
   Hell's wild groan reaches not the sky.
God spread his joyous heavens above,
   And set his saints like bright stars there:
Then, further to accentuate love,
        Doomed some souls to despair.

Christian.

All doubts are swallowed up in praise:
   Jesus is Lord of all for me.
Upon the pierced hands let me gaze
   That bled upon the accursèd tree!
Emmanuel rules my heart to-day:
   Wife, parents, children,—all are gone.
Pale stars are they! they fade away,
        And Jesus reigns alone.

Satan.

Through era on era, age on age,
   The great world's giant drama ran.
The actors' feet upon the stage
   Were slippery with the blood of man

R

Greece shivered.   Rome called out to stop.
  All hearts were wearied out in fact.
Man would have let the curtain drop.
     Then God sent Christ to act.

CHRIST.

And me, who would have quietly played
  A peasant's part upon the boards,
They dressed in purple robes and made
  Rich from their Church's secret hoards.
The trick worked swiftly, once begun :
  They changed the child (man's reasoning's odd!)
Of Mary and Joseph to the son
     Of Mary and of God.

A VOICE FROM HEAVEN.

A VOICE FROM HEAVEN.

Each evening on the ethereal canvas wide
   I paint new sunsets, colouring all the air.
When Turner failed and flung his brush aside,
   I touched the heaven,—the longed-for tint was there.

Yet who will gaze each evening at the sky?
   Who cares to contemplate my work supreme?
Unnoticed, shade by shade, the bright tints die.
   Man lusts for gold, while God and poets dream.

When my sonorous thunder-pæans sound,
   What audience have I in the heights of space?
When my stars fill the air for leagues around,
   Frail man is staring in some harlot's face.

Alone I travel o'er the shoreless sky ;
   Alone in labour, and in pain and strife.
I cross the surges of eternity
   While man sails round the land-locked bay of life.

What genius-loneliness is like to mine ?
   Man shapes one statue, or he paints one face :
A poet's soul lives in one single line,
   A woman's beauty in one curve of grace :

Upon one earth ye suffer and ye groan :
    Your Jesus for one suffering sad world died :
But I—for ever past my lonely throne
    Sweeps the great stars' illimitable tide.

I rule new nations in vast star on star :
    My thought creates new eras, one by one.
I steer across the blue sky's harbour-bar
    Daily the giant ship ye call the sun.

Nor only one sun.   Through the waves of space
    Millions of sun-ships plunge upon their way.
I am the sole spectator of their race :
    My touch upon the helm they all obey.

And yet my love can pulse through space and time.
    Does one sad woman in the wintry gloom,
Despairing, maddened through another's crime,
    Wait, while the dark waves tempt her to her doom ?

Does one frail heart of woman long to die,
    Hurling her sorrow deep into the wave?
There is the God of all things.   There am I.
    There is the love that even yet can save.

There is the love that from the central throne
    Listening can hear the accents of despair :
Can hear through all the stars a woman's moan ;
    Answer the strong man's agony of prayer.

Aye, if hell's ocean seeks to swallow one
    Frail human sinner, blood-stained though he be,
The love of God will bid the mighty sun
    Rescue the sinner, and dry up the sea.

BOOK IV

NATURE AND HUMANITY.

I.

NATURE.

SONG OF THE FLOWERS.

But Satan's word reached not the tender flowers
    In deep green bowers :
They bloomed and loved and sang, and praised their King.
" Rise from your rest, O sisters sweet, for soon
    It will be June,
The world will need our fragrant comforting ! "

        So spake the rose ;
        And from repose
The countless hosts of sister-roses woke.
        They filled the air
        With fragrance rare,
As morning after summer morning broke.

Then came the violets in their myriads too,
        Arrayed in blue,
Save some, the tenderest, who were robed in white.
All sang to heaven their song of perfect praise,
        And filled the ways
With scent divine by day, though most by night.

        Yes, most by night,
        For then the light
Of the enchantress moon is over each :
        And then you hear,
        Low, silver-clear,
The tender murmur of the flowers' soft speech.

Then rose to rose, lily to lily, speaks.
     Then by the creeks,
Whereover pours a flood of moonlight pale,
Gentle forget-me-not and iris bold,
     Blue, streaked with gold,
Converse, and love lifts from their hearts its veil.

    " Lo ! God is good "—
    In the green wood
Thus spake a wild rose to its sister nigh :
     " Seest thou up there
     Those star-flowers fair ?
Those are what roses come to, when they die !

 " Yes, sister, roses die,—and then they light
     The whole wide night ;
They change to what men call the ' stars ' above :
And then for endless ages they shine through
     The endless blue,
And thrill the souls of men to dreams of love.

    " No blossoms die :
    The whole wide sky
Receives, and turns to stars their silvery bloom.
     The fields of air
     That gleam up there
Receive us, sister, in their azure tomb.

 " Just for one little moment here we dream,
     And then we gleam
For ever set upon the brow of space :
Aye, then with exultation we shall find
     —God is so kind !—
Another and a deathless dwelling-place.

"Here we delight
For one sweet night
One pair of lovers with our breath most sweet :
But when we die
We shall supply
Light to a thousand fond hearts when they meet."
    *   *

So spake to a sister-flower the pale pink rose,
Like one who knows
The secrets of the stars and of the night.
And then two lovers came, and plucked the rose—
And now it glows
Doubtless amid the stars, and gives man light.

What once was breath
Most sweet, in death
Has been transfigured into higher bloom :
The rose once flowered,
But now is dowered
With light, to gleam across the purple gloom.

Praise, love and praise.   This ever was the word
The flower-souls heard :
They caught no distant note of Satan's psalm.
The fragrant wondrous flower-world's vast content
With joy was blent,
And infinite repose, and ceaseless calm.

"O sun gold-red,"
The daisy said,
"Thou art so grand, and yet thou copiest me !
My heart of gold
I now behold
In the blue waves, reflected back from thee !"

The violet whispered, as it gazed on high,
    " O deep-blue sky,
Thou steal'st my hues.   I love thee for the theft ! "
The sky laughed out to hear the violet's speech ;
    Pure love filled each :
" Love," sang the green ferns in the granite-cleft.

    " Love," sang the sun ;
    And from his throne
To fill the daisy's heart he sent down rays,
    Till it became
    One golden flame,
A golden sunflower flashing back his gaze.

    *   *

And then a lily in the garden-bed,
    Lifting her head,
Said to her sister, " Happiness is ours,
Indeed.   We live but for a little while,
    And yet our smile
Is deathless.   Yes : the good God loves his flowers.

    " In pale sick-rooms
    Some lily blooms :
The sufferer's sad eye kindles as it sees
    The dainty stem,
    White diadem,
And fragrant heart that maddened once the bees.

" Nothing is lost.—We bloom but for a day,
    And yet we stay
For ever in the soul that found us fair.
We lift and comfort ; we redeem and save :
    Yes, even the grave
Grows beautiful, when lilies enter there.

"The ghost-moths white
That flit by night
Around our stalks, and through the grass-blades dry,
Were lilies.   Now
From bough to bough
Their white wings carry them.   We shall not die!

"Nothing can die.   All things but shift and grow,
With progress slow :
The lovers we have seen beside us stand
Will grow to angels—as the lilies change
To ghost-moths strange—
And win their gold wings in another land.

"Praise God, who makes
The hills and lakes ;
Whose hand can guard whate'er his heart hath given :
The golden air,
The sun up there,
The stars that whisper, 'We are flowers of heaven.' "

SONG OF THE RIVERS.

· I.

With ripples tuned to silver song
Our current foams and leaps along.
On either hand the green reeds close :
We see the brown bee rob the rose.

Upon the hedge its petals gleam :
The red rose closed its eyes to dream.
Into its heart the quick bee goes,
And sucks its sweetness from the rose.

Within our safe strong-timbered locks
The painted shallop sways and rocks :
Beneath our waves the pike darts by,
And all the timorous grey roach fly.

The white-sailed ghostly cutters glide
Along our curves and reaches wide :
And now the river-steamer too
Cuts with keen keel the waters blue.

Fleet racing-boats with eager force
Along our current steer their course.
Past piers and London wharfs we flow :
We lap stone walls with ripples slow.

We hear love whispered on the breeze,
And underneath our neighbouring trees.
White hands lean from the boat's bright edge,
And draw up lilies draped with sedge.

The spotted trout flash through the deep,
And up the weir great salmon leap.
The angler's fly says, " If you dare,
Snap at me ! " to the dace down there.

Along the stream gold fields of corn
Shine underneath the sun at morn :
And in the afternoon they seem,
Mist-clad, like corn-fields in a dream.

We, rivers light of heart and gay,
Chant through the whole long summer day;
And, when the harvest moon is up,
We make love to the cowslip cup.

The ragged-robin on our edge
Whispers " Good evening " to the sedge.
The red kine come to cool their feet
In our clear waves in August heat.

The country girls wash clothes, and laugh,
And hollowing hands, our waves they quaff.
A thousand slight things fill the day—
Then, when the sunset fades away,

The yellow moon above our banks
Rises, discerned through tall green ranks
Of rushes on the water-line :
Then one by one the bright stars shine.

All is so lovely in our life :
So free from labour, sorrow, strife.
We thank the God who gave his streams
Their day of toil, their night of dreams.

Dreams very tender,—seldom sad.
We watch the eyes of lovers glad :
We hear the maiden's whispered " I
Shall love you, darling, till I die."

We hear the strong man answer : " Love,
Our love will last till heights above
Receive us.   True love cannot die :
It shares the stars' eternity."

We hear, and we are glad.   We float
More buoyantly the lovers' boat. ·
With tender thoughts we watch it gleam
Adown the darkness of the stream.

II.

The memories of our mountains still
Are with us.—Each was once a rill,
Swift, foaming down some mountain's edge,
And tumbling on from ledge to ledge.

Then large the greatening river grew,
And deeper yet, and yet more blue.
Great towns it passed,—and then began
To carry out the schemes of man.

The white-sailed ships pursued their course
Along the river,—used its force.
It floated lilies in past hours,
But now it floated ships for flowers !

Yet, deepening ever in our flow,
As we bear commerce to and fro,
We feel, if youth's first dreams are lost,
The gain is worthy of the cost.

In countries many, mighty and great,
We aid man's tasks, we share man's state ;
Where were the glory of the Thames
Without its steamers' iron stems ?

What were the grandeur of the Seine,
Unshadowed by the historic fane ?
Highly the Seine 'mid rivers ranks,
For Notre Dame is on its banks.

And Westminster's grey stately towers
Are worth the loss of early flowers
That Nuneham flung, or Oxford threw,
From golden fields on waters blue.

III.

Thus, deepening onward, carrying ships,
Kissing the air with statelier lips,
Stream after stream must ever tend
On towards its God-appointed end.

The end is grand, the end is sure :
In front, a heaven of waters pure
And vast and stainless waits the stream—
A waste wherein its soul may dream

Dreams kinglier far than dreams that sped
About it in the days long dead ;
Old dreams of mountains robed in mist,
Far meadows by the sunlight kissed.

This waits us when our work is done :
A night wherethrough can pierce no sun ;
A depth no starlight from the air
Can traverse,—nor can moon gleam there.

This waits us.　Deep our souls shall rest
Within the mighty ocean's breast.
Rill, river, stream—We all shall be
Lost in the greatness of the sea.

SONG OF THE SEA.

I.

Bright sunsets come and go
Above my waters' flow :
The gold stars rise and set :
But I am young as yet.

I saw the first star gleam
Above my grey-blue stream :
Before the race of man
I, the great sea, began.

When man's race dies away,
My green waves still will play
Round granite echoing shores
That echo not to oars.

God dwells upon his throne,
And I on mine, alone.
Though all things else should die,
We could not,—he and I.

*   *

The sun has amorous hours
With golden plains of flowers.
He flashes through the trees :
He gilds the emerald leas.

His are the inland nooks,
The birch-trees, and the brooks :
The orchids, white or pied,
The daisies, golden-eyed.

His are the birds that sing
His praises in the spring :
The larch is his,—the fir,
The rainbow-gossamer.

His is the hazel-copse ;
His are the mountain-tops,
And valleys green and sweet
Where flocks in thousands bleat.

His heart can find repose
In kissing the red rose.
He fills with love-desire
The newly blossomed briar.

The gem-like humming-bird
Is gladdened at his word.
What birds and flowers love me,
The ever-ravening sea ?

Only the sea-weed red
Upon my wild floors spread :
The sea-bird fierce and strong
That loves the billows' song.

Strange, through the murky night,
Glitter my storm-birds white :
My gulls and petrels flit
Above my waste, moonlit.

Moonlit, or lightning-rayed :—
When strong men pale, afraid,
Then all my heart delights,
In the mad winter nights.

Sweeter than grass to me
Is tangle of the sea :
The rough brown weed that floats
Among the spars of boats.

Sweeter than fields of corn
The sea-gull's cry forlorn,
As on the wave he rests
Or rises on its crests.

A giant ship is tossed
Upon my waves and lost.
To-night its course is done :
I greet to-morrow's sun.

Or, with a laughing smile,
I greet some coral-isle.
Weary of dripping ghosts,
I kiss its golden coasts.

In depths that were a grave
My crimson sea-fronds wave
Most gently.   In a rill
The star-wort is less still !

Then, when night sinks again
Upon my boundless plain,
I chase the glimmering ships,
Foam flashing from my lips.

Where all was peace before,
My white-maned lions roar :
The ships' planks part and crack,
And spot their manes with black.

II.

When first God made me, he
Set peace upon the sea.
My waters all were calm,
Like windless isles of palm.

But soon my strength arose ;
I sprang up from repose :
And now two giants fight—
God, and the ocean's might.

Daily I gain more strength :
It may be I at length
Shall overwhelm and merge
The whole earth in my surge.

God's angels shall despair
When the tornadoes bear
My angels, through the night
Glittering,—my sea-birds white :

Above the dying ship
Fast in the black rock's grip
They hover, and they shine,
These angel-hosts of mine.

Lo ! at my mad waves' shriek
Blenches the sailor's cheek.—
To-night is dark. The shore
Will never see him more.

His wife may wake and pray,
And watch the waste of spray :
I thunder to her prayer
One answering word—" Despair."

" Despair : for God is far.
He cannot light one star !
I've drowned them one by one,—
As I will drown the sun.

" Despair : for God is weak.
He cannot cry, nor speak.
What if he spake ? Could he
Out-thunder the whole sea ? "—

IV

SONG OF THE STARS.

Across the solemn purple plains of night
        The starry light
    Falls in a million gold and silver rays.
Within the arch of heaven the star-flowers sing :
        Yes, these too bring
    Their ceaseless tribute of deep love and praise.

God sowed the fields with daisies—so they say :
        With many a ray
    Of golden light he sowed the heavens on high.
We are the blossoms of the purple air :
        We blossom there,
    The buttercups and cowslips of the sky.

One law pervades our being.   We arise
        Upon the skies
    In sudden fiery light and fervent heat :—
Then grass and herbs upon our surface grow,
        And after lo !
    The varied countless life we find so sweet.

Some stars are tulips of the deep-blue sky,
        And others vie
    With snow-drops in their whiteness as they gleam.

There are fierce warrior-hosts of ardent stars,
              Decked out like Mars ;
  But other orbs are gentle as a dream.

All are swayed justly by the high God's hand.—
              Our sea and land
Are duly parted, and our living things
All render homage unto God who made
              The sun and shade,
  And gave the fish its scales, the bird its wings.

All, all is good.—The viper in the fen,
              The worst of men,
  Can bring to pass the high God's perfect will.
No single ray of light from any star
              Can wander far ;
  Each has some fruitful purpose to fulfil.

Storm, thunder, terror, blood-red war, white peace,—
              Hopes that increase,—
  Fears that wax strong, or passionate joys that wane,—
These all achieve their end: Fierce pain and woe,
              Sunshine or snow,
  Thin fields of corn, or leagues of golden grain.

On each star at its great appointed hour
              God sends the power
Of some redeeming saviour-soul indeed.
All stars shall know in turn a saviour's face,
              And woman's grace
  In each to woman's serfdom shall succeed.

On one small star that swings in dark-blue air
              A saviour fair
Was born in a far Eastern land, they tell.

Great marvellous deeds he did with loving hand
　　　　　In that far land,
　And lifted souls from sin, and saved from hell.

But ah ! small star, in regions past thy dream
　　　　　Star-legions gleam :
　Thy resurrection-tale is also ours.
In every star Christ died : in each Christ rose.
　　　　　Each planet knows
　Its Saviour crowned with thorns,—then crowned with flowers.

All stars move slowly towards their destined fate,
　　　　　Small stars and great :
　Each star was born, and each shall find its tomb.
Yes : the Eternal power whom we obey
　　　　　Shall sweep one day
　All stars and strong suns into lampless gloom.

Then He, the Eternal power, shall build again
　　　　　The dark night's fane,
　And fit the dome of heaven with lamps quite new.
Just as earth's blossoms wither in a night,
　　　　　So all our light
　Shall pass, and fresh lamps burn against the blue.

A million, million years are but a day
　　　　　To God, one ray
　Of wandering sunlight thrown against the dark.
And yet the Eternal power shall never lose
　　　　　One white star-rose,
　One pale moon-petal, or one red sun-spark.

The tiniest flower the living God's hand made
　　　　　In the first glade
　In the first star he flung upon the sky

Is living yet in some unknown fair mode
In some abode :
God hears the hidden violet's faintest sigh.

Beyond all highest poets' highest dreams
The sweet truth gleams,
Gleams out resplendent.   Nought can pass away.
What God has once inspired with living breath,
This knows not death :
Sunset predicts another golden day.

The sunset of the stars when all things end,
This doth portend
Another sunrise on the seas of space ;
Another vision of more stars than ours,
And fadeless flowers,
And deathless beings of a lordlier race.

So, ever, living God, we worship thee.
Each galaxy
Of moons and suns and stars that veer and change
Worships with endless worship at thy shrine :
For they are thine,
And thou art theirs, in union sweet and strange.

II.
HUMANITY.

I.
VOICES OF HUMANITY.

I.

CHANT OF POSITIVISTS.

I.

All early dreams have passed away :
The golden heavenly skies wax grey :
　　The sunset of the Lord has come.
Now first we find the green earth sweet :
The grass is cool to tired-out feet :
　　The sweet earth is indeed a home.

We know our own true home at last :
The gorgeous dreams of heaven are past :
　　No angel's harp sounds on the breeze.
Gold wings are gone.　We mark instead
White wings above the dahlia bed,
　　And blue wings o'er the clover leas.

These are our angels.—Butterflies,
Blue as the cloudless azure skies,
　　Or white-winged as the clouds at morn,
Dance o'er the garden-beds, and gleam
Above the hedges.　Now we dream
　　Of other crowns than that of thorn.

The pale-browed Jew who ruled so long,
By virtue of his priestly throng
　　Of worshippers, has passed away.
T

The long night of the race is done :
Now in the East behold the sun,
　　The herald of man's glorious day.

Man first made God, but now retakes
The sceptre from God's hand,—unmakes
　　What once with fiery thought he made.
God is a dream of mankind's brain :
But man dethrones God ; man must reign ;
　　Not God, but man, must be obeyed.

This earth is all.—Then add new worth
To our one home, our fair old earth :
　　Love every flower in every vale.
The fancied flowers of heaven were grand.
Yet pause : look round.　Stretch out thine hand.
　　Gather that snowdrop pure and pale.

Was ever heavenly bloom so white ?—
Did great stars glitter through the night
　　Of heaven, as on our earth they gleam ?
Had heaven a million lamps, as we ?
Or white birds on a dark-blue sea ?
　　This is the truth.　Heaven was the dream.

Heaven was the dream.—But now we know
How man is made, where man must go :
　　We seek no opening to the tomb ;
Content to pass, content to be
At rest for all eternity
　　Within the deep and flameless gloom.

The flameless gloom—for once hell-fire
Roared up to heaven, aye flickered higher
    Than heavenly towers that rose sublime.
If heaven we've lost, we've lost as well
The flamelit under-realm of hell :
    We cannot either sink, or climb.

We cannot climb to heaven, or sink
Below old hell's fierce ravening brink :
    God cannot plunge man in his deeps.
Nor can we climb the mountains high
That used, we thought, to pierce the sky
    And beckon with their sombre steeps.

The earth is left.—We can adorn
Her beauty,—drape with fields of corn
    The plains that fill her ample breast.
Now heaven has past, our souls are free
To love the green earth and the sea :
    Now hope is dead, we are at rest.

II.

And woman too is left to love :
She brings us dreams of things above
    The common daily life she scorns.
Woman makes all things beautiful ;
For from the hedge her hand can pull
    The blossoming rose, and leave the thorns !

Our angel stands beside us. She
First made man of a certainty
    Dream of a life beyond the tomb.

And, now we seek that life no more,
Woman is left us to adore,
　　　And woman's worship to resume.

The force we wasted on the sky
Returns to earth.　We put it by ;
　　　We store it up for better things.
The noblest angel after all
Is woman : sweeter if she fall
　　　At times, for very want of wings !

Great were Isaiah, Peter, Paul :
Our poets can transcend them all ;
　　　And, now they sing of earth alone,
They'll rise to lordlier heights of song.
Yes, man himself shall reach ere long
　　　The steps of the Eternal's throne.

For that eternal force is ours :
It brings forth man, it brings forth flowers
　　　And life and death, in it, are one.
It shines in stars : in man it lives :
Its colour to the rose it gives,
　　　And gives its red flame to the sun.

One force through all things works its way :
Through joy and sorrow, night and day :
　　　Is gentle in the blue-bell's breath :
Is soft within the snow-flake white :
Fierce-hued within the lightning's light :
　　　One power speaks " Life," or whispers " Death."

But all beyond is wrapped in gloom.
Nought answers from beyond the tomb :
    No starlight travels from that sky.
No eye can pierce the solemn veil :
Each soul exploring comes back pale
    From contact with eternity.

Man's heart must fail, man's head must reel,
In searching heights where cloud-ranks wheel
    For ever through the space profound.
Christ climbed death's mountain long ago :
He vanished 'mid the mists and snow
    Without a look, without a sound !—

III.

Therefore the earth is ours alone :
The sun sits on its flame-red throne ;
    The stars sit on their thrones in space ;—
We have this earth whereon we stand :
We have the thrill in woman's hand ;
    We have the love in woman's face.

We have the force to win a flower
Of love, and wear it for an hour,
    And for an hour to find it sweet.
Aye, sweeter is our love for this—
In that there is no second kiss,
    And even the first is over-fleet.

In that to-morrow's frost will slay
The violets, passing sweet are they !
    Life is so short.   Let it be grand !

Let every deed of man be true :
There is no heaven in which to do
    The noble deeds we only planned.

Great peace is ours ; a peace beyond
The reach of those who hope, despond,
    And snatch at heaven, and shrink from hell :
The peace of those who hope for nought
Save what each long day's toil has brought,
    And, hopeless, feel that all is well.

CHANT OF CHRISTIANS.

I.

He brought no flowers, he brought no gems,
No jewels of earth's diadems;
    Within a stable he was born.
With us he suffered day by day;
Upon his brow no gold crown lay,
    But only mocking points of thorn.

Not on divine soft banks of rose
Where souls of lovers may repose
    Rested the Lord of earth and air.
He found not where to lay his head;
Was cradled where the oxen fed;
    A rock-tomb was his sepulchre.

No gifts of love, or power, or fame,
Or earthly rank, were his who came
    To lift the humble soul on high.
Though not one star without him shone,
Uncrowned he came, he came alone,
    He brought no star-wreath from the sky.

Though, long before the first star g'eamed,
Within God's bosom Jesus dreamed,
    He was content that dream should pass.

He entered, here, a woman's womb,
And let her sacred flesh entomb
          All that he felt, all that he was.

The maiden's womb by God so blessed
Bare Jesus, and the maiden's breast
          Suckled the living King of kings.
The infant Mary brought to birth
Was king of heaven, and lord of earth
          And air, to where the last star swings.

This was God's condescension great :
To enter by that sacred gate
          The land of woe, the land of pain.
And, having reached this land of ours
Where thorn-points peer from fairest flowers,
          What was the fashion of his reign?

He reigned in sinful hearts and weak :
The sinner's soul he came to seek ;
          He came to dry the sufferer's tears.
He came to tell the worn-out heart,
" Be of good cheer.   Lo ! mine thou art,
          And shalt be through the endless years."

He came to bid the harlot rise :
To pour God's sunlight through her eyes,
     ·   And bid her dark night wane and flee.
He came to bid the whole wide earth
Partake, with man, a second birth ;
          To soothe to rest the restless sea.

He came to bid the waters sink
To quiet on the blue lake's brink ;
  To say to wild waves, " Peace. Be still ! "
He came, that wind-tossed souls might find
A haven for the weary mind :
  He came to do the Father's will.

The will of him who sends the rain
To touch to green the parched-up plain,
  Or sends the sun to charm the air :
The will of him through whom night's hours
Glitter with ceaseless starry flowers
  That make the boundless dark fields fair.

The will of him through whom began
The cycle of life that ends in man,
  And who in Jesus ended all :
Making in Jesus man complete ;
Devising evil's full defeat
  Through him, and Satan's abject fall.

The will obeying which he died
Thorn-crowned, a spear thrust through his side
  And red nails through his feet and hands :
The will of God through which he rose
And passed into supreme repose,
  Peace God's Son only understands.

II.

He came to make the blind eyes see ;
To show that human will is free ;
  That God's will underlies the whole :

That, past all weary winds that roar,
Sweet sunlight gilds a golden shore
    Where harbourage waits the storm-tossed soul.

He came and suffered here on earth
That man might win the second birth :
    His spotless flesh and blood he gave
That man, partaking, might be fed
With heavenly wine and heavenly bread,
    And, haply, so elude the grave.

He healed disease that man might know
That pang and torment, throb and throe,
    Are not to last for ever such ;
That God, who works in every place
Through his own laws of time and space,
    Can change those strait laws at a touch.

God binds the laws. They cannot bind
The Lord of nature and mankind.
    Can God's own star-crown bruise his head ?
Can God, who made both life and death,
Who breathes through dust a living breath,
    Not raise the righteous from the dead ?

Can God, who makes the storm arise
And hurls the thunders through the skies,
    Change not, at will, his mode and style ?
God, who controls the lightning's fire,
Can he not change, if he desire,
    Winter to summer by a smile ?

Can he not change man's March to May?
Weave jessamine in December grey
  Around his temple-porch at will?
Change ice that stiffens into blue
Calm water, where the reeds renew
  Their whispering courtship of the rill?

This is what Jesus came to teach :
That God's sure hand is over each ;
  That waves may rise, and winds may roar,
But God the King is Lord of all,—
Nor shall a single sparrow fall
  From his safe hand for evermore.

Our hairs are numbered—so he said :
Each bright ray of the sunset red
  God paints with thoughtful conscious hand.
The sunset, be it gold or rose,
Just as he wills it, shines and glows,—
  And every wave he leads to land.

Not endless law, but ceaseless will.
This is Christ's gospel-message still :
  Will at the heart of all things made.
Not Chance at the world-vessel's helm,
But loving Will throughout the realm
  Of life, eternally obeyed.

III.

So he who, ere the world began,
Was God, became in all points man :
  God's Son was of a woman born.

God took account of woman then,
And honoured the sweet slave whom men
        Have lowered and saddened with their scorn.

God honoured woman.—None can say
Since that far-off first Christmas-Day
        That woman hath no share nor part
In God's eternal great designs.
Woman and man God's thought combines :
        They dwell together in his heart.

So, thus this stormy world of ours
Was entered.   Christ's hand gathered flowers ;
        He watched the sunset and sunrise :
He wandered by the inland sea,
The blue calm Lake of Galilee ;
        Earth spread her gifts before his eyes.

God, who had made, in epochs long
Anterior to the first bird's song,
        Our fiery bright home spin through space,
Appeared, himself, to test the whole :—
The unexplored vast cosmic soul
        Was obvious in a human face.   .

God came himself, his work to try :
To test his sunlit dome of sky ;
        To see that all had turned out well.
Through Jesus' searching eyes he viewed
The desert waste, the green-leafed wood,
        The rocky height, the watered dell.

Through Jesus' eyes he gazed on man :
And here he chiefliest found his plan
   Primordial marred and wrenched awry.
Man whom he made divinely free,
Ruler of earth, lord of the sea,
   Was veriest slave beneath the sky.

And woman, whom God made so sweet,
Was trampled by tyrannic feet :
   The queen was harlot now, and slave.
The love that God designed of old
Man's love should win, the women sold :
   They bartered now what once they gave.

So, looking on this world of sin,
God saw no hope without, within,
   Nought left save only, dying here
At man's own hands, so to restore
Woman—that man's heart might adore ;
   And man—that woman might revere.

Christ,—having entered by the gate
Of birth the world he made so great,
   He found so small, so dark, so sad,—
By one path could return to God :
The grim cross pointed out the road,
   And Jesus saw it, and was glad.

By woman Christ was born. Through men
He reached his Father's home again,
   The realm corruption may not see.—
When woman's God so longed to save
That he assumed the flesh she gave,
   What was man's answer ? Calvary.—

CHANT OF POETS.

Sweeter than dreams of moon or star,
Or dreams of heaven—aye, fairer far,
  The dreams of woman's beauty born!
God, when he toiled in heaven alone,
Grew weary. Now she shares his throne
  And brings him rapture, night and morn.

What was the whole of heaven most fair
Without the love of woman there—
  Without her eyes, without her look?
In heaven the soul of woman grew,
And still her eyes retain the blue
  Of that deep heaven which she forsook.

Still something sweet, and something strange,
Is in her eyes that gleam and change,—
  A something not of earth or sky:
A something maddening hearts that gaze;
Requickening thoughts of ancient days,
  Dreams of a past eternity.

Half angel she—and yet not quite :
Woman,—with neck and bosom white;
  Woman,—who gives, gives overmuch.

An angel's heart; a woman's frame;
She brings us peace; she burns with flame;
  Destroys a life's work at a touch.

Within the sick-room dark and dread
The glory of her golden head
  Brings sunlight. Nigh the grave she stands;
And man forgets the flowers they bring
In gazing at that sweeter thing,
  The heavenly lilies of her hands.

Yet passion fierce and passion strong
She wakes. She thrills all hearts to song:
  She crowns the poet with the bays.
In dreams of her his life goes by;
Her glances fill with stars his sky,
  And fill with thoughts of fire his days.

God made her soul. Then Satan took
The sweet thing and he changed her look
  And set some light of evil there.
She who was wholly angel then
Is half a temptress now to men;
  Aye, half a fiend, and wholly fair.

But wholly fair,—for ever fair.—
The mere slight fragrance of her hair,
  The least soft thrilling of her hands,
Has served ere now, again will serve,
To make the course of history swerve,
  And ruin souls, and ruin lands.

Aye, God and Satan well may fight!
She is so sweet, she is so white;
　　　She is so good to touch and hold.
Love is the only thing that well
May outlive heaven and outlive hell:
　　　This one joy never groweth old.

Still fresh as in the early day
When Eden heard the first rose say,
　　　"A sweeter mouth than mine is born,"
She treads the earth.　Since time began
She has given herself away to man,
　　　With rapture half, and half in scorn.

The magic in her voice and gaze
Is still the same as in old days
　　　When Eden found her very fair.
Till time itself shall change and die
Some marvel past man's speech shall lie
　　　Within the sweetness of her hair.

The sympathizing world has worn
On its own brow Christ's crown of thorn
　　　For nigh two thousand years to-day:
But, ages ere he lived and died,
Woman could lure man to her side;
　　　Her mouth could melt man's will away.

A mere girl's eyes of hare-bell blue
Can thrill a strong man through and through
　　　Whom Jove's own thunders would not bend.
And man will win a world, and this
In turn will barter for a kiss:
　　　And so it will be to the end.

Long ages ere man's history spoke
Woman could win man's heart. She broke
  Man's heart in many a star that shone
Uncounted ages ere our star,
Crossing its own birth's harbour-bar,
  Spread sail, and dared the void, alone.

And, when Christ's life is but a dream,
A fairy legend, a star-beam
  Past, almost, from the race's view,
Woman will rise up like a flower,—
Born as it were that very hour,
  Fresh as that far-off morning's dew.

Gods pass : men pass : but she abides.—
Death fades, and time. But love derides
  The years whose wrinkled faces flee.—
Not deathless is thy crown of thorn,
Lord Christ. The flower thy followers scorn
  Will outlast this, and outlive thee.—

IV.

CHANT OF WOMEN.

I.

Man brings us flowers, and brings us grief ;
He twines for us love's myrtle leaf,
  And wreathes about our brows the thorn.
We crave for love ? Man gives us this ?
Nay, he bestows but passion's kiss,
  And tinges passion with his scorn !

Ten thousand years have passed away,
Or more years yet, the wise men say,
  Since history on this earth began.
In all those years, what have we gained ?
Deceived, misunderstood, disdained,
  What shall we render back to man ?

Love.—This our great prerogative,
Eternally we gain and give :
  We bring God's sunlight from on high.
The earth was dark until we came ;
We fill the earth with love's bright flame,
  And steal the gold dawn from the sky.

By love we grow ; by love we gain
The right to live, the right to reign :—
  When man's wild wayward course is done

We then shall say to man : Behold,
While thine hand delved amid the mould
    Our souls caught glory from the sun !

While thou wast watching earth with eyes
Most dim, we watched God in the skies
    With gaze that daily grew more clear.
To conquer earth was all thy dream :
To build thy mills on every stream ;
    Through unconjectured waves to steer !

Where once were fields made bright with flowers
Grew grimy towns and sullen towers :
    By river-banks great wharfs arose.
Where once were alder green and oak
Black factories loom, and chimneys smoke,
    And engines break the morn's repose.

O maker of all hideous things,
'Twas well God sent us without wings
    To dwell upon thine earth with thee—
Else, long ere this, our souls had fled
Beyond the waste of sunset red,
    Beyond the green-blue waste of sea :

Else some remembrance of our home
Had lured us forth to soar and roam
    Through silent leagues of star-sown air,
Compelling us to search for flowers
In airy fields and heavenly bowers,
    Man having stripped earth's meadows bare !

II.

How couldst thou, having hid with steam
And smoke the skies where sweet stars gleam,
　　　Discern the starlight in our look?
How couldst thou, having choked all flowers
In fields and woodlands, care for ours?
　　　What cares the boulder for the brook?

Thou, slave of thine electric light,
Hast even invoked perennial night
　　　To brood above thy city's spires;
Lest one vast arrow of the sun
Should pierce the fog, and leave not one
　　　Unquenched, of thine ephemeral fires!

But we, who dreamed of higher things,
Were happy where the brown lark sings
　　　Above the fields of golden grain.
At peace with God, we saw the showers
Rejoice the pale sun-stricken flowers,
　　　And blessed God for his bounteous rain.

The poor fish panting out of reach
Of the cool water, on the beach,
　　　With death's hues glittering on his side,
Him would we save: him back we threw,
And, smiling, saw the water blue
　　　Receive him safe.—You would deride.

What pity for the tortured horse
Has man? He goads him on his course:
　　　There is no mercy in his soul.—
God, when he made the dumb things, erred.
If he had let them speak one word,
　　　Just to repudiate man's control!

And God, who made our womanhood
And made it at the outset good,
    Erred too, in that he made us weak.
The strength was man's : the soul was ours.
God should have guarded his pale flowers
    In heaven, and let man come to seek.

And yet . . . . . . God hardly could have known
That man would claim us for his own ;
    Would hound the thought of God away :
Would change the form God made so sweet
Into the harlot of the street ;
    Teach those to curse, who once could pray.

Ah, piteous story of our wrongs !—
And yet to God the whole belongs :
    We give to God and Christ the whole.
We trust God, till all sufferings end :
We have in Christ a deathless Friend,
    An helper sweet, a kindred soul.

Christ by his perfect womanhood
Hath power to make all women good :
    The fallen to lift, the sad to save.
Women who met his glances knew
That here at last was manhood true :
    Fearless, to him their hearts they gave.

They called him "God"; for God was here.
The Godhood in a man makes dear
    The man to woman.   Woman's kiss
Is never given as mankind deems,
Absorbed in its own narrow dreams.
    God *in* man—woman worships this.

Not all the flowers man brings to her
Make her forget Christ's sepulchre.
      She whispers, " Lord remember me !"
In every crown her brow has worn
Woman in secret plants a thorn,
      In homage to Gethsemane.

Not by the flowers he brings her shrine
Will man draw forth that deep divine
      Strange thing he calls a woman's heart.
Not by his wordy gifts of praise—
(They win for poets crowns of bays,
      But woman differs, here, from Art.)

The old same story still goes on :
Man ever wins, he wins alone,
      By Christhood in his mind and soul.
Would he from woman's heart and head
Drive out the Christ ? *Be* Christ instead :
      And thou shalt reach the self-same goal.

Be Christ, O man ! Let old dreams flee.
Lo ! woman asks no gift of thee.
      Better than flowers she loves Christ's thorn. —
Be thou with Jesus crucified,
And thou shalt win an heart-whole Bride,
      And meet her on thine Easter morn.

II.

BALLADS OF HUMAN LIFE.

I.

BLUE-BELLS.

" One day, one day, I'll climb that distant hill
   And pick the blue-bells there !"
So dreamed the child who lived beside the rill
   And breathed the lowland air.
"One day, one day, when I am old I'll go
And climb the mountain where the blue-bells blow !"

One day ! one day ! The child was now a maid,
   A girl with laughing look ;
She and her lover sought the valley-glade
   Where sang the silver brook.
" One day," she said, "love, you and I will go
And reach that far hill where the blue-bells blow !"

Years passed. A woman now with wearier eyes
   Gazed towards that sunlit hill.
Tall children clustered round her. How time flies !
   The blue-bells blossomed still.
She'll never gather them ! All dreams fade so.
We live and die, and still the blue-bells blow.

II

THE TOURNAMENT.

The trumpets' blare
Rings through the air :
The glittering lists are bright with sword and shield.
A hundred gallant knights,
Known in a thousand fights,
Mix and engage upon the mimic field.
But one towers o'er them al
A noble knight and tall,
With giant form in armour black concealed.

In vain, in vain,
The thick blows rain,—
He dreams of her whose heart has wrought him wrong.
With little heed of all,
He lets the swift strokes fall :
His war-horse steers a way with onset strong.
He gazes up above :
Where is his lady-love ?
He marks her not amid the courtly throng.

And yet at last,
When hope was past,
Flashed on his eyes the wondrous eyes he sought.

She wore his colours too,
White, twined with tender blue—
"She loves!" His strength rushed on him at the thought.
Then knight on knight fell low:
Aye, always it is so!
By woman's hand a true knight's sword is wrought.

III

CHRISTMAS FAIRIES.

Ah ! dear old Christmas-tides of long ago.
   Around the creaking roof-tops roared the blast :
The streets and hills and fields were draped in snow ;
    Across the ice the glittering skates shot past.
                Youth was not dead !
                Bright green and red
The holly-leaves and holly-berries gleamed.
             The merry church-bells rang ;
             Our young hearts laughed and sang ;
Of joyous years to come our spirits dreamed.

But years to come bring trouble and despair.
   If childhood brings its simple dream of joy
Youth brings love's holier dream, a dream more fair
    Than dreams which haunt the bright heart of the boy.
             But all dreams melt
             As soon as felt,—
They fade into the mist of things unseen.
             Youth's dream of love, alas !
             Must likewise pale and pass :
Sweet love must be as if it had not been.

And yet—the holly-berries still are bright ;
The bells chime merrily across the snow :
A thousand Christmas-trees will give delight,
   Green as the Christmas-trees of long ago.
               Why are we sad ?
              The young are glad ;
They dance around the fir-tree hand in hand.
           Outside, white miles of snow :
           Inside, the red fire's glow ;
And children's smiles and dreams of fairy-land.

TWO NIGHTS.

Last night he kissed my hair, and kissed my face,
And laughed, and praised my figure's supple grace.
My soul was dazzled as with sudden flame :
Star behind star my sweet star-bridesmaids came :
       To-night, to-night,
       No soft starlight,
But gloom profound that veils the heaven and sea.

Last night the world was full of light and fire :
Star throbbed to star, and burned with sweet desire.
There was no heaven,—for earth was heaven instead !
No immortality,—for death was dead !
       To-night, to-night,
       Dead is delight,
And pain awakes and lives eternally.

Last night I thought before God's throne I stood
And knew, knew once for all, that God was good.
To-night how vast a darkness clothes me round :
I madden for love's footfall.   Not a sound !—
       Last night, last night,
       My love took flight :
Cloud sobs to cloud, and whispers, "Where is he?"

LOVE'S ETERNITY.

Love's early honey-moon is passing sweet.
  The enraptured lovers wander hand in hand
Through the wild roses and the golden wheat,
  And passion's glamour clothes the sea and land.
          Her eyes outvie
          The starlit sky :
Love is so full of light that nought else gleams.
          Love would give light,
          Were the world black as night !
Love would create its heaven of stars and dreams !

Then come maturer days.   Glad children glance—
  Upon the tree of life love's blossoms blow.
And yet some element of old romance
  Has vanished, melted in the long ago !
          The husband says,
          " Think of the days
When hand in hand we wandered, you and I ;
          The nights of June ;
          The marvel of the moon :
In later days must love's old glory die ? "
          x

But with the voice that charmed his heart of old
　　And made the whole of life one moonlit dream
The true wife answers, "Life's tale is not told :
　　In front of us new starlit skies will gleam.
　　　　　　　When toil is o'er,
　　　　　　　Love as before
Will find us, sweetheart, claim us for his own.
　　　　　　　Love's autumn day,
　　　　　　　Aye ! though our hair be grey,
Shall match the sweetness of our summer flown."

VI

MIDNIGHT AT THE HELM.

"What see'st thou, friend?
The frail masts bend,
Thy ship reels wildly on the tossing deep;
Thy fearless eyes
Regard the skies
And this broad waste wherethrough white chargers leap;
See'st thou the foam?"
Pilot.—·   " I see my home,
And children on a white soft couch asleep."

" What see'st thou, friend?
The tiller-end
Thou graspest safely in thy firm strong grip;
Thine eyes are strange,
They seem to range
Beyond sea, sky, and clouds, and struggling ship,
Beyond the foam."
Pilot.—   " I see my home,—
Brown cottage-eaves round which the swallows dip."

" What see'st thou, friend?
Black leagues extend
On all sides round about thy bark and thee;

Not one star-speck
Above the deck
Abates the darkness of the midnight sea ;
The waves' throats roar—"
Pilot.--   " I see the shore,
And eyes that plead with God for mine and me."

VII

THE GHOST AT THE WHEEL.

Off Beachy Head the vessel wrestles hard :
　In vain the captain's eyes would pierce the gloom.
The great grim cliffs, foam-belted, iron-barred,
　Through the wild wreaths of scudding sea-fog loom.
　　　　　No stars shine out.
　　　　　Put helm about?
Nay ! this one ship will hold her lonely way !
　　　　　Though death be near,
　　　　　Her captain's deaf to fear :
His voice out-thunders wind and hissing spray.

Yet at the rudder, see this lurid light !
　A form takes shape amid the wind and spray :
A white face glitters through the jet-black night.
　Why falls the captain on his knees to pray?
　　　　　His brother's form
　　　　　Shines through the storm,
His brother drowned where these same mad waves flow
　　　　　Round Beachy Head :
　　　　　The strong man shakes in dread :
When dead men steer, where will the doomed ship go?

The dead man steered.   The labouring ship veered round.
　The awe-struck sailors watched without a word.
The waves and threatening thunder ceased to sound :
　You might have caught the carol of a bird.
　　　　　　Then slowly grew
　　　　　　The sky pale-blue ;
Morn showed that when the spectre took command,
　　　　　　Ten yards away
　　　　　　Were deadly reefs and spray :
Love outlasts death, and aids with living hand.

VIII

THE SENTRY.

Along his path the sentry paces slow ;
  Above the field of battle soars the moon : ,
The night is silent, save for wailing low
  Of wounded men who will be silent soon.
          The sentry stands
        With ready hands
And eyes that peer far out into the gloom.
        The hostile hosts,
        Like groups of ghosts,
Upon the distant shadowy hill-tops loom.

But not on these the soldier's gaze is set ;
  His heart is gazing elsewhere than his eyes.
He sees a garden sweet with mignonette ;
  He hears a voice that to his own replies.
        O'er leagues of sea
        In thought flies he ;
He stands beside a window wreathed with rose.
        Sweet eyes of blue,
        Pure, soft, and true,
Gaze in his own, till his heart overflows.

Ha ! guns flash out.   The dream is over then.
  The vision vanishes.   It melts away.
Lo ! plumes, and neighing steeds, and throngs of men,
  And rattling rifles, in the morning grey.
          No cottage door—
          Mad guns that roar !
No tender glance from maiden's loving eyes.
          Yet pity not
          A soldier's lot :
He well has loved, who for his country dies.

IX

THE ENGINE DRIVER.

Through sleet and snow
The wild wheels go :
Across waste wolds with purple heather bright,
O'er many a bridge,
Through tunnelled ridge,
Flinging weird fires along the startled night,
The engine flies,—
And one man's steady eyes
And hands must guide the thundering force aright.

What trust we place
In that one face,
In those stern lips and dauntless hands that steer :
Bridegroom and bride
Sit side by side,
And trust their lives to him without a fear.
Through sun and snow
The flashing wild wheels go :
He guides those flashing wheels from year to year.

Through storm and sun
The wild wheels run ;
Blue skies o'erhead, or murky midnight gloom :

Through summer showers,
Past woodbine-bowers,
Past steep banks yellowed with soft primrose-bloom.
Yet one man's skill
Makes the end good or ill :
He holds the keys of pleasure—or the tomb !

X.

ON THE RAMPARTS.

The gold sun sets above the solemn sands ;
  The strained sight aches across the yellow sea :
In front, around, the solitude expands,
    Grim, terrible, devoid of flower or tree.
          The waste seems dead ;
          No line of red
Upon the horizon brings the city cheer.
          Fierce foes surround ;
          Their trumpets sound ;
No answering English bugle-note rings clear.

Upon the ramparts lo ! one paces slow ;
  From time to time he gazes o'er the sands :
If morning brings not help, all hope must go.
    He lifts to silent heaven strong urgent hands.
          Is help not nigh,
          O starlit sky
And Eastern moon whose white orb glitters past ?
          Black looms the night.
          No help in sight !
Must the beleaguered city fall at last ?

Morning!   The thin mist rises in the air:
  Not yet the great sun flashes from the sky.
That grim and silent watcher still is there.
  To-day must bring relief, or all must die.
          Gaze once again
          Across the plain:
One last wild look, for now the sun shines clear.
          Ha! bayonets gleam;
          It is no dream;
Our England's help can reach us even here!

XI

THE EXPLORER.

Through forests deep,
Where serpents creep,
The fearless strong explorer threads his way :
'Neath tropic moons,
Past dim lagoons,
Depths where the sun can never send a ray.
His life is in his hand :
He treads the burning sand :
His labour ceases not from day to day.

And yet at night
His soul takes flight :
He seeks another country in his dreams.
He wanders through
Lanes fresh with dew
And corn-fields where the scarlet poppy gleams.
He sees the spotted trout
From the dark bank flash out :
He sees green willows fringing English streams.

At morn he wakes :
His road he takes :—
Upon mud-banks vast crocodiles repose.

The trout's quick gleam
Was but a dream :
The poppy was a dream, a dream the rose !
Yet England's viewless might,
Stretching through day and night,
Follows wherever English valour goes.

XII

THE BURNING SHIP.

The transport ship pursues its lonely way
  Across the purple moonlit Indian deep.
Above, the stars shine out with tender ray :
  The waveless far-spread ocean seems asleep.
        All, all was well,
        When evening fell,
And well at sunrise all shall surely be.
        There's nought to fear !
        Steer, keen-eyed helmsman, steer,—
Steer the great ship across the silent sea !

But ah ! what piteous sudden cry rings out ?
  " Fire ! "—" Fire ! " again.—Oh, can this dread thing be ?
Yes, once again the wild heart-rending shout
  Troubles the bosom of the peaceful sea.
        " Fire ! "—Red flames rise
        And stain the skies :
The fire spreads o'er the sails, and licks the mast.
        The ship's consumed !
        The passengers are doomed :
Each agonizing moment seems their last.

But ah ! the steady soldiers form in lines :
   Athwart the fire the regiment's old flag floats.
The fire upon men's fearless faces shines :
   The sailors pass the women to the boats.
        The boats recede ;
        Wild eyes give heed—
Their death-watch on the deck the soldiers keep.
        One strange last cheer,
        Which England's heart shall hear—
And then the sun rose on a sail-less deep.

V

THE SONG OF ABOU KLEA.

Our English manhood's still the same
   As in the days of Waterloo ;
The sons uphold their fathers' fame,
   Beneath strange skies of burning blue.
The race is growing old, some say,
   And half worn out and past its prime ;
But English rifles volley " Nay,"
   And English manhood conquers time.
         Then fear not, and veer not
         From duty's narrow way :
         What men have done, can still be done,
         And shall be done to-day !

The broad wild desert stretched away
   For many and many a weary league ;
Our soldiers suffered day by day,
   Enduring hunger, thirst, fatigue.
But still, when their fierce foes they met,
   They fought and conquered as of old :
The sun of England has not set ;
   Our nation's story is not told.
         Then blench not, and quench not
         High hope's glad golden ray :
         What men have done, can still be done,
         And shall be done to-day !

"ENGLAND, HO! FOR ENGLAND."

A FEDERATION SONG.

Old England needs her children,
　　She needs them every one,
From India's morning-bugle
　　To the last sunset-gun :
North, East, and South, she needs them,
　　And in the furthest West,
And where the Channel waters
　　Storm round her rocky breast.

The day is surely coming
　　When all alike she'll need,
All far-off true descendants
　　Of the old island-breed.
The day is surely coming
　　When all may have to strike
For England, ho! for England—
　　So all must fare alike !

" For England, ho ! for England "—
　　The great deep-throated cry
Rings far across the waters;
　　A million mouths reply,

" For England, ho! for England,
  Till England's work be done,—
And England's work is timeless
  And measured by the sun."

III.

THE WORKMAN-KING.

I'm only a working man, my boys,
    I toil in the London smoke,
But when a holiday comes, my boys,
    I cease to grind and choke.
The garden of England's mine, my boys,
    Its valleys and woods and plains,
For the people rules the whole, my boys,
    The people votes and reigns!

The democrat rules the whole, my boys,
    The forests of larch and oak ;
We never need cough and sniff, my boys,
    In the great towns' soot and smoke.
The heather-bud swells on the moors and fells
    And the sea is blue and wide ;
Do you know how sweet the country smells ?
    You never can tell till you've tried !

A noble heritage this, my boys,
    To possess and rule and sway !
Now the people votes and reigns, my boys,
    We speak, and our lords obey.

The garden of England's ours, my boys,
  But to rule ourselves remains,
For the man who governs and rules himself
  Is ever the man who reigns—
The man who can govern and rule himself
  Is ever the king who reigns !

IV

RETROSPECT.

"O conquering poet, thou that hast
   The whole world at thy feet,
What laurel-garlands crown thy past !
   Is not the present sweet ? "

Poet.

" I'd fling away my crown of bay,
   Lose it without one throe,
To feel beside my own to-day
The tender heart I flung away
         Long, long ago ! "

" O statesman, thou that guidest things
   With godlike strength of will,
Thou art more regal than earth's kings ;
   They hear thee, and are still."

Statesman.

" I shape the world continually,
   I lay its monarchs low,
And yet I'd give the world to see
The dead eyes smile that smiled at me
         Long, long ago ! "

"O warrior, thou that carriest high
   Thy grey victorious head,
What pæans echo to the sky
   At thy war-horse's tread!"

Warrior.

"I heed them not. I long to hear
   The child's speech, soft and slow,
That used to sound upon my ear,
So sweet, so pure, so silver-clear,
Many and many and many a year
              Ago!"

V

TWO NESTS.

In the leafless sycamore
   Lo ! a winter nest.
Round it all the ceaseless roar
   Of the storm's unrest.
Here love's palace once was seen
   Swinging to the breeze,
Roofed and guarded by the green,
   Full of melodies.
Here the sunset loved to rest,
Smiling on the thrush's nest.

In yon London attic room
   Once a painter wrought ;
All our dense November gloom
   Darkened not his thought.
Woman's love was here as well ;
   Woman's loving eyes
Met the painter's when they fell
   From the pictured skies.
Love forsook his fiery quest,
Pausing at the painter's nest.

Both are changed alike to-day.
　When the thrushes flew,
Sorrow turned the green leaves grey,
　Robbed the heaven of blue.
Painter, sweetheart, both are dead,
　But the room remains,
And an easel smeared with red,—
　Dusty window-panes.
Death destroys with equal zest
Painter's bower, or thrush's nest.

VI

THE PATHWAY OF LIFE.

In every heart a story;
　　In every heart a grief;
The sorrow of a lifetime;
　　A pain or rapture brief.
Old hearts and young together,
　　All hearts alike, are one;
All harden in black weather,
　　All soften at the sun.

All hearts have had their burden;
　　Romance has come to most,
Has entered life with trumpets
　　And vanished like a ghost.
Each heart is like an album
　　With blossoms therein dried;
Sweet blossoms, pure love-blossoms,
　　That bloomed a day, then died.

Oh! brothers, Oh! strong brothers,
　　And sisters sad and sweet,
Wives, daughters, fathers, mothers,—
　　In suffering all can meet.

The path of pain in common
  We all alike have trod,—
May that one pathway lead us,
  Lead all alike to God!

THE PILOT'S WIFE.

"The moon shines out with here and there a star,
 But furious cloud-ranks storm both stars and moon :
The mad sea drums upon the harbour-bar ;
  Will the tide slacken soon ?
O Sea that took'st my youngest, wilt thou spare ?"
—And the Sea answered through the black night-air,
  "I took thy youngest. Shall I spare to-night ?"

"The thundering breakers sweep and slash the sands ;
 To westward lo ! one line of cream-white foam :
I raise to darkling heaven my helpless hands ;
  I watch within the home.
O Sea that took'st my eldest, wilt thou save ? "
—And the Sea answered as from out a grave,
  "I slew thine eldest son for my delight."

"The giant waves plunge o'er the shingly beach ;
 The tawny-maned great lions of the sea
With pitiless roar howl down all human speech ;
  Is God far-off from me ?
O Sea that slewest my sons, mine husband spare ! "
—The Sea's wild laughter shook and rent the air :
  Lo ! on the beach a drowned face deadly white.

THE DEAD CHILD.

But yesterday she played with childish things,
   With toys and painted fruit.
To-day she may be speeding on bright wings
   Beyond the stars! We ask. The stars are mute.

But yesterday her doll was all in all;
   She laughed and was content.
To-day she will not answer, if we call:
   She dropped no toys to show the road she went.

But yesterday she smiled and ranged with art
   Her playthings on the bed.
To-day and yesterday are leagues apart!
   She will not smile to-day, for she is dead.

THE SHADOW AT THE DOOR.

What adds a beauty to the rose?
The thought that, when the night-wind blows,
The petals white or petals pink
At his cold touch may fail and shrink.
This gives its beauty to the flower—
That it but blooms and lives one hour.
The sun gives charm.   What gives it more?
The Shadow waiting at the door.

The sweetest hour must swiftly pass :
Brown are these blades, that once were grass.
Blue eyes, gold hair, they are but shows ;
Death takes them, as it takes the rose.
Love draws such eager passionate breath
Because he's followed fast by death.
What makes us value Love's kiss more?
The death-like Shadow at the door.

O love, our bower of love is sweet ;
The white rug nestles round your feet.
Your brown eyes watch the bright fire's glow ;
I watch your eyes.   I love them so !

The pictures watch us from the wall :
I'm king, and you the queen of all.
Does aught else watch? Aye one thing more
That ghost-like Shadow at the door !

SADNESS AND GLADNESS.

Our tired hearts gather sadness, as we grow
     In care and thoughts and pain.
The sweet spring sunlight that once charmed us so
     Will never gleam again.
The grey mists thicken as the sun declines:
A deepening shadow clothes the mountain pines.

But our tired heart sees not the whole of things.
     Still over the brown stream
Flashes the kingfisher with rapid wings,
     One sudden azure gleam.
Because our souls are weary or are sad,
We quite forget that half the world is glad!

Some lover just has won his lady's smile,
     As we won long ago:
The wild hedge-blossoms cluster by the stile,
     Gold buttercups a-row:
The silvery minnow darts along the stream:
Life is not all a trouble or a dream.

NEAR AT HAND.

The dead are with us through our nights and days ;
They have not journeyed far,
Beyond the clouds, beyond the golden haze
That shrouds the furthest star.
Our earthly flowers
Are still to them most dear,
And still they hear
The songs of merry birds in hawthorn bowers.

Friends who have passed are never far away,
Beyond the warmth of June,
Beyond the sights and sounds and scents of May,
Beyond our waters' tune.
They linger still
To watch the warm moon rise
Behind the hill,
And still take pleasure in the sunlit skies.

They nearest are, just when we need them most.
They help with living hands ;
No spectral shape, no fruitless pallid ghost,
Peers from the unseen lands.

They watch and heed;
Their legions fill the air;
They never speed
Beyond the cry of pain, or reach of prayer.

XII

LOVE AND DEATH.

An angel watched the world rejoicing :
  The flowers sang in the morning light ;
The blue sea sang its tender love-song
  To golden-girdled stars at night.
All seemed so full of peace and gladness—
  Till lo ! a sudden ice-cold breath
Passed over hill and wave and meadow :
  A stern voice whispered, " I am Death ! "

Alas ! in all that angel's dreaming
  His loving heart had never dreamed
That only for one single moment
  The fairy blossoms sang and gleamed.
He turned, and in despairing sadness
  Would have resought the heavens above,
When, softly sounding through the shadows,
  A sweet voice whispered, " I am Love ! "

And then the angel saw that fairer
  Than heaven with all its strifeless calm
Is earth, for Love makes sorrow lovely,
  And plucks from grief the victor's palm.

Aye, Love with its undying sweetness
    Can soothe the weary, cheer the lone :
If Death's voice threatens through the darkness,
    Love whispers, " Death is overthrown ! "

III.

LYRICS OF LOVE AND PASSION.

COCK MILL.

Upon the bridge beside the mill
 Two lovers paused, and watched the stream :
The golden autumn woods were still
 With all the stillness of a dream.
They gazed into each other's eyes ;
 They loved—they felt that life was sweet ;
So still the woods, so calm the skies,
 They almost heard their own hearts beat,
   While flowing, ever flowing,
    The clear stream sought the sea,
   As love-sweet moments going
    Mix with eternity.

Beside that grey old Yorkshire mill
 A hundred hearts have paused to dream :
Have watched the shadows on the hill,
 And watched the foam-bells on the stream.
And all have found the present fair,—
 Have found the future—who can say ?
But still that same old mill stands there,
 And still the stream goes day by day
   Flowing, for ever flowing,
    Bearing dead hopes along
   Like dead leaves, all unknowing,
    And changing not its song.

And in the future hundreds more
   Will pause and watch the rippling stream,
And hope as others hoped of yore,
   And dream as dead hearts used to dream.
A sadness hangs about the mill
   And broods above the waters' flow ;
So many hearts must now be still
   Who watched those bright waves long ago,—
      Those bright waves ever flowing,
       Singing to hill and sky,
        "Seize each love-moment going,
       For even love must die ! "

A LOST LOVE.

I would have died to win her:
    I loved her past a dream.
Ah! hand in hand we wandered
    Beside the mountain-stream.
I kissed her raven tresses:
    I kissed her gentle hand:
I was the proudest lover
    In all the wide wide land.

But ah! the rich man sought her;
    He bribed her with his gold.
He changed her heart. He bought her.
    Her love for me grew cold.
And now my life is over—
    In vain the sun may rise;
I never loved the sunshine,
    I only loved her eyes!

Ah! my lost love, my darling,
    Will your heart one day see
That when you won your heaven
    You purchased hell for me?

Ah ! my lost love, my beauty,
  His soul is fierce and mean.
He loves you like a plaything :
  I loved you like a queen !

III.

A SUMMER DAY.

The broad blue sky above me,
   The sunshine on the corn
(Oh, had I you to love me,
   This perfect August morn !)
Green tall trees overslanting,
   With sunlight flashing through
(And yet one thing was wanting ;
   My heart cried out for you !)

Oh, were you with me, darling,
   This perfect summer day,
Its glory were completer
   Than tongue of man might say.
The green trees of the forest,
   The bright flowers of the dell,
All longed for you, my darling ;
   And oh, I longed as well !

And then the eve came slowly :
   Soft moonlight glittered down
With tender light and holy
   Upon the seaside town.

(Oh, were you only with me,
　All longing, love, would cease :
The day that dawned in sadness
　Would close its eyes in peace!)

IV

THE DANCE.

Weary I am this winter night,
  Sleep presses on my brain ;
But you will dance till morning light
  Gleams at the window-pane.
Yes, you will dance, while I shall sleep—
  So it must ever be !
This winter night is starry-bright
  For you, but dark for me.

Yes, you will dance, while I must sleep,
  And many a heart will thrill
As through the dance your Spanish glance
  Flashes its magic still.
Yes, you will dance, while I shall rest,
  And so it ought to be ;
For you the night, ablaze with light !
  The lampless dark for me !

And ah ! I read the lesson through ;
  I read and grasp it all.
The day may come when sleep more deep
  May on my spirit fall.

I shall be sleeping very sound
And very still, maybe,
While life is yet one merry round
Of dance and song for thee.

"WILT THOU REMEMBER?"

Dost thou remember me?   It matters not!
   My heart revisits every spot
   Which, sweetheart, we have trodden together
   In this blue perfect summer weather.

Dost thou remember me?   Wilt thou forget!
   Mine is the deep regret ;
Mine the undying pain.   It sometimes seems
   That love comes only in dreams!

Wilt thou remember?   Will thy girl's heart keep
   Treasured in store-house safe and deep,
   Soft memories of the days soon-dying
   Before love's laughter changed to sighing?

Wilt thou remember?   Must it only be
   That I shall think on thee?
Ah ! through my heart shoots swift an arrowy pain . . . .
   We shall not meet again !

FOR EVER YOUNG.

The wild world hastens on its way;
   The grey-haired century nears its close;
Its sorrow deepens day by day;
   The summer blush forsakes the rose.
But, darling, while your voice I hear
   And while your dark-brown eyes I see
Sad months and sunless, seasons drear,
   Are all the same, all glad, to me.
       Despair can never reach me
        While your soft hand I hold:
       While your eyes love and teach me,
        I never shall grow old!

They say that love forsakes the old;
   That passion pales and fades away;
That even love's bright locks of gold
   Must lose their charm and change to grey.
But, darling, while your heart is mine
   And while I feel that you are true
For me the skies will ever shine
   With summer light, and tenderest blue.
       Yes, let old age deride me!
        I scorn his mocking tongue.
       Dear love, with you beside me,
        I am for ever young!

AUTUMNAL LOVE.

Fair is love whose footstep wanders
   'Mid the sunny meads of spring ;
Love that smiles and laughs and ponders
   While the swallow's on the wing ;
      Fair and tender,
      Full of splendour,
Full of thoughts the roses bring
—— Full of dreams the roses bring.

Sweet is love when fervent summer
   Fills the fields with flowers and fruit ;
When strong passion, swift-winged comer,
   Wakes wild echoes with his lute ;
      Songs of sweeter
      Note and metre
Make spring's softest music mute
—— Make spring's sweetest music mute.

Yet life's autumn brought *my* treasure.
   I was sad and tired and old,
Worn and weary beyond measure,
   When thy face I did behold :

Sweet love found me,
Saved and crowned me,
When the corn was turning gold
—— When the corn was turning gold.

"GIVE ME THAT ROSE!"

Give me that rose!
It rests, it blows,
Next to your heart, my sweet.
Oh give me, give me,—give me for mine own
That flower to which such favour has been shown,
That flower whose petals feel your warm heart beat ;
Give me that rose!

Give me that rose,
Whose white repose
Is like your soul so white!
Give me that rose. You have not given me much ;
A glove to kiss, a finger-tip to touch,
A glance of laughter, or a glance of light :
Give me that rose!

Give me that rose :
Our moment goes ;
What now might chance, again may never be !
If I have loved you with a love supreme,
For just one wild mad moment let me dream
(And die within the dream) that *you* love *me !*
Give me the rose!

IX.

A TUFT OF MEADOW-SWEET.

A tuft of withered meadow-sweet,
  Just that and nothing more :
And yet what hosts of memories fleet
  The dry old fronds restore !
A tuft of withered meadow-sweet,
  No gaudy pink or rose ;
And yet the dried-up leaves I see,
Long scorned of butterfly and bee,
Are holier, dearer, unto me
  Than any flower that blows—
Than any flower that blows, my love,
  Than any flower that blows !

For once—ah heaven ! how long ago—
  You have forgotten quite—
Where over the blue waters' flow
  Wild sea-birds' wings shine white,
You picked a tuft of meadow-sweet
  (This very tuft I hold) :
You plucked the flower, and quite forgot
The flower, the scene, the youth, the spot ;
You chose to share another's lot,
  And share another's gold ;
You scorned the flower, but I did not,
  And do not, though I'm old !

A HEART IN ARMOUR.

I show the world my armour,
  All marred and bent with blows.
Let men complain!—I never deign
  My true thoughts to disclose.
I show the world my armour,
  Clinched close in every part.
To you I show my weakness:
  To you I show my heart.

I show my strength to others;
  My tenderness to thee:
An ironbound rock, I stand the shock
  Of life's tempestuous sea.
But at thy touch, my darling,
  All hardness melts away:
Tears stain my cheek, if you but speak,
  And lo! the rock can pray.

How little mankind knows me!
  All chained and barred in steel
They find my heart. Then they depart,
  And think I cannot feel.

Yet heights and heart-depths hazy
  Are sometimes clear to one:
The sun's one favourite daisy
  Can understand the sun !

XI

AT REST.

Your dark eyes win a glory
  From every passing day ;
The longer grows love's story,
  The sweeter 'tis, I say !
We conquer Time together ;
  For every flower we've seen
Has passed into our kingdom,
  And made you ten times Queen !

We win the wealth of summers ;
  We rob the winter days ;
You're Queen in your fur tippet,
  Queen of the fireside blaze.
Strong love defies all weather :
  While you and I are one,
While we walk on together,
  We always see the sun !

More beautiful and holy
  You are to me, my Queen :
Life's vistas lengthen slowly,
  And scene melts into scene.

But life's old strange heart-hunger
Has ceased—I am at rest :
And daily you grow younger,
And I more deeply blest.

XII

LOVE THE CONQUEROR.

O love, if life should end to-night,
　How short our life would seem !
One little flash of summer light ;
　One brief and passionate dream ;
One glimpse of roses on the wall,
　Or blue-bells in the lane,
Then, love, the end, the end of all—
Aye, buds might swell, and leaves might fall,
　But not for us again !

The stream we used to watch and love
　Would ever onward flow ;
From the dark pines the grey wood-dove
　Would call—we should not know.
Ah ! not for us the pines would wave,
　For us no stream would run ;
We should be silent in the grave,
Unable even to hoard and save
　One little glimpse of sun !

Yet is not this a sombre view
　Of life and all it brings ?
Thank heaven, the bright waves still are blue,
　And still the throstle sings !

And oh, before love's conquering song
  Death's voice sinks quite away ;
For life is short, but love is long,
And death is fierce, but love is strong,
  And love shall win the day !

XIII

"MY ALL!"

Thou art my all ! The golden sun
   Runs on its course by day,
Till sombre clouds and vapours dun
   Fold round its chariot gay :
Yet without thee the world were dark,
   The sun would never shine ;
It would be just a wandering spark,
   Were not thy hand in mine !
Yea, even the golden sun above
Owes all its glory to thy love.

Thou art my all ! The flowers are fair
   When summer comes to reign :
But bind the sweet buds in thy hair ;
   What sweetness new they gain !
The rose is rich, the lily white,
   Yet sweeter each one grows
For soft communion with thy bright
   Soft mouth, that richer rose.
Thou art indeed the loveliest thing
That passionate summer steals from spring.

Thou art my all upon this earth ;
   And thou wilt surely be
My all, when heavenly stars shine forth
   On heavenly shores and sea.

My all on earth, my all in heaven,
  My earthly summer's rose,
My perfect flower in that strange hour
  When earthly summers close—
My light on earth, be still, sweet soul,
My light when life has reached its goal.

XIV

"LOVERS STILL!"

From lands where Love for ever dreams
   Thy soft eyes took their light ;
No moon with quite such magic gleams,
   Nor any star by night.
There is a light that from the soul
   Flows forth, and that is thine ;
The only light that can control
   So wild a heart as mine !

Thou bindest all my heart in chains,
   Sweet chains, as sweet as strong ;
Love sometimes for one moment reigns,
   But thou hast reigned so long !
In truth I now begin to see
   That we shall never part,
But that God's vast eternity
   Will link us, heart to heart.

The thought is strange and solemn, love,
   Yet sweeter than 'tis strange :
Grand is the love time cannot move
   And life's cares cannot change.

Love me with changeless love like this—
  Then let time work its will,
It cannot steal or mar our bliss
  If we be lovers still !

XV

"AH! ONCE I THOUGHT I LOVED THE ROSE."

Ah! once I thought I loved the rose
   And once I loved the sky,
Its calm yet passionate repose,
   Its blue eternity,—
But now I love thy lips and eyes,
   Thy beauty I adore,
I worshipped flowers and summer skies
   But thee I worship more.

I know not whether love is pain :
   It sometimes brings despair :
Then blooms the summer rose in vain ;
   In vain it scents the air.
If thou dost wrap my soul in doubt
   And bid bright hope fly far,
Though all night's countless stars shine out
   I never see one star.

And yet with pain I would not part,
   Not even with despair,
If only I may win thine heart
   And find my solace there.

A thousand faces meet my eyes,
And yet I see but one,—
As silent leagues of starlit skies
Dream only of the sun.

XVI

"IF ONLY THOU ART THERE!"

Why seek for love beyond the sky,
  In stars that swim through space?
Behold! sweet love is very nigh,
  And very close his face.
On purple fells, by forest-wells,
  By our blue ocean's side,
Love lives and smiles, and dreams and dwells;
  He lords it far and wide.

Not in the shining distant space
  Where faint star-clusters gleam
Does Love reveal his sovereign face,—
  Nay, here he loves to dream.
Our dim old earth can hear his mirth
  Through forest-arches ring;
Aye, English lake and Scottish firth
  Have heard Love's red lips sing!

But most of all, O love of mine,
  Does Love reveal through thee
His look superb, his touch divine,
  His matchless sovereignty.

All stars may die in depths of sky,
　All dreams fade out in air,
Earth will be heaven if thou art nigh,
　If only thou art there !

NOCTURNE.

SLEEP.

NOCTURNE.

SLEEP.

I.

Not for joy and fiery pleasur
  Would our spirits ask :
Weary past all mortal measure
  With our ceaseless task,
All too weary even to weep,
  All our inmost grief confessed,
All we ask is rest and sleep,
              Sleep and rest.

Surely, if the world-wide nations,
  If these spake as one,
Endless sorrowing generations,
  All beneath the sun,
North and South and East and West,
  All alike in anguish deep,
All would yearn for sleep and rest,
            Rest and sleep.

Lovers who loved on undaunted,
  Till they met Despair :
Poets, dreamers, ever haunted
  By the spectre Care ;

If the truth be told indeed,
   One prayer throbs through every breast—
"Give our weary souls for meed
             Sleep and rest."

II.

In the far-off heavenly places
   Lo! God hears man's cry
Piercing through the starry spaces
   And the untroubled sky.
To the sufferer's restless pillow,
   To the sailor tossing on the deep,
To the weary sea-bird on the billow,
   God to all his creatures sendeth sleep.

When the golden sun has vanished
   And the glare of day
From the hot blue sky is banished,
   Gentle ray by ray
Gleam the stars upon the ocean,
   Soothing all the hearts and eyes that weep:
Rest succeeds to daylight's fierce emotion.
   Even the murderer God can rock to sleep.

Even the soul, whom on the morrow
   The black gibbet waits,
God can visit in his sorrow.
   Through the prison-gates
Passing unopposed and fearless
   God can touch his eyes with slumber's wing;
Make that one last sleep most sweet and tearless;
   Wander with him through the fields of Spring.

III.

To the lark that nestles 'mid the clover,
 After daylong worship of the sun ;
To the brown thrush when his song is over,
 To the swallow when his flight is done ;
To the eagle on his eyrie,
 To the robin in his nest,
When the wings of each grow weary,
     God sends rest.

To the happy bride and bridegroom lying
 In the first long love-sleep side by side ;
To the aged, when life's hopes seem dying
 And when Death is longed for like a bride ;
To the heart of Summer darkening
 Slowly at the Autumn's breath,
God, from his far blue skies hearkening,
 Sends his angels, Sleep and Death.

To the heart that starts with happy dreaming,
 When the first long days of summer shine ;
To the soul that sees the red sun gleaming
 Through the autumnal groves of larch and pine ;
To the heart of Winter wailing,
 When no corn is left to reap,
God with tenderness unfailing
 Sends twin angels, Death and Sleep.

IV.

Grey-grown nations, when they weary,
  When their course is run ;
When their shortening days grow dreary
  For the lack of sun ;

Hebrew, Roman, Carthaginian,
Syrian, Grecian, when their day is past,
God removes to Death's dominion :
Even the longest record ends at last.

As the sacred night descending
Covers all the sky,
Its vast purple robe extending
Downward from on high,
So the night of time has swallowed
Endless nations, cities, one by one.
Greece passed first, the Roman followed.
England too will pass beyond the sun.

All the towns that press and hustle
In the modern maze :
London with its stormy bustle ;
Paris' gaslit blaze :
All will pass :—till, leaning lastly
From his throne within the heavenly deep,
God will work once more, more vastly,
Sending on the whole earth rest and sleep.

—

BOOK V

EXIT SATAN.

SATAN.

[

SATAN

I.

Before me stretches out creation vast :
The future and the present and the past
　　　　　Are unveiled at my gaze.
I pass at will beyond the furthest skies ;
Beyond the land of sunset and sunrise ;
　　　　　Beyond the dim sea's haze.

I hear the psalm that all creation sings,
Praising with heart and tongue their King of kings ;
　　　　　I stand aloof, alone.
My heart is lonely like the lonely sea ;
Aye, lonely, ever lonelier, I would be
　　　　　Upon my mighty throne.

I hear the lowing of the joyful herds,
The lisp of waters and the song of birds ;
　　　　　I hear the Christian's prayer :
I see the scarlet wings of butterflies ;
I see the raiment of the sunset skies
　　　　　That crimsons all the air :

I see the green-blue bright waves as they leap
Along the furrows of the sunlit deep ;
      I breathe the thyme-tuft's balm :
I hear the enraptured song the maiden sings
When tender first love to her pure heart brings
      Its passion, or its calm.

But far beyond these things my gaze can pierce.
I see War's sanguine arrows, swift and fierce,
      Fly through the battle-gloom :
Where Love was yesterday, to-day I see
Vast struggling warrior-hosts advance and flee,
      Black blood-stained chargers loom.

I see God's failure written on all things.
I know the weakness of the King of kings :
      Behind the scenes I gaze.
I, lurid Satan, whom he thought to quell
Am victor ever, for I know too well
      The great Lord's works and ways.

I know how he leads mortal spirits on, —
Then leaves the souls in darkness quite alone
      Whose faith was strong to dare.
Ah ! I was in the sombre clouds that heard
On Calvary pale Jesus' dying word,
      And that word was " Despair."

You human beings have passed from hand to hand
The story of his life. I understand
      That life : I watched it too.
I heard the curse that from his heart arose
When, dying in the midst of fiends and foes,
      He found his God untrue.

You see just what you hope for.—But I see
Despair enthroned from all eternity
                        Behind the Lord of all.
Behind the form of Jesus I discern
Pale Death's shape dogging him at every turn,
                        And plotting for his fall.

He rose! yes, in your hearts and in your brains.
Him ever the cold marble tomb retains;
                        Him,—and his tender heart!
He rose and lived—within your paintings grand—
But never entered an immortal land
                        Save that of deathless Art.

Beyond all hopes of yours I see the end.   .
I see your wild faith in your heavenly Friend:
                        I know that faith is doomed.
Have there lived not, on other stars than this,
Christ-kings betrayed by some foul Judas-kiss,
                        In other vaults entombed?

Ye deem your Man-God central God of all:
Fools! I have watched a million Man-Gods fall;
                        Yes, I have laughed to note
Faith even as yours in stars and moons destroyed
Millions of ages ere the viewless void
                        Felt your earth's young keel float.

A million Christs have risen before my eyes:
A million Marys with their tears and sighs
                        Have followed to the tomb.
Dreams such as yours have waved their fairy wings
And then been ushered, by your King of kings,
                        Into eternal gloom.

2 C

Behold ! in God's great hand a million stars
Are but as floating sparks.   He makes and mars :
                He builds, and then with blows
Terrific he destroys what he has built :
His sword is blood-red to the very hilt :
                He spares nor friends, nor foes.

Trust him, and mark the issue.   Once his sky
Held no more loving spirit even than I :
                But now I know his ways
He shapes with cunning hands a rose-bower sweet ;
Then tramples all its blossoms with his feet,
                And blasts it with his gaze.

To-night . . . to-night . . . the moon is full and fair :
A thousand lovers in the enchanted air
                Will meet.   " O love," saith one,
" How tender must the Lord of lovers be !
Praise God, who gave my moon of love to me
                And gave the world the sun."

" Praise God," says she, " who gave your loving heart
To mine.   Praise tender heaven for what thou art !
                Lo ! this star-lighted place
Hath one star sweeter than all stars to me :
God's own starlit and sweet eternity,
                O love, shines through thy face."

Behind the boughs I lurk.   I hear them speak.
I, Satan, mark the love-flush on each cheek.
                I laugh, the while I hear.
I draw quite close.   " Your love is like the rose ;
'Twill bloom just till the first cold strong wind blows,"
                I whisper in her ear.

But that is little! Far beyond such scenes
My stern gaze pierces. No cloud intervenes :
            I see your star's last hour :—
I see the hour when all you hold most grand
Will be crushed into nothing by God's hand—
            Just as I crush this flower.

Fools—ye who think because ye think and love
That therefore in your wisdom ye can prove
            God thinks and loves as well!
God loves.—And therefore in a thousand stars
What lovely things he makes, his same hand mars.
            God thinks.—His thought is hell.
         *   *

O fool who prayest to God, dost thou not think
The wagtail pausing on the waters' brink
            Has its own right to care?
Thou deemest that thy cry will answered be :
Think of the white wild sea-gulls on the sea,
            The swallows on the air!

Think of the countless herds in desert plains,
Starved, hunted, battered by the fierce mad rains,
            Or stricken by the sun :
Have not these perished fatherless? Thy cry,
Could it have reached and pierced the farthest sky,
            What aid would it have won?

Think you the flowers have not their various right
To call on God their Father through the night
            Made fragrant with their bloom?—
What does he give to these? One single day.
Then languor,—then pale death, or slow decay,
            And, 'mid wet leaves, a tomb.

One soul succeeds.   A million toilers fail.—
Your cities teem with faces sad and pale,
                    Worn-out with work or sin.
What of your harlots ?   Ever I laugh to see
A young girl's brown eyes full of purity :
                    So let her life begin !

It will not end so.   God will see to this.
God shall eternalize the harlot's kiss :
                    He would not lose its thrill.
Where there are women, still will harlots be ;
Aye, harlots fresh to all eternity ;
                    Such is the high God's will !

I watch and laugh.   I know the girl will change.
Something within her eyes of new and strange
                    Wild light will soon appear.—
Yes.   Soon the gas-lit dreary streets are graced
By a new dark-eyed wanton therein placed
                    By this God whom ye fear.

God withers flowers, I said.   He does far more.
He withers women-flowers whom men adore :
                    Withers them, one by one.
He gives them weary streets by day and night
Wherein to wander,—gives them gloom for light,
                    Aye, gas-jets for the sun !

Those who in country lanes once gathered bloom
Sweet with the dews of morning, through fog-gloom
                    Now wander, pale and weak.
Yes—once a mother in the bright June air
Thanked God who made her girl so pure and fair,
                    And kissed this rouge-pink cheek.

These are your God's great doings.—How I stand
Night after night within your gas-lit Strand,
                    Or nigh your mud-stained stream—
How night by night I think, " Yes, God is good."
Often I've watched, as on some bridge I stood,
                    A drowned girl's gold locks gleam.

" O great successful God!   O King and Lord,
By countless churches incensed and adored,
                    Worshipped by all but me !
This is thy greatness—that a girl should drown,
Friendless, unpitied, in this church-packed town,
                    Cursing thy priests and thee ! "

II.

I love the English.   They are so devout.
It cheers my heart to see them sallying out
                    On Sunday, clothed in black.
They like to hear their preachers preach of hell,
But they forget its fierce fumes in the smell
                    Of soup, when they get back.

The whole long week they swindle and they cheat,
Then on the Sabbath in the church they meet
                    And gabble through the creed.
They start at naked sculpture.   Naked lust
Attracts them, and a fat Frenchwoman's bust
                    Excites their amorous greed.

I love their sports.   I love to see the fox
Bound over ditches, bushes, streamlets, rocks,
                    And pant his life away.
When the dogs rend him piecemeal on the ground,
I love to see the bright girls crowding round,
                    Gazing with interest gay.

Fishing ?   Delightful !   By a purling brook
To stand, and fit the worm tight on the hook
              (The women do **it best**) :
Then, when your fish is caught, slowly to drag
His guts out with the hook, red rag by rag ;
              This gives the sport such **zest** !

Dove-shooting ?   Better **still**.   The birds fly out :
Soon bloodied plumes are scattered all about
              Upon the grass and walls.
A lady looking on, with soft dove's eyes,
Applauds each bird demolished,—and she **cries**,
              " Well shot, sir ! " **when it falls.**

But best I love when autumn's leafy gold
Showers o'er the fields, to follow and behold
              The gallant shots perform.
I watch the wounded pheasant 'mid the **briars** ;
And in the rabbit's blood, as it expires,
              I keep my fingers warm.

            *   *

Think how God sports **with sorrow** !   Once he sent
A Deluge to submerge a continent,
              To ravish life's best bloom.
Once ?   When the Yellow **River** burst its **bank**
Last year, straightway seven million toilers sank
              Unpitied to their **doom.**

Seven million Chinese toilers !   (God is love).
Upon their swarms he poured down from above
              The giant river's wave.
Helpless they **were** and harmless.   As he chose,
As he commanded, the great river rose
              And whelmed them in one grave.

For countless miles their bodies lie and rot.
Is this the whole of God's scheme ?   It is not.
                    Soon pestilence will spread.
Those who rebuild the river's Titan dyke
With fever's poisoned spear-points he will strike,
                    And lay new thousands dead.

Then he will tempt fresh toilers.   Millions more
Upon the Yellow River's fertile shore
                    Will toil, and sleep, and wake :
Till suddenly Jehovah will arise,
With the old keen amusement in his eyes,
                    And bid the barriers break.

Then, in a month, where will those myriads be ?
Whelmed all once more beneath the tossing sea ;
                    Drowned,—with their fruits of toil.
They make a garden with their countless hands.
God makes a waste of rotting reeds and sands
                    And putrid yellow soil.

              *   *

And can God compensate for horrors done
Beneath the starlight or beneath the sun ?
                    Do dead men reach the skies ?
Think you that at his palace-door he waits
To usher seven millions through his gates ?
                    Think you these dead will rise ?

(On the first day upon your dead one's face
Ye gaze.   Ye say, " What pure angelic grace !
                    What peace divine ! what calm ! "
Wait till the second day—or till the third.
The tenderest turns aside without a word,
                    And with a stomach-qualm.

Life I prefer to all your empty dreams.
I love the good old sun that glints and gleams
    Upon the good red rose.
The scent of angels is too strong for me !
Angels—in climates hot—take less than three
    Short days to decompose).

Seven million Chinamen !   The river's rush
That whelmed them would be slight beside the crush
    Among God's mansions grand
If all these crowded on the big main street
Of heaven (and what an ugly crowd to meet
    In the sweet heavenly land !)

Or think you, when the Roman circus steamed
With blood, that blood-red lion-torn fragments gleamed
    At once in heaven again?
Think you that Jesus gathers in his bag
First bony morsels, next a fleshy rag,
    The relics of the slain ?

Think you that, surgeon-like, at heaven's high gate
He stands, ready to bind or amputate?
    Think you he can restore
A maiden ravished in an Apache raid
To virgin pureness, ere the next night's shade
    Falls over hill and shore ?

Where are the countless myriads, monkey-faced,
Who strove and lusted, frolicked and grimaced,
    Ere man sprang forth from these ?
Are all these monkeys angels ?   Do they stand,
Winged monkey-seraphs, in the heavenly land,
    Or climb the heavenly trees ?

Did all the ancestors of man survive ?
If one soul conquers death, all souls must live,
          Yes, plants and flowers as well.
Ants must turn angels : crabs and parrots too.
There must be mice in heaven (if this be true)
          And cats, perhaps, in hell.

There must be lion-angels at the gate
Of heaven, and angel-elephants sedate,
          And angel-sharks malign.
See unto what the Christian's faith would lead !
A saner faith than this the nations need ;
          New bottles for new wine.

When Nero lit live torches, did the tar
That smeared them also splash with many a star,
          Deep-black, heaven's hangings white ?
Can God make angels out of melted grease ?
Can God, when at the stake the fierce flames cease,
          Bid ashes stand upright ?

Oh, that were wonderful, most grand indeed !
If God can make the limbs that frizzle or bleed
          Or sputter in the air,
If God can make these fragments live again,
Then hath he surely won the right to reign
          And I may well despair.

If God can snatch the drowned from out the sea,
Find room for them in heaven's halls instantly,
          Rub burnt fat from the stake
And change it to an angel in his sky,
It matters little where or how you die—
          You're bound in heaven to wake !

III.

Cease ye, poor fools, to trust your "Lord of hosts."
Trust rather in the aid of fleshless ghosts,
          Pale spirits of the air :
Trust in the storms that range the skies for prey,
But trust not God.   Trust in the wild sea-spray ;
          The rocks that rend and tear ;

Trust these things as ye will.   But trust not him
Who having made the sun, made all things dim
          Beneath the black night's veil :
The God who made the lips of woman fair
And, that the soul of man might quite despair,
          The heart of woman frail.

Lo ! what is woman ? just a lovely flower.
Through beauty's gift alone she wields her power,
          And, when that beauty goes,
She is as worthless as the violet, white
With the fierce frost that struck her fronds last night,
          Or as the wind-torn rose.

Pleasure she gives.   One moment's rapturous glow :
Sorrow for ages.—God has made her so.—
          Ice-cold is woman's breast
When true man worships.   Yes ! she loves the fool
Who loves her not,—becomes lust's ready tool,
          And serves the tyrant best.

Think ye, if Christ had tested woman's kiss,
That still he would have dreamed of heavenly bliss
          And of a Father's care ?
The nearer that the soul of woman grows,
The less you love the daily fading rose,
          The more you will despair.

Ah ! Christ was wise.   Far-off his spirit held
The soul of woman, and he thus compelled
    A distant love from all.
How little would have lasted of his fame,
Had he known woman more than just by name !
    She would have planned his fall.

This is the wise path.   Just to love your flower
While scent is sweet around it in its hour
    Of comeliness supreme :
Then to seek other blossoms, and to say—
" I kissed with rapture gold locks yesterday ;
    To-day it is a dream !

" To-day dark hair allures me.—What is love ?
One gleam of azure from the skies above :
    Then sharp the hail-stones sting !
And what is woman ?   Just a model sweet :
Sweet arms, sweet lips and breast, and dainty feet :
    A soulless perfect thing.

" Who loves her, loses her.—Who hates her best,
Who treats her love and passion as a jest,
    Who crowns her brow with thorn,
He wins her worship.—Who despises most
Woman, of amplest victories can boast.
    Man wins her by his scorn."

IV.

There is a peace in absolute despair :
I hate the God who rules the starry air
    With hatred so profound
That even to ravish, while long ages roll,
One bright star from his heaven affords my soul
    A rapture beyond bound.

Because God hates me, and has set my heart
In lonely heavens—a planet leagues apart
      From all, a blood-red star—
I hate God with a hatred like his own ;
Had I the power, would hurl him from his throne ;
      What he makes, I would mar.

I cannot reach him ! None the less, I reach
The creatures he has made.   I study each.
      He made the humming-bird.
I set beside its plumes the deadly snake.—
He makes the spotless lily.   From the brake
      Springs night-shade at my word.—

He moulded, grand with all its mighty limbs,
The horse, subservient to man's slightest whims,
      The white or coal-black steed.
I, still defiant, made the desert groan
As my gaunt lion wandered forth alone,
      His jaws agape with greed.—

God makes the salmon, and I make the shark.
He makes the hound that saves with watchful bark :
      I make the wild wolf prowl.
While God is painting plumes of butterflies,
I send a shiver through blue Indian skies
      That hear my tigers howl.

God fills the summer air with scent of rose :
I send the creeping aphis-brood that goes
      Along the stalks and leaves.
God shapes the grapes that yield the purple wine :
I send a sudden blight upon the vine,
      Or on the golden sheaves.

I watch the murderer's stroke, and laugh to feel
The blood-drops almost down my own hands steal,
   Hot from the knife I gave!
God plans his Beatrice. I change her face
By slow degrees: I sell to man her grace:
   I change her to a slave.

I plot for ages,—well content if one
Gold ray be wrenched from moon-rim, or from sun,
   While past those ages fleet.
I revel in the strong adulterer's bliss
When, after years it may be, the wild kiss
   Brings virtue to his feet.

Because my own despair must wax and grow,
I would infuse in all hearts even so
   A growing deep despair;
Despair of man, of woman, and of all.
My soul rejoices at a woman's fall;
   The frailest are the fair!

I lurk within the room when lovers meet.
Behind the white bed-curtains I retreat;
   No light is in the room:
And yet—though fierce with passionate desire—
The woman pauses, as like sudden fire
   My eyes flash through the gloom.

Then I withdraw. I would not harm the pair!
I pass into the fragrant forest-air
   And wait the golden light
Of morn,— for in the morn man's blood must flow:
I watch the duel in the morning glow
   Who watched love in the night.

This is my life, my rapture, my one aim :
To hurl against the Lord my tiny flame,
                    My match's thin blue ray,
Content,—for Satan's match, so slight and small,
May burn till forest after forest fall
                    If one branch leads the way !

CHORUS OF SPIRITS OF DARKNESS·

CHORUS OF SPIRITS OF DARKNESS

I.

O Satan, lord of hell,
Through whom the darkness fell
    First over land and sea,
Beyond all dreams of light
We worship thy black night,—
    Beyond all blackness, thee.

Thou only, thou alone,
Upon thy mighty throne
    Art seated in mid space :
The clouds and thunders flee,
Lord, at the sight of thee ;
    Stars tremble at thy face.

Thou only didst withstand,
Thou, with thine own right hand,
    The Father-God and Lord :
Of him thou hadst no fear ;
Thou threatenedst him with sheer
    Bright lightning of thy sword.

Thou with thy mighty wings
O'ershadowest living things ;
      Thou art the lord of hell :
Thou art the lord of earth
That shudders at thy mirth ;
      At thy word woman fell.

Through listening, lord, to thee
From primal purity
      The soul of woman bent.
Through thee the storm-clouds rose
On Eden's first repose,
      And heaven's blue veil was rent.

We listen for thy voice
That ever says, " Rejoice,
      Ye spirits of the night :
Who loves my work to see
Is ever friend of me
      And foeman of the light.

"Not yet are ye exempt
From labour.   Seek and tempt
      The righteous and the just.
Where woman's love is sold
Bring ye your gauds and gold,
      And frenzy man with lust.

"Where woman still is pure
Struggle, hope on, endure :
      Her strength of soul is slight.
Extends she virtue's shield ?
To-morrow she will yield ;
      Or, it may be, to-night !

" Encourage man to wait.
Time opens every gate :
     The gold key can unlock
The wards of woman's heart ;
To-morrow she'll not start
     If he forget to knock !

" To-night the girl will dream
Of rubies as they gleam
     And diamonds as they shine.
I heard the man's heart pray ;
Comfort my servant : Say,
     ' To-morrow she is thine ! ' "

II.

And what can God proclaim
In letters as of flame
     Of punishment for sin ?
All follows certain law ;
And Nature has no flaw
     To let its Maker in.

For ever the blue seas
Will hearken to the breeze ;
     And, when it turns to storm,
The breakers fierce and white
Will hunt like hounds at night
     The pale ship's flying form.

Prayer never saved a ship
From the reef's ravening lip :
     God has no ear for prayer.
Or, if he hath the ear,
He dares not interfere ;
     All things rest as they were.

The lightning-stroke by law
Falls. No man ever saw
          God's golden sceptre wave.
Whatever live souls say,
There is no gleam of day
          Beyond the darkling grave.

When Jesus slowly died,
Smitten through hands and sidë,
          Where was his Father high?
What had this Jesus done
That God should leave his Son
          In agony to die?

Death held him fast. He ne'er
Rose into heavenly air,
          Though some hearts dreamed he rose.
Nay, he was hardly missed
By soft lips he had kissed:
          How soon a girl's love goes!

The shoreless depth of night
Soon swallowed up the light
          Of Jesus' face and eyes.
Call ye! He will not hear.
He is most deaf of ear.—
          Weep ye! He will not rise.

In some wild women's dream
He rose. A ghostly gleam
          Of starlight o'er his grave
Made fond and frail hearts think
Their Master could not sink
          In cold corruption's wave.

But yet he sank indeed :
His body served to feed
  The gnawing worms below :
And, whither Jesus went,
With cursing or content
  All men shall surely go.

Why should the high God save
One atom from the grave
  Even if he had the power ?
What is the race of man
In God's great world-wide plan
  Save just one wayside flower ?

A poppy by the way,
Such is man's race to-day :
  To-morrow's sun may strike—
The poppy's scarlet head
Falls like a rag of red
  Into some ditch or dyke !

God cares about as much
For mankind, as for such
  Red poppies whom he slays
By myriads every year,
Without a thought or tear,
  In the long summer days.

Thou wilt survive ? O fool,
The weak reed by the pool,
  Compared with thee, is strong.
No note of Shakespeare's lyre
In God's ears reaches higher
  Than one brown linnet's song.

Your mighty of heart and hand,
Your bay-crowned genius-band,
    Your Dantes, Hugos great,
Crumble to dust and rot :
God recognizes not
    Your kings, for all their state !

They crumble alongside
Some fool who lately died :
    Their bones with his grow white.
God's mocking laughter sounds
O'er their sepulchral mounds,
    And rings along the night.

III.

Seeing that this is so,
Those are most wise, we know,
    Who apprehend the whole :
Grasp pleasure while they may,
And live but for the day,
    And seek the moment's goal.

Moreover highest of men
Turn back, and back again,
    To pleasure, though it pall.
The statesman's work fatigues :
Pleasure with pain intrigues,
    And they befool you all.

The statesman quits his task ;
The priest throws off the mask ;
    The poet fails to soar ;—
With feigned surprise they meet,
In some convenient street,
    Beside the brothel-door.

They find a rest supreme :
Each flings aside his dream,
  With all its stately charms.
Away each high thought goes !—
Each sinks into repose
  Within a harlot's arms.

This is your life, ye fools ;
A life that Satan rules ;
  . The prince we love and serve.
Ye need not fret, nor chafe :
Your flesh and blood are safe ;
  Your every bone and nerve.

The things ye see and hear
And taste and feel are clear
  And true, and these alone.
A bosom sweet and white
Appeals to sense and sight,—
  But not God's great white throne.

Earth's joys will surely last
When dreams of heaven are past,
  And Satan still will sway
The earth till all things end—
Man's best and truest friend,
  And safest to obey.

For God gives joys ideal :
But Satan gives man real
  And present joys to hold.
God pays with heavenly cheques—
So fails with either sex,
  For Satan pays in gold.

III.

CHRIST.

.

CHRIST.

I.

O Satan, thou art strong, and yet behold !
Thou shalt not snatch one sheep from out my fold,
　　　　Nor one star from the star-bright air.
Wherever thou canst pass, God goes before :
Seek thou the lonely heart, or lonely shore,
　　　　And thou shalt find my Father there.

The saddest soul is his.—The loneliest rose
That all unloved upon the hillside blows
　　　　He guards and tends with loving hand.
The least frail rose-pink shell is in his care,—
Though it be least of all the shells that were
　　　　Tossed last night on the golden sand.—

All sinful souls are his.—He can redeem
The tiger-heart and tiger-eyes that gleam :
　　　　The hands that seek for human prey.
Plunge down to deepest hell. Yet God is there.
He passes unscorched through its burning air,
　　　　And turns its lurid night to day.

From evil blossoms good.   The God who fills
With flowers the hollows of the green-robed hills
            And fills with bloom the lap of spring
Is the same God who at the helm presides
When the wild vessel plunges through white tides :
            The reckless waters own their King.

Through me the thought of God that underlies
The hills and vales and woods and clouds and skies,
            That, ever unseen, works its will,
Became just for one moment plain and clear :
God spake once, so that every soul might hear :
            Judge of the ocean by the rill.

The ocean, deep, eternal, rolls along :—
Lifting its billows, foaming, stormy, strong,
            It plunges on from shore to shore.
But yet the silver rill that all men see
Has its own waves.   God's image was in me,
            The human god whom ye adore.

            *   *

Did I make still the waves, and raise the dead ?
This I achieved—that all men since have said,
            " The God who acted once on law,
Can ever act so.   God can still the waves,
And bring the dead in graveclothes from their graves : "
            And all men worshipped God with awe.

This I achieved.—What men believe that I
Once did, God ever does.   He from the sky
            Stoops down to make the blind man see.
God's miracles are one long endless chain.
He changes drought into the fruitful rain :
            He sets the ironbound prisoner free.

Starlike and grand, God's noiseless angel glides
Between black prison-bars. Wild ocean-tides
      Meet God, and find his force too strong.
God casts out Satan from the world at large.
I stilled the waves upon Gennesaret's marge :
      God stills the waves through centuries long.

The world is ever blind. God makes it see.
Blind Bartimeus waits continuously
      For constant God to intervene.
My love redeemed one woman : God redeems
Each night some woman from her wanton dreams,
      And saves anew the Magdalene.

I died once on the hill. Men ever die.
They see no more, ye think, the starlit sky :
      They watch no more the waving trees.
Ten thousand saviours on their gibbets hang :
Vast, multitudinous, is the great death-pang :
      There are ten thousand Calvarys.

I rose once from the grave. Men ever rise.
Each soul that leaves you in appearance dies,
      Or wanders into ghostly ways.
But death exists not. There are many suns :
Mine is but one among ten thousand thrones :
      There are ten thousand Easter days.

II.

Nor, Satan, hast thou learnt with all thine art
The subtle secret of one woman's heart :—
      She serves, thou deem'st, the tyrant best ?
She yields herself,—as freely as the snow
That lets the passers by tramp to and fro
      Above it, baring its white breast ?

Thou deem'st that true love fails, and lust succeeds ?
That love may whisper to the river-reeds,
   But cannot reach a woman's ear ?
Thou deem'st the tyrant's plan the plan that wins :
That woman courts man for his very sins,
   And worships best in abject fear ?

But for a moment she shall love the base :
Nor is this true love.   Then her sweet sad face,
   Divine through deepest agony,
Shall seek the presence of a heavenly friend :—
Who suffers anguish to the very end
   Must, ere that end comes, worship *me*.

I win her love by my own wreath of thorn.
O Satan, thou canst hate, and thou canst scorn ;
   Thy vaunting words are fierce and strong :
This thou canst never do—by love redeem
One woman; change wild passion's sin-stained dream
   Into an angel's sinless song !

Man deems I loved not.   Yes, and woman deems
My soul was swallowed deep in passionate dreams
   Of heavenly hills and golden towers.
Ah ! more than poet's rapturous soul I felt
Love's sweetness, when the lips of woman melt
   To sweetness as of tenderest flowers.

But yet I knew that flowers must pass away :
The love I gave should last not for one day ;
   Then darken into black despair.
Because the soul of woman was so sweet,
She must ascend to highest heaven and meet
   Her thorn-crowned strong redeemer there.

No poet's task of gathering flower and flower
Was mine,—but just to deepen hour by hour
   Man's faith in woman's soul, and hers
In her own soul.—All womanhood became
My Bride, and called me by love's holiest name :
   The prophet who loves one bride, errs.

I yielded up the tender marriage-kiss,
The common lot of love, content with this—
   That in far days beyond my dream
All women of all nations should agree
That man's most noble love sprang first from me :
   The stars I lighted, daily gleam.

No flower of love in your wild world to-day
Blossoms, save for love-seeds I flung away
   Upon the breeze of Palestine.
New life to woman—this it was I gave.
She passed with me the portals of the grave,
   And rose with her white hand in mine.

Never she weeps to-day, but I too weep.—
I send the stars to guard true lovers' sleep.
   I make the bright sea blue for these.
The Father hath put all things in my hand :
I make the emerald grass adorn the land,
   And gem with ruby fruit the trees.

O Satan, Satan, thou shalt pass away !
A million years are but one single day
   Before high God's eternal gaze.
Two thousand years have passed since Calvary's gloom
Deepened around me,—still thy sins consume
   Thyself, and all who seek thy ways.

O lonely spirit, who hast no power to see
The deathless spirit of love that shines in me
          And in the Father of all things ;
O spirit, who feedest on thine own despair
And see'st alone the shadow in the air
          Of thine own form and sombre wings :

O spirit, who see'st in woman just a flower,
White, fragrant, sweet to pluck in pleasure's hour,
          And who would'st have man share thy creed ;
O spirit, who on the blood-red battle plain
See'st nought but wet heaps of the newly slain,—
          In corn-fields see'st alone the weed :

O spirit, to whom the stars are blots on space ;
Who tarriest in thy dreary dwelling-place,
          Despairing, doubting, and alone :
How would it be if from the highest air
A voice said : "Thine ineffable despair
          Is ended. Thou too hast a throne.

"Thou hast a throne, but not the lonely seat
Whereon thou sittest while the storm-winds beat
          Around and o'er thee through the vast."
How were it with thee if the high God said :
"O Satan, raise unto the stars thine head ;
          Thy woes and sins lie in the past."

There is a loneliness divinely sweet,
My Father's ; his in whom all spirits meet,
          And yet who dwells apart, alone.
In every petal of each new-born rose
His sweet creative bounty blooms and glows :
          All seas make music round his throne.

The purple depths of the eternal space
Serve him for home and boundless dwelling-place ;
   Yet dwells he in the humblest heart.
His loneliness is ever unlike thine,
For Love creates the loneliness divine,
   And Hate is regnant where thou art.

The eyes of Love are those alone which see.—
When the great English warrior followed me
   And passed into the land divine,
What sawest thou, Satan, with thy lurid eyes ?
Thou thoughtest death came like a fell surprise ;
   That Gordon's thoughts were even as thine.

Thou sawest his body flung into the wave.
" The Nile," thou thoughtest, "is this soldier's grave.
   He toiled. God hath rewarded well.
His faith in God,—what was it but a dream ?
Soon will his corpse grow rotten in the stream."
   Such was thy thought, when Gordon fell.

But I, the spirit of God beyond the gloom,
Knew that for love there is no grave, no tomb :—
   God dies not. Those who live in him
Share the eternal life that was before
The first wave rippled on earth's first green shore ;
   That will be when all stars wax dim.

This is the eternal life I came to show :—
The life all men may share in here below,
   And carry out in heights above :
The life that through God's veins with great throbs burns ;
The life whose rapture thrills him when he turns
   Weakness to strength, and hate to love.

This, God's own life, was, ere one sea-bird flew
Above the primal ocean faint and blue
    And dull and lifeless, stretching far :
Before the deep primordial dark was lit
By the first golden fire-spark piercing it
    With flame that gathered to a star.

And this the life of God beyond all creeds,
Beyond the thoughts of frail men and their deeds,
    Beyond their stars, and dreams of space,
Extends for ever towards the eternal gloom
Where solar systems plunge into their tomb
    As cataracts plunge, and end their race.

When over the last purple steep of sky
The gold star-cataracts plunge themselves, and die,
    When heaven is left again alone,
God's heart will still be starful, and supreme :
Across his soul's sky still the stars will gleam,
    And through his thought the winds will moan.

The heart that said, "Let light awake and be!"
That bade the first blue billows of the sea
    Arise and laugh in dawn's bright air:
The heart that said, "Let golden sunrise flame!"
Will still abide unchangeably the same
    When suns nor moons nor waves are there.

The heart that bade the storm-winds wail or roar
Along the rocks of many an iron shore
    And summoned thunders from the deep
Will still abide the same, when the last breeze
Dies in a whisper in the dying trees,—
    When the tired thunder sinks to sleep.

CHORUS OF SPIRITS OF LIGHT.

CHORUS OF SPIRITS OF LIGHT.

I.

However sad man's lot,
Despair should enter not
    The suffering heart of man.
God by one single stroke
Can heal the heart he broke,
    So carrying out his plan.

For no man sighs in vain :
The humblest creature's pain
    Is known to God on high.
He hears the horse's neigh ;
He hears his red-breasts pray ;
    He hears his throstles sigh.

He hears his violets plead,
And on the thirsty mead
    He sends the gladdening rain.
The golden buttercup
That sighs its sweet heart up
    To heaven, sighs not in vain.

No bright marsh-marigold
Is withered by the cold
    Of late tempestuous May
Without a pitying thought
Of God, who hastening brought
    At last the warm sun-ray.

The trefoil owes to him
(Just as the cherubim
    Receive from him their crowns !)
Its crown of fairy gold
That lights the wind-swept wold
    Or glitters on the downs.

The daisy once was white
—Until it caught a sight
    Of angels in the air.
Such rapture flushed the flower
That, ever since that hour,
    Its glad pink blush is there !

      *   *

So with the sons of men.—
God often and again
    By sudden stroke can change
The most unequal lot :
Aye, oftentimes his thought
    Takes roads and courses strange.

How often has he sent,
To bring some soul content,
    An angel all in white—
When on the window-sill
A snowdrop by his will
    Has blossomed in the night !

How often has he brought
From sorrow beyond thought
    A peace exceeding praise.
Though daylight bring despair,
There shall be starlight fair
    And hope in the moon's rays.

Above the weary town
The silver moon smiles down :
    The towers and turrets shine.
The fog-clouds roll away
In banks of sullen grey
    Along the river-line.

Though man's vast cities breed
Deep misery indeed,
    They yield their joys as well.
Not all the city life
Is one long round of strife,
    Or one grim coign of hell.

With song and laugh and shout
The children sally out,
    Poor hoarse-throat London rooks !
They leave the streets dull-grey,
And seek the meadows gay
    Where gleam the silver brooks.

We follow where they go :
Pale faces all a-glow,
    And hearts no longer sad.
See ! one child's fingers hold
A kingcup. Crown of gold
    Would make a queen less glad.

They paddle in the brook :
They strive—in vain—to hook
    With crooked pins and thread
The minnows flashing through
The waters clear and blue,
    Or roach with eye-rings red.

Their laughter is divine !
Their merry glances shine !—
    Oh, God is good to these.
They make grand holiday
Amid the fragrant hay
    And under the elm-trees.

What could an angel need
More than this grassy mead
    Which buttercups enstar?
The blue sky shines out clear :
Heaven seems so very near,
    And hell so very far !

Their London life is hell
Maybe. To-day this dell
    Where white wild roses bloom
Is heaven indeed, and God
Is in the golden-rod
    And in the yaffle's plume.

God speaks to children thus :
And he commissions us
    To guard them as they go.
In God's great endless park
From daylight until dark
    They wander to and fro.

Then, when the night sinks down
The white moon o'er the town
　　Shines out, and points the way.
The children's feet have trod
Sweet country roads with God
　　For one long summer day.

II.

Moreover things men dread—
War's reckless sword, stained red,
　　And trumpet-bearing hand,—
The thunder of the seas,—
Swift arrows of disease,—
　　The thirsty wastes of sand,—

Blue leagues of glittering ice
That crushes in a vice
　　The ship that tempts its grip,—
All evil things and strange,—
The loves that pale and change,
　　That once lay lip to lip,—

All these things God includes
In his vast rule.　Man broods
　　On ceaseless plan and plot ;
But under and above
Is the eternal love,
　　The God who changes not.

God does not dread the storm
That shakes the ship's frail form :
　　He sees beyond the night.
The sailor fears, for he
Sees darkness whelm the sea—
　　But God's eye sees the light.

The lover's broken heart
Sees all sweet dreams depart,
    For all his dreams were one.
He sees to-day's black gloom,
And thunder-clouds that loom—
    But God's eye sees the sun.

God hears to-morrow sing,
And voice of birds that wing
    Through future boughs their way.
Man only marks and sees
The chill and leafless trees ;
    Man only sees to-day.

Man only sees the earth
To-day. God marks the birth
    Of blossoms yet to be.—
Man sees the storm-drum swing.
God sees the white gull's wing
    Upon a stormless sea.—

Man sees the earthquake's shock
Rend house and tower and rock,—
    Feels horror over all.
God, 'neath to-morrow's sun,
Sees the green lizard run
    Along the shored-up wall.—

Man worships in one star.
In globes that near and far
    Whirl in their maddening race
God brings forth ever-new
Life, thrilling the strange blue
    Unsounded depths of space.

God, in that he is God,
Upon the winds hath trod
   And rested on the storm.
The stars are in his fold ;
Nor plunges from his hold
   One comet's angry form.

And yet the God who counts
The stars on the dark mounts
   Of heaven, nor loses one,
Will let no frail heart break ;
And for one daisy's sake
   He would create a sun.

www.ingramcontent.com/pod-product-compliance
Lightning Source LLC
Chambersburg PA
CBHW052343110726
47901CB00005B/1343